PAY OUT AND PAY BACK
The next installment from the author of
the award winning mystery
CAUGHT IN THE WEB

"PAY OUT AND PAY BACK is a wonderfully twisty, high-
tech crime mystery with many roads, branches, turns and
discoveries. Enjoy the journey!"
Jodi Wyner-Holmes
The Bookplace, Elk Grove, CA

"CAUGHT IN THE WEB is a fast-paced, literary
roller-coaster of an action/adventure mystery. Barbara Scott
is a gifted storyteller with a flair for the dramatic."
THE MIDWEST BOOK REVIEW

Other Books by

Barbara A. Scott

ALWAYS IN A FOREIGN LAND

CAUGHT IN THE WEB

To: Lisette

Enjoy the mystery!

PAY OUT
AND
PAY BACK

Barbara A. Scott

By Barbara A. Scott

ZENAR BOOKS

All characters in this book are fictitious, and any resemblance
to actual persons, living or dead, is purely coincidental.

Published by:

> *Zenar Books*
> P.O. Box 686
> Rancho Cordova, CA 95741-0860

Library of Congress Number 99-90043

ISBN 0-9637134-2-6

Manufactured in the United States of America

Original cover photo © Trevor Burrows Photography,
Plymouth, UK

Cover design and photo manipulation © Tamara L. Dever,
TLC Graphics, Orangevale, CA

I would like to thank Richard John Kneebone, retired Police Inspector for Devon and Cornwall Constabulary for his invaluable help with research for this book; Jill and Peter Bunce for their gracious hospitality during my stay in Plymouth; John and Gwen Reekie for their continuing support and interest in my work and for their boundless patience and generosity while acting as guides and chauffeur while I was in England; Arlene F. McClung and Judy Goss who reviewed and commented on the manuscript; and Bob who works undercover on the team.

Team Members and Friends

Bradley Cover-Rollins British	Brad - team leader
Mary Cover-Rollins British	Brad's wife
Paul Artier Thai-American	Second in command of team
Peter Kononellos Greek	Team member - known as Kon
Geilla Kononellos Italian	Kon's wife and team member
Jack Barrons American	Team member
Nea Cortlin British	Dress designer, artist, and business partner to Mary
Bridget British	Nurse on rescue team in Devon
Edgar Marné Swiss	Bank owner and manager Mentor and father figure to Kon
Charlotte Marné Swiss	Edgar's wife who hired Peter as a handyman, but raised him as her son

Chapter One

Adam Willard hurried down the steps toward his boss, Roger Dremann, who lay groaning at the bottom.

"Mind the slick, Adam," Roger called over his shoulder. "It would really please the blackguard who set this up to bring down two of us."

Thus cautioned, Adam held the handrail tightly as he carefully skirted the pool of clear oil, barely visible in the middle of the second to last step.

"It's good you happened along when you did, Adam. I think everyone else has gone home."

"Don't you remember? I always go up to accounting this time of day. Do you think I should send for help? You might be seriously hurt."

"I don't think it's all that bad, Adam. I'll probably be fine once I stand up. I just need a hand to get started."

"If you say so, but you should see a doctor," Adam said, extending his hand and pulling Roger up.

"I imagine I'll be stiff tomorrow," Roger said, rubbing his back. "But I don't believe I've broken anything."

"Well, it certainly looks as if someone was deliberately trying to cause an accident. This oil doesn't resemble anything we use here at the plant."

"It doesn't, does it," Roger agreed, stooping down rather stiffly to have a closer look. He dipped his index finger into the oil and studied its consistency.

"I think you'd best fetch a caretaker whilst I guard the stairs, Adam. Marcolm and Blake would have to pay an insurance claim if anyone besides myself slipped on the stairs."

"If you ask me, it's time we fetched the police. All these little *accidents* are becoming too frequent to ignore."

"If you remember, I did call them about the tyres that were slashed, and precious little was done about it. Although I did take their suggestion to install more lights in the yard. No, Adam, I think we all just need to be on our guard until we find out who's behind all these little incidents."

"Seems to me that somebody has it in for Marcolm and Blake. I think we should do something about it before anything more serious happens."

"You could be right," Roger allowed. "I shall alert security of course, but for now let's just clean up the mess and go home. I could use a long soak."

"As you wish, Mr. Dremann, but if a brick had come crashing through my window, I wouldn't be so calm about it."

Roger sighed wearily. "If you remember, I wasn't in at the time so no harm was done. We shall all have to be more cautious in the future."

Brad turned off A386 at Plymbridge Road and drove southeast toward the industrial park where Marcolm and Blake, Ltd. was housed in a rather unpretentious two-story brick building. From the outside the building didn't appear substantially different from the other businesses in the area. The car park in front was not fenced and there was only a single strand of barbed wire stretched along the top of the brick wall surrounding the delivery area.

Brad noticed the police car as soon as he turned into the drive. It was Monday morning and he wondered immediately if some other accident had happened over the weekend, something so serious that it couldn't be fixed quietly. Brad parked his car and went in through the front door. Security guards had been on duty around the clock at the plant for years, but the video monitors had only recently been installed upon Brad's recommendation. Since he had been issued an employee badge, he didn't need to sign the visitor's log on the huge security counter. He was keeping up the charade of being Randolph Chillingsworth, Ph.D., but he was beginning to hear grumbling from the staff as to why he never attended meetings. People also wanted to know why he was given high-level security access when many of them did not have it. He decided he had better ask the CEO, Roger Dremann, to arrange an all-staff gathering and pack the agenda so there wouldn't be time for him to say anything of substance.

2

As Brad entered the lobby he called "Good morning," to Tony Schaffer, the young, daytime security guard, who looked up from his morning doughnut, grinned broadly, and called out, "Morning, Doctor Chillingsworth!" Brad decided it was best to curb his curiosity about the police car in order to keep his cover and went straight to his desk in the tiny office that had been allotted to him. Before he got his coat off, however, he saw the message from Roger asking to see him as soon as he came in.

Marcolm and Blake had been developing a series of complex electro-optical imaging systems that Roger envisioned would eventually replace the photographic camera for remote scanning applications. Although the resolution properties had not yet been perfected, the systems had tremendous potential. They had developed a digitizing component which, when linked to an in-flight display device, could locate questionable areas with pinpoint accuracy, eliminating the need to wait until film had been retrieved and developed. If there was need to investigate a certain portion of a field more closely, the pilot could to do it right then and there. Also, since the information was on magnetic tape, a computer could be used to correct geometric errors and enhance patterns in the original image.

Roger had been effusive in his praise of the new system for determining moisture content in soils, and mapping wetlands and flooded areas even through atmospheric haze or clouds. He was noticeably silent about the military applications for Marcolm and Blake, but Brad was aware that with proper adjustment, the equipment could be used to spot enemy ground forces with incredible accuracy even through camouflage.

It had been only two weeks since Dremann had called Brad in desperation after having been underbid by a French Company called Centre pour le Développment de la Télédétection (CDT). He was convinced that someone at the plant was stealing Marcolm and Blake technology and causing them to lose their edge on the market. Dremann had related to Brad that three months previously at an industrial seminar in London, Martin Trevone from CDT had presented a paper on Infrared Applications. Afterwards Martin had shown Roger some 'as yet unpublished' photos that Roger recognized as having originated at Marcolm and Blake. Then three weeks ago Marcolm and Blake was bidding on a government contract to develop an across-track scanner which can collect radiance data simultaneously in multiple spectral bands. Their proposal had made the short list and they heard some favorable rumors that they were certain to get the award. Suddenly, however, they were out in the cold and the award went to CDT.

Roger had been astounded and went to the review committee personally. When they would not tell him anything, he threatened to file an appeal which would have caused a significant delay in the final award process. Pressure was brought to bear on Marcolm and Blake that if they followed through with their appeal, all the government contracts they presently had would be withdrawn. The situation was extremely critical. Finally one of the ministers who believes in British industry told Roger that CDT had submitted a proposal almost identical to Marcolm and Blake's except that their bid was lower. Roger was desperate. If he said nothing, Marcolm and Blake technology would be stolen piece by piece. But if he admitted to the government that there had been a breach of security, all his government contracts could be canceled immediately. After a consultation with his local MP, Roger had withdrawn his appeal and called Bradley Cover-Rollins. Although the international organization Brad was associated with did most of its work on contract for various governments, they did take private clients when the matters at issue crossed jurisdictional borders. Keeping British defense-related trade secrets out of the hands of the French was deemed worthy of a confidential investigation by Brad and his team of specialists.

Brad grabbed two reports at random and walked carelessly towards the CEO's office as if he intended to present the latest production figures. He smiled and called a greeting to two of the secretaries who quickly stepped away from the window. He knew they had been discussing the police car. It's too bad those two don't work security, he thought. They never miss an opportunity to eavesdrop.

Brad was prepared to find a local constable in Roger's office, but he was surprised to see Harvey the senior security officer. Harvey had always impressed Brad as taking his job seriously. It's true that he managed to read the paper between his rounds, but he was thorough and regular about making his building checks and had never been caught sleeping or using the company shower during his shift.

"Ah, Chillingsworth, do come in," Roger said, looking up as Brad stepped through the door.

Brad nodded as Roger introduced Inspector Timothy Tomlin and Constable Bob Grigley or maybe it was Greenly. Brad decided to confirm it later so as not to interrupt Roger and to give himself an excuse to talk to the man again if necessary.

"Apparently," Roger continued, "Harvey has recognized an unidentified body these two gentleman found out on Cornwood Road. He insists the woman worked here, but I have no recollection of her. Inspector Tomlin suspects that foul play was involved in her death. I thought you might assist them in going through the employee files."

"Certainly, Mr. Dremann," Brad answered quickly, thinking how smoothly Roger had given him the right to be part of the investigation without ever stipulating what his position was with the company.

"Harvey, why don't you carry on and quietly take these gentlemen out to your desk. No need to upset everyone until her identity can be verified."

"Right, Mr. Dremann," Harvey agreed quickly. He opened the office door and led Brad and the police officers out to the security area. Tony was sitting behind the desk, his attention divided between a chocolate covered doughnut and the computer screen. Harvey dismissed him quickly with a casual wave of his hand. "Mr. Dremann wants me to find some information for these gentlemen, Tony. Why don't you go make your rounds so I can have your chair."

"It's not time for my regular check, Harvey. Are you sure it's all right for me to leave my post unattend . . ."

"It will hardly be unattended with a police inspector and a constable standing here, Tony," Harvey countered sharply.

"Well, I'll leave, but I think I should let Mr. Willard know that you said I could leave."

"That's fine, Tony. Go right ahead. And don't forget to add that you're slowing down an official police investigation. I'm sure he'll want to know that part."

5

"I didn't mean to get in the way, Harvey. You said I need to pay more attention to the rules," Tony mumbled dejectedly. When Harvey ignored him, he nodded to Brad and the police officers and went away without further objection.

"It might take some time, but I'm sure I can find her signature on the sign-in sheet," Harvey continued. "She came in almost every weekend—Sunday mostly—if I recall correctly . . . and real early. I figured she wanted to get her work done without being interrupted."

"How did you happen to hear that her body had been found?" Brad asked casually as he thumbed through the stack of logbooks that Harvey had piled on the counter.

"Last night after my shift was over, I decided to go on down to the station house. The Missus was away visiting our daughter so I figured I'd go exchange insults with the men. I used to be on the force with ol' Bob here," Harvey added, waving an arm carelessly in Grigley's direction. "I was doing right well 'till I hurt my back. I was out of commission for a time and got put on disability. I finally landed me this job and it really helps out. I still share a few beers with the men now and then and they fill me in on what's happening in the glorious world of crime fighting." He paused and gave Bob a playful punch on the arm. "Anyway, they got to telling me about this woman they found on Saturday morning, and how nobody seems to know who she was or where she came from. They was describing her and the more they said, the more I thought I'd seen her here at the plant. Young, good-looking woman—you don't forget a face like that. She always had her hair and makeup just right, even at six-thirty Sunday morning. Most people who . . ."

Harvey stopped abruptly, apparently having found what he was looking for in the logbooks. "Here we are . . . Elizabeth Duncan. She was in on 7 June. Goodness how time flies. That was about three months ago." Harvey turned the logbook around so that Brad and the police could see the entry just below his stubby finger. "And see, here she is the week before, and the week before that. I can ask Mr. Willard to run a computer printout of the card key logs to see how many times she was in."

"That would be very useful," Brad answered, but Inspector

Tomlin objected. "I don't care if she was working overtime. All I need to get is a full name and address so we can check it out."

"Well, Mr. Willard can get you that too once we have the key card number. I'll jot down times she came in and I'll match them against the printout. It shouldn't be hard. Like I said, she always came in at off hours."

Harvey grabbed a clipboard and began making notations on it as he ran his hand across the column. He had barely started before the door to his left opened and a man hurried through. Brad recognized him as Adam Willard. "What's up, Harvey? Tony came rushing into my office complaining that you sent him away and that the lobby was full of . . . well, I guess he was exaggerating," he concluded when he saw only two strange men. "What's this all about?" he asked more politely.

"I'm Inspector Tomlin," Tomlin said extending his hand. "We're trying to identify the body of a young woman we found on Cornwood Road. Harvey here seems to think she worked for Marcolm and Blake. We need to check this log-in sheet to find an address."

"Oh dear . . . " Willard said, looking startled. "A dead body?"

"I'm afraid so," Tomlin answered quietly.

"Oh my. Have you found a name, Harvey? I'll have to run a printout. It'll take me a few minutes. I have to cross-check several lists in my database. Can I call you when I'm finished?" he asked hopefully.

"We would prefer to wait," Tomlin answered.

"Oh . . . I see . . . well, yes, of course," Willard mumbled. "Harvey, could you give me a hand back at my desk. Lilla always does the data run," he added lowering his voice, "but she knows everyone and can't be trusted not to blab. I'd prefer to keep this quiet, if you know what I mean."

"Certainly, Mr. Willard," Harvey answered. "I'll be right back, Tim," he continued, turning toward Tomlin. "Why don't you and Bob make yourself comfortable. Just don't let any suspicious characters in while I'm gone."

"I'd like to come with you," Brad put in. "I am Mr. Dremann's representative on this matter."

"Oh . . . I suppose it's all right," Willard said reluctantly. He put his own key card against the scanner on the wall, and jerked the door handle as he heard the click. "Really . . . if all the other troubles we've been having lately aren't enough, now it's dead bodies. I just don't see how we can keep this quiet," he muttered shaking his head.

Willard mumbled nervously to himself all the while he led Brad and Harvey back to his office. Lilla was working at the computer, but Willard made some excuse about an urgent memo and sent her to a corner office to type it up.

With Harvey's help it didn't take Willard long to generate the printout of the key card numbers, but when Harvey checked it against the employee lists the name that kept coming up was Stanley Pommer. Finally, in frustration, Harvey pulled up the complete employee list and ran a search for Elizabeth Duncan. The third time "No match found" flashed on the screen, Harvey's ears turned red and he slapped the desk. "Bugger the bitch!" he muttered as the truth struck him.

Chapter Two

It was hard for Harvey to traipse back to ol' Bob and Tim and admit that he had been fooled by a woman, but he did it. They were professional about it, however, and didn't make any derisive remarks, at least not in front of Brad. Harvey knew they would get him later though, over a pint at the pub.

For the moment Tomlin and Grigley were all business and suggested there was no time like the present to talk to Stanley Pommer. Stanley's office was judged too small and too open for such a delicate conversation, and at Brad's suggestion, he was discreetly called to a large conference room in another section of the building. Stanley shuffled in, slightly stooped, as usual, seemingly physically apologizing for the fact that he was so tall and lanky. He greeted everyone openly.

"Mr. Pommer, we need to talk to you," Inspector Tomlin began once the door was closed.

"What is this about?" Stanley asked without showing undue concern.

"I'm Inspector Tomlin and this is Constable Grigley. Why don't you sit down, Mr. Pommer?" The remark was more of an order than a polite offer and Stanley sat.

"What? . . . what can I help you with?" he asked innocently.

"Mr. Pommer, we are investigating the disappearance of a young woman. Her name is Elizabeth Duncan and we have reason to believe you knew her."

Stanley scratched his head, but didn't look particularly disturbed. "I don't know an Elizabeth Duncan. I don't know anyone named Elizabeth. Why would you connect her to me?"

"She was using your keycard to get into Marcolm and Blake at weekends."

"My card? But that's impossible. I don't know anyone by that name."

"Do you still have your card? Did you loan it to anyone?"

"Yes, I still have it, and no, I didn't loan it to anyone. It's against the rules to do that."

"Well, she used your card to get in here Mr. Pommer. The numbers match. Now how do you think she got your card?"

Stanley looked nervous for the first time and wiped his eyeglasses with his tie. Then suddenly, he looked hopeful. "I lost my card a while back. I had to sign in and wear a visitor's badge for a few days. I didn't think anything about it at the time. I'll admit I'm not the tidiest person . . . maybe someone took my card on purpose."

"Did you report that your card had been stolen?" Harvey asked, bringing his face close to Stanley's.

"No. I . . . I didn't want to pay for a new one. I figured it would show up again and it did."

"Are you sure you didn't give it to anyone?" Harvey asked trying to sound tough, but only partially succeeding.

"Yes, I'm quite sure. What is this all about, Chillingsworth? Why do you think I am involved?"

"It's about a possible murder, Mr. Pommer, so I advise you to take it seriously," Brad answered.

"Murder!" Stanley gasped in shock. "Why . . . ? Why do you think I'm involved?"

"She was using your key card to get into the building, Mr. Pommer. If you didn't give it to her, how did she get it?"

"I don't know," Stanley wailed. "I told you it was missing for a while. Maybe she found it."

"I would like you to look at some pictures of her belongings, Mr. Pommer," Tomlin said opening a large envelope he had been carrying tucked under his arm. Carefully he set three black-and-white photos on the table in front of Stanley. "Do you recognize anything? Her jewelry, her dress—anything?"

Stanley leaned forward slightly as he looked at each of the pictures. Brad saw him tense as he glanced warily from one to the other and noted that he did not touch them.

"Do you recognize any of these items?" Tomlin asked.

Stanley looked up from the pictures and noticed that Brad was watching him intently. He looked away immediately. "I . . . I've never seen any of these things before."

"And you've never met a slim blonde woman, about 5' 6" tall, with brown eyes who kept her makeup and nails perfectly groomed?"

"No! I . . . I've never . . . where would I meet someone like that? What . . . what happened to her?" he added weakly.

"As near as we can figure, it was set up to look like a hit and run. But it seems unlikely that a woman would be hiking along Cornwood Road in her evening dress and high-heeled shoes."

"Oh, no . . . I don't suppose she would."

"So you have no idea who she is?"

"No, none at all," Stanley affirmed.

"Well, I guess that's all for now, Mr. Pommer." Tomlin began, but Brad cut him off.

"Before you finish, would you mind stepping into the hall for a moment?"

"Me? Well, certainly, if you have something to add."

"Yes, please . . . "

Brad was nearest the door. He stood up quickly, opened it, and motioned for Tomlin to follow him into the hall. Brad closed the door behind them and waved Tomlin away from the door.

"What's this all about? Are you holding something back, Chillingsworth?"

"No, but I do think Mr. Pommer is lying. He knows that woman. We . . . that is, you have to search his residence quickly before he can remove anything."

"Well hold on now, Chillingsworth. What's your interest in all this? We would have to get a warrant to search his place and without any evidence, except your suspicions, that doesn't seem likely."

"My interest in this matter as a company representative is to get it cleared up as quickly and quietly as possible. Correct me if I'm wrong, but you wouldn't need a warrant if he agrees to let us in. Why not do it now, quietly, before the gossip starts? I would rather settle it now than have you and Grigley showing up here every day, asking questions and setting everyone's tongue to wagging," Brad declared forcefully.

Tomlin nodded as if he understood the point, but remained quiet.

"I see your point, but I hardly think Mr. Pommer is about to roll out the red carpet for us. He keeps insisting he doesn't know the woman."

"Do you believe him? I don't."

"I'm not exactly sure, but I figured I would let it rest for a while. Sort of not tip him off that we're suspicious."

"I say, let's investigate right now. If he's clean, we end the gossip right here."

"Do you have something in mind to make him change his story?"

"I think so. At least let me have a go at it. Let me do the talking when we go back in. Just don't contradict anything I say. After all, I'm not with the police. I have more latitude to maneuver."

"All right then, but be quick about it. This doesn't seem to be leading anywhere."

Brad nodded and led the way back inside the conference room, but this time he took a seat next to Stanley and looked directly at him. "Look, Mr. Pommer," Brad started, but stopped. "May I call you Stanley? We are co-workers after all, although we work in different departments." Without waiting for an answer, Brad hurried on. "This matter has gotten very sticky, Stanley. Inspector Tomlin didn't want to bring it up since you say you didn't know the dead woman, but there was a certain memo in her handbag."

Stanley continued to look at Brad with a blank look. "What are you driving at?"

"It was on Marcolm and Blake memohead, Stanley. The handwriting appears to have been washed off in the rain, but the printing is still clear. Inspector Tomlin here is planning on having the memo analyzed in the police lab. Now this handwriting business isn't very accurate, but if he even suspects that the handwriting is yours . . . well, you could be arrested, Stanley."

"Arrested? But I didn't . . ."

"Of course not," Brad assured him quickly, "but it will look bad for you if you don't cooperate."

"But I am cooperating. I just don't know the woman."

"Well, maybe if you agreed to let these gentlemen look around your flat they would be satisfied and let you alone. Otherwise . . . with that memo and all they are just going to hound you to death, both at home and at work. Now we both know that Roger isn't going to like having the police hanging about all day asking questions. He takes a very dim view of that kind of publicity. That's why he asked me to kind of smooth things over for you."

"My God! Mr. Dremann knows they're here to talk to me?"

"Of course, Stanley. These men needed his permission to pull you off the job. He agreed this morning, but he won't take kindly to doing it every day. You could save yourself a lot of trouble by letting them look at your place right now."

"But I . . ." Stanley began, but Brad cut him off. "Oh come on, Stanley. What's the harm in letting them have a quick look 'round right now so we can send them packing? I for one would like to tell Mr. Dremann that the matter is finished so things could get back to normal."

"Well . . . I guess . . . I haven't done anything wrong."

"That's the spirit, Stanley! I'll ride with you and the police can meet us there so no one here will be any the wiser where we're off to."

Brad stood abruptly and took Stanley by the arm. "We'll drive out first, Inspector Tomlin, and wait for you at the bottom of the road, beyond the first turning."

Tomlin seemed a bit surprised by the suddenness of it all, but he mumbled his agreement.

"I'll call someone to collect prints," Tomlin whispered to Brad as he was shepherding Stanley out the door.

After seeing Stanley's flat, Brad was undecided whether it should be declared a public menace by the health department, an aluminum recycling center by local government, or a bomb scene by the police. It took talent or years of neglect to make four small rooms look as if 30,000 screaming rock fans had just staged a riot. Even Stanley admitted diffidently that he had been letting things slip lately.

A systematic search seemed a daunting endeavor. Anything from Marcolm and Blake trade secrets to the crown jewels could be hidden in the waist high accumulation of aluminum and cardboard containers, and Tomlin didn't seem of a mind to go exploring. He was very professional, however, and directed the fingerprint expert to follow the narrow path that was cleared from the couch to the stereo and also advised examining the edge of the dresser in the bedroom. He told Brad that he would leave a further search of the premises until after he learned if the fingerprint search turned up anything unusual.

Brad stayed with Tomlin until the print expert finished his work. He decided that he would assign Kon, one of his team members, to do surveillance on Stanley. After all Stanley's key card was the only clue concerning the dead woman's identity.

Stanley's peace was short lived, for by Thursday morning the police were back at Marcolm and Blake with an arrest warrant. Elizabeth's prints had been found on several of Stanley's plastic tape cartridges and on Stanley's dresser. There were also some very suspicious dents on the front fender of Stanley's car. This time Stanley was taken to the police station for questioning. Brad was not allowed to be present at the official interview, but he recommended a barrister to Stanley. Still believing that Brad was associated with Marcolm and Blake, his long-time employer, and desperate for some friendly advice, Stanley jumped at Brad's suggestion.

Langston Crist had worked with Brad on other cases. Although he rarely appeared in the courtroom himself, he was a master at treading the fine line between seeing that justice was done and being charged with betraying client-attorney privilege. He often set Brad onto various tracks of investigation, but if evidence could not be produced by other means, he would not allow Brad to make use of any information a client had told him in confidence. Langston could be trusted to tell Brad what happened at the interview, but anything Stanley said in private would be kept from Brad.

As reported afterwards, Stanley had confessed to knowing Elizabeth Duncan, but not under that name. He knew her as Christine Saunders. He had met her four months ago during one of his frequent lunchtime runs in the open fields that surrounded the Marcolm and

Blake building. He had noticed her iridescent green shorts and shapely legs immediately, but he was too shy to say anything. After a few days of passing her without a word, he began to nod and smile as he roared past. Then one day, just as he came panting past, she fell.

Stanley had stopped to help, but was so shy, it took him a while to realize that she wanted him to drive her to the emergency room to get an x-ray of her ankle. Fearing that he would be late returning from lunch, he had offered to call an ambulance to take her. She had whimpered that she couldn't afford the cost, and that surely he would be forgiven for doing a good deed. Stanley acknowledged that as a single male he ate mostly take-out, and he had been embarrassed by the state of his car, but she had smiled at him all the way to the hospital. He stayed with her while she was being treated and his life was never the same after that.

He began to meet her at out of the way places and take her to U-2 concerts. He was a devoted fan and she seemed to like their music as much as he did. He had wanted to introduce her to the staff at Marcolm and Blake, but she kept putting him off. He didn't mind. He enjoyed the adventure of meeting Christine at a pub called The George after work and going to hotels. It was an inconvenience though, and it seemed quite natural when she suggested they go to his flat. He thought it strange that she never commented or complained about the disorder.

Since the police would not permit Brad to visit Stanley in jail, Brad sent Paul Artier, second in command on the team, who gained access on Monday by playing the role of Langston's clerk. It was Paul who questioned Stanley about his role in stealing Marcolm and Blake secrets. Stanley steadfastly denied knowing anything about stolen secrets, but did admit that he suspected someone had been tampering with his computer. Paul questioned Stanley doggedly, trying to determine whether Christine was more interested in Stanley or his files. Stanley finally admitted that Christine had seemed more than casually interested his work. Even though she had broken off with him months ago, Stanley was loath to admit that Christine had never truly cared for him. After lengthy questioning he confessed that he knew where Christine lived and that he had gone there one night after she had broken off their relationship. He maintained that he went to Christine's flat with the intention of begging her to reconsider, but that he had lost his nerve and left without talking to her.

Paul knew that the police should be told where Elizabeth's flat was, but he decided that he would wait until he had had a chance to check out the scene. He would tell Langston about the flat and have him advise Stanley to tell the police. In the meantime, Inspector Tomlin was back at Marcolm and Blake circulating Elizabeth Duncan's photograph and systematically questioning Stanley's co-workers about his habits. Lilla was not able to identify Elizabeth from the photo, but she was quick to report that Stanley had undergone a personality change several months ago.

"Oh yes, I remember. He started wearing a tie to work and coming in with his shirts pressed. He had never done that before. And humming in the hall—more than once, mind you. Everyone commented about that! All the girls giggled that Stanley must have a love life. I asked him once myself, and he grinned and wiped his thick glasses with the end of his tie. He said he did have a new lady friend. New lady friend! As if Stanley had ever had a lady friend! Take my word for it, Stanley was researching something totally new to him."

Chapter Three

The address Stanley had given for Christine's flat was in a moderately expensive section of Plymouth. Under Paul's persistent questioning, Stanley had admitted that he knew very little about Christine and was unaware that she went by the name Elizabeth Duncan. She had told him she was an estate agent, but he didn't know if she was connected to an established firm or ran her own business.

Because he was required to interface with the police on the case, Brad decided it would be too great a risk for him to go to Christine's flat in person. Instead he provided Paul with the necessary papers and assigned him the task. Although all the team members were skilled at impersonations and made various role changes as their jobs required, Paul was a master of disguises. Jack often joked that Paul was the best liar on the team. Armed with his fake police I.D., Paul knocked on the door of the building manager's office at mid-morning on Monday. No one responded until Paul's second knock, but a man finally opened the door.

"Yes? What can I do you for?" he inquired with a politeness that fit the respectability of the building.

"Are you the manager of this complex?" Paul asked.

"Yes. I'm David Lawrence and you are?"

"Inspector Starks, London CID," Paul answered. "I'm looking for Christine Saunders."

The man stared blankly at Paul for a moment until the name registered. "Ah, yes, Saunders. I'm sorry, but she left."

"When?"

"Oh months ago. I would have to look it up if you must know the exact date."

"It would be helpful."

"Oh, all right then. Well, come in. Come in." The manager waved Paul inside and closed the door.

"And I'd like the forwarding address," Paul added.

"That I can't give you," the manager answered heading toward a file cabinet in the corner of the combination living room-office. "She just up and cleared out one day—no notice, no forwarding address."

"Was she behind on the rent?"

"No, nothing like that. She was all paid up. I just like to know so I can inspect the flat and arrange to have it cleaned."

"Was the flat untidy after she left?"

"No, neat as a pin, hardly looked lived in. If you ask me, she didn't spend much time here. She didn't have but three pieces of furniture. Said she was going to be bringing in more, but she never did. Ah, here we are . . .," the manager said with satisfaction as he drew out a thin file. "On the 11th, almost three months ago now."

"Do you have any idea where she worked?"

"She said something once about being an estate agent. Say, what is all this about anyway? Is she wanted for something? She was always quiet and respectable while she was here."

"She was murdered, Mr. Lawrence and I'm trying to figure out who might have wanted to do it."

"Murdered! Oh dear me. I've . . . I've never had anything like that happen here. But she left so it's no one here."

"I'm not suggesting it was, Mr. Lawrence. I'm just trying to learn something about her. Do you suppose I might talk to her former neighbors?"

"Oh dear. I hate to have anyone know about this. It's not good for business. The complex has a good reputation, you know."

"I understand, but this is serious business and so far I have very little to go on. I thought perhaps someone in the building might be able to fill in some details about her life."

"Yes, I see. Well, Mrs. Burnell lives next door to the flat and the Kellys are across the hall. The Kellys are on holiday, but I do believe Mrs. Burnell is in. If you insist upon talking to her, I would like to ring her up first and sort of explain the situation to her. We don't get many police investigators coming by and I don't want to upset her."

"I understand." Paul nodded, resigning himself to the amount of time it was taking him to dig out a few facts. He glanced at his watch and hoped he could finish with Mrs. Burnell before the Plymouth police showed up.

"Well, just a minute then," Mr. Lawrence said and drifted off to another room. From the snatches of conversation Paul overheard, he assumed that Mrs. Burnell was in and had agreed to see him.

"Mrs. Burnell says she doesn't mind helping the police. I'll take you up," Mr. Lawrence said as he came back to Paul.

"Thank you," Paul replied.

"Don't thank me yet. Mrs. Burnell is a widow. She doesn't get much company and she can talk your ear off. Best not to take your coat off and whatever you do, don't sit down or you'll be stuck in there for hours."

"I appreciate the warning. And I would like to ask you one more thing, if I may. I know it sounds strange, but if you get a visit from the local police, I would appreciate it if you wouldn't mention that I've been to see you. They get a bit put out when inspectors come down from London to handle matters—territorial disputes and all. You understand."

"Oh dear, you mean there will be more questions?"

"Well probably not as many. I'll show them my report, of course, but they'll want to do their own follow up. I hate to put you on the spot because of regional politics, but that's the long and short of it. You don't have to lie if they ask you a direct question. Just don't volunteer any information."

"I'll be quiet. I don't want to waste any more time on this matter."

Mr. Lawrence rode up to the third floor with Paul and directed him to Mrs. Burnell's flat. A frail woman who appeared to be in her mid-seventies opened the door promptly in response to his knock.

"Sorry for the intrusion, Mrs. Burnell. This is Inspector Starks. Like I said, he's down from London investigating Miss Saunders' . . . um . . . er . . . demise."

"Oh, do come in Inspector Starks," Mrs. Burnell said warmly. "I'm afraid I didn't know Miss Saunders well, but I will be happy to help in any way I can."

"Thank you, Mrs. Burnell. I appreciate your taking time to see me."

"That's quite all right, Inspector. Would you like some tea?"

"No thank you, Mrs. Burnell. I don't have much time."

"What about you, Mr. Lawrence? I bought a fresh tin of biscuits this morning."

"No thank you, Mrs. Burnell. I must return to guard the door. Seems especially important, what with people getting themselves murdered, if you get my meaning."

"I understand. Hearing about Miss Saunders does make one feel more vulnerable. Perhaps you'll stop by some other time, Mr. Lawrence."

"Yes . . . right then. I'll be off, Inspector Starks, if you don't need anything else."

Paul nodded silently, but Mrs. Burnell looked a little disappointed as she closed the door. "I was sorry to hear about Ms. Saunders. Poor dear . . . such a lovely girl. How could anyone do such a thing? Please sit down Inspector."

"No thank you. As I said, I don't have much time."

"Won't you at least take off your coat?" Mrs. Burnell said hopefully.

"I'm sorry, but I really don't have much time."

"Such a lovely girl . . . do you have any suspects yet?" Mrs. Burnell asked brightly.

"The local police have made an arrest, but the case is still being investigated. I thought that Miss Saunders' neighbors might provide some background about her. Mr. Lawrence seemed to think you knew her."

"Well, I wouldn't say I knew her. We talked a few times. I live alone, you see, but I don't like it. I'm always eager for a bit of company, so I go out of my way to meet the new tenants."

"Was Miss Saunders here a long time?"

"Oh, no. She was just in before she was out again. Oh, do sit down, Inspector."

"All right," Paul agreed and reluctantly followed Mrs. Burnell into the sitting room. As soon as Paul entered the room, he knew Mrs. Burnell was a dedicated rose fancier for in addition to the smaller vases of roses that graced every end table and bookcase, there was a massive arrangement of rose buds that appeared to have completely overgrown the mantle. Paul wondered fleetingly how Mrs.

Burnell could afford the expense of so many fresh roses until he realized that all the flowers were dried. He was drawn forward by the need to examine the display more closely. It was obvious that it was hand crafted for each dried bud had been attached to the mantle's bricks with very fine wire.

"Did you do this?" he asked with admiration.

"Yes," Mrs. Burnell answered modestly.

"How long did it take you to do it?" he asked, feeling that her incredible skill deserved some response.

"Oh, I've been working on it, on and off, for years. I miss having a real garden, you see. The colors are not as brilliant as live flowers, but it does cut out the pruning. Do you like it?"

"It's absolutely beautiful! I'm impressed with your patience," he said, wishing he could take a picture to send to his mother who was a devoted gardener. He stood for another moment admiring Mrs. Burnell's craftsmanship and then quickly sat on the edge of a couch. He pulled out a notebook he seldom bothered to use and pretended to study it in order to prevent himself from being drawn into a lengthy conversation about the merits of roses. His mother could go on for hours with her lectures about plants. As a chemist he was curious about the exact chemical mixture Mrs. Burnell had used for drying her flowers, but he had no time to waste at the moment.

"Did Ms. Saunders ever mention where she worked?" he asked abruptly, looking across at Mrs. Burnell who had perched on the couch across from him. She was silent and crinkled her brow as if in deep thought. "She mentioned once that she was an estate agent."

"Do you remember the company name?"

"Oh yes. Frankly I didn't think it was very creative. It was simply *Select Estate Agents.*"

"Do you have any idea why she left?"

"Not exactly. She never discussed it with me, but I have my own ideas."

"Would you care to share them with me?" Paul prodded.

Mrs. Burnell smiled a sly smile. "Perhaps you'll have some tea now, Inspector. It helps me think, you know."

Paul was silent for a moment. He wondered if her feelings would be hurt if he glanced at his watch. On the other hand, if he didn't indicate that he was in a hurry, he might be trapped for hours. He decided an official look was in order and studied his watch as if weighing how much time he could trade for her ideas. "I guess I have time for one cup," he said and smiled to indicate that he would play her game a while longer.

She beamed back at him. "Good, I'll just put the kettle on." Paul nodded and she moved slowly into the kitchen.

He heard water running and cupboard doors being opened and closed, but it seemed a long time before she appeared bearing a huge silver tray holding a teapot and two delicate cups. Seeing the size of her burden, Paul stood to help her. "You really didn't need to go to all this trouble. I usually gulp my tea whilst standing."

"Well, this morning you shall have a proper tea," she declared. She poured tea and plied Paul with tiny biscuits, arranged artfully on a delicate china plate that matched her cups. It did not surprise him that the china pattern featured pink and yellow roses. Paul noticed also that her hands, though wrinkled, were as small and fine as her china. How lonely she must be to waste her fine china on such a fearful occasion as a murder investigation.

"Now, Mrs. Burnell," Paul began after a polite interval of sipping tea, "before I have completely emptied your tin of biscuits, please tell me your theory as to why Miss Saunders left so suddenly."

Mrs. Burnell drew herself straight and held her cup in mid-air. "You must understand that I am not a gossip, Inspector Starks, but I am, as you can see, alone and . . . shall we say 'underutilized.' I took an interest in Miss Saunders. She was so pretty and had the most beautiful clothes. She was not like most of our tenants and I was curious. We spoke only a few times. I often invited her to tea, but she came only once. She was rarely at home and kept to herself."

"But?" Paul put in to hurry her along.

"There was some sadness in her life and something she was afraid of. She never admitted it, but I think someone was abusing her."

"What made you think that?" Paul prodded.

"She was skillful with makeup, as most young women are these days, but I noticed the bruises. Then one evening I heard a row in the hall."

"A row?"

"Yes. I recognized Miss Saunders' voice. She and a man were talking rather loudly."

"Could you make out what they were saying?"

"She told him several times that she didn't want to see him again, but he kept begging her to reconsider. He said he loved her and that his life would fall apart without her. She was very firm with him. I was beginning to be afraid for her, but suddenly I heard her door slam shut. I heard him bang a few times, and then everything was quiet. I opened my door a crack and peeked out. I saw a man standing by the lift at the end of the hall."

"Can you describe him?"

"I had my glasses on but, I didn't really see much of his face. He had his head down. I do remember that he was tall and wore wire-frame glasses. They caught the light from the lamp next to the lift."

"Did he see you?"

"I don't believe so. He seemed very upset and kept striking the lift button with his palm."

"So you think this row had something to do with Miss Saunders' decision to move?"

"Of course. I think she was afraid of him and ran away. Three days later the removal company came and she was gone with never so much as a good-bye."

"Did you see the removers?"

"I didn't actually see the men, but their lorry was parked outside when I got home from shopping. Mr. Lawrence said she didn't have much furniture. They must have had everything loaded, because they pulled away before I got inside."

"Do you remember what company it was?"

"Yes. It was Watson's Limited. I always notice their lorries because one of the tenants had a relative who was a driver for the company. He used to come see her whenever he could manage to slip away. It was a little joke among her neighbors, because he always parked the lorry on the street and everyone knew when he was here."

"And how long ago did Miss Saunders leave, Mrs. Burnell?"

"It was the 11th of June. I remember the day because it was just before my grandniece's birthday. I had gone shopping for a gift."

"Did Ms. Saunders ever have any other visitors?"

Mrs. Burnell looked thoughtful, but before she could answer, Paul felt the unmistakable pulse of his specially-tuned watch signaling that Jack had spotted the local police. He knew he had to clear out fast. He regretted that Mrs. Burnell had taken so long to give him a lead on Christine that he had lost his head start on the police. In another five minutes, Mr. Lawrence would be calling to say the police wanted to talk to Mrs. Burnell. He would have to race to Watson's Limited and hope they could dig out Christine's new address before the police arrived.

He stood to make a dash and then suddenly smiled at Mrs. Burnell. "You have been a great help to me in my investigation. I wish I could do something to repay you . . . wait a minute. Perhaps there is. I have not yet had the opportunity to visit the gardens at Saltram House. If you would agree to act as my guide, I would be happy to invite you to lunch with me."

For a moment Mrs. Burnell looked as startled as if Paul had asked her to runaway to sea with him. But then the sincerity of Paul's smile and his charming interest in her simple tales of the neighbors overcame her reserve. It had been a long time since such a handsome young man had invited her anywhere and Saltram House was one of her favorite places. She was a long-time member of the National Trust, but she rarely got out to see any of the properties anymore. Going with a stranger seemed wildly daring, but after all, he was with the police.

Paul noticed her hesitation and quickly pleaded, "We'll have to go immediately so I can work in a visit before I track down the leads you've given me. Please say you'll come."

Suddenly she felt very important. She had helped with a murder investigation and now a police inspector wanted her to show him a garden she knew and loved. This was rare excitement in her lonely life. "I'm not really dressed for . . ." she began.

"You look fine. Please . . . I must hurry. I don't have much time for escorting ladies down garden paths."

"All right. I'll go," she conceded almost guiltily. "Just let me get my coat."

Paul had his hand on the doorknob when she returned with her coat and handbag. A moment later as he followed her through the door, the phone rang. "Oh dear, I wonder who that can be?" she asked in surprise.

"I'm sorry . . . I really can't wait any longer," Paul insisted.

She hesitated. A phone call was an event in her dreary life, but it could not compare with the excitement of a visit to Saltram House with a handsome young man. "I suppose they'll call again," she said reluctantly.

"I'm sure they will. Would you mind if we went out the rear door? I would like to check something in the garage." Paul asked in a serious tone.

"Oh no," she said with a laugh. She had a delightful sense of sneaking off on a secret adventure.

Once in the garage, Paul made a show of counting the parking spaces and measuring their width, but it was only to put Mrs. Burnell off the real reason he didn't want to leave through the lobby.

As planned Jack was waiting with the car around the corner, out of sight.

"Oh my, there's two of you," Mrs. Burnell said hesitantly when Paul opened the rear door for her. Suddenly realizing that perhaps she would feel less as though she were being kidnaped if she sat in the front, he quickly pulled open the front door for her. "On second thought why don't you sit in front and act as co-pilot. Mrs. Burnell, may I present Inspector Barrons my cohort in crime. He's big, but I promise he won't bite."

"How do you do, Inspector? It's a pleasure to make your acquaintance," she said following social ritual, but she truly did feel pleased when Jack displayed a smile that seemed to radiate from every inch of his six-foot-four-inch frame.

"Jack, Mrs. Burnell has agreed to give me a tour of Saltram House Gardens but we have to hurry to work it in."

"How convenient that she could spare the time right now," Jack said and grinned at Paul.

By late that afternoon, Mrs. Burnell was almost breathless with excitement from visiting Saltram House and sharing an elegant lunch with two sophisticated young men. They had been extremely courteous about slowing their pace to a crawl so that she barely felt self-conscious about her shuffling pace. She had been happy to share her knowledge of local plant lore with Paul for he seemed as interested in the gardens as he was about learning the minute details of Christine Saunders' life.

He guessed that she would want to tell the details of the afternoon outing to anyone who would listen, and he hated to disappoint her. However, he knew he must. He instructed Jack to stop the car in front of her building and opened the door for her, but he declined her invitation to come in. "I must ask a favor of you, Mrs. Burnell," he began seriously. "If the local police come to question you about Miss Saunders, please don't mention that I was here. I'm afraid they might think I was being lax about the investigation if they knew I spent the afternoon strolling down garden paths and dining with a beautiful lady."

He had expected her to be disappointed, but instead she put her china-white hand to her mouth and smiled mischievously. "Oh, Inspector Starks, you do know how to charm a lady. It will be hard, but I will keep your secret, on one condition," she added as if suddenly struck by a wicked thought.

"And what is that?" Paul asked feeling puzzled.

"That you let me know if I was right about why Miss Saunders moved away."

"Agreed," Paul said and they shook hands to seal their bargain.

Chapter Four

"Let's get back to business, Jack," Paul said as he slid into the front seat. "I've got to get to Watson's Limited before they close. Did you find the address?"

"Yes. While you and Mrs. Burnell were having tea, I looked it up."

"Good man! I just hope we can locate Saunder's flat and get some leads before the real Inspector Starks gets back to his office."

"Quit worrying. Brad said the guy will be gone for three days."

"Yeah. I'm covered unless someone asks for a description of Starks. Even if I grew a beard, there's no way I'm ever going to look like him," Paul said, referring to his jet black hair and dark, almond-shaped eyes he had inherited from his mother.

Luckily for Paul no one at Watson's Limited knew that the real Inspector Starks had freckles and a full reddish-blonde beard. The assistant manager was on hand and authorized a clerk to search the files for June 11 and 12. She seemed bent on demonstrating her efficiency to the assistant manager and produced the new address in less than fifteen minutes.

Paul didn't bother to caution the staff at Watson's Limited not to mention that he had been in to see them. He figured it would be another day before the local police got to Mrs. Burnell, and even then they might not realize that behind all that superficial chatter, she was a keen observer.

According to the information gained from Watson's Limited files, not only had Christine moved to Saltash, which was across the Tamar river in Cornwall, she had started using the name Elizabeth Duncan. Jack took off going west on A38. He found the address quickly, but the landlord was unimpressed by either Paul's charm or his police I.D. He seemed to take it as a personal insult that a police inspector from London was bothering the good citizens of Cornwall. Paul's statement that he had come to check out a report of a missing person called forth a barrage of rude questions.

"Why did they send you all the way from London? Aren't our

locals good enough? Don't take no hot shots from London to ring doorbells and bother folks with questions."

"They didn't *send* me. I came in person because I am a personal friend of Ms. Duncan's father," Paul lied to avoid being drawn into a jurisdictional dispute. "She was supposed to meet him in London, but she never showed up. She hasn't answered her phone and he's worried."

The landlord considered Paul's reasoning for a moment before beginning to grumble again. "Your Ms. Duncan ain't no innocent young girl, yer know. She goes out and no one catches sight of her for days."

"Regardless of how old and or guilty she might be, her father is worried and it's my job to find missing people. Now, will you let me and my assistant check out her flat or do I have to come back with a SWAT team and bust the door down?"

"All right! Ain't no cause to get nasty. That the way you big time operators do it in London? We're peaceable folks here in Cornwall."

"We don't like to get rough, but you are wasting valuable time if Ms. Duncan has come to grief."

"Yeah, yeah. What 'bout my time? I'll open her door, but I'm going in with yer. I don't want to be accused of stealing if she comes back and finds things a missin'."

"That suits us fine," Paul agreed. "Just don't touch anything."

"Bloody nuisance to have coppers crawling' all over the place," the landlord mumbled as he shuffled out of his flat and up the stairs. "Who do yer expect to find up there, Jack The Ripper?"

Jack and Paul followed him without comment.

Ms. Duncan's flat was small and Mr. Lawrence had been right about her three sticks of furniture. One of them was a large mahogany desk and a brief glance at it told them that someone had already searched the premises. The middle desk drawer had been forced open disengaging the locks on all the other drawers which now hung open. Papers were scattered over the top of the desk and thrown hastily to the floor. Using a pair of long, thin tweezers, Paul picked carefully through the mess. "Did you know that someone had been in here?" he demanded, turning toward the landlord.

The landlord stepped backward. "No . . . I don't see how . . . she must have given someone a key. The door's fine. Honestly, I never saw anything."

"We'll have to talk to the neighbors when we're done. Perhaps someone in the building saw something," Paul added, turning back to the pile of papers. He moved each sheet aside carefully as though playing a bizarre game of pick-up-sticks. Suddenly, among the phone bills and miscellaneous news clippings, Paul spotted the Marcolm and Blake logo. He pulled the sheets clear one by one and realized they were all of the same diagram of lens systems made at different copier settings. Together they told a tale of copies made rapidly on a machine the operator was not familiar with. Digging through the pile, Paul also unearthed an organization chart for Marcolm and Blake and an access card he suspected to be a duplicate of Stanley's. At the bottom of the middle drawer he found a Marcolm and Blake photo I.D. badge listing the name Elizabeth Duncan.

While Paul sorted papers, Jack searched the rest of the flat with the landlord trailing close behind. He noted that Ms. Duncan's closet was full of clothes for every occasion. All of them had labels from expensive shops in London. He took down the names of Elizabeth's five bottles of perfume, noting the one that seemed to be her favorite. There was a wooden jewelry box on the dresser, but the drawers were hanging open and empty, indicating that someone had emptied them in a hurry. Jack also made note of Elizabeth's phone number to check the records. Numerous dates were circled on the calendar which might indicate meetings, but no explanation was filled in.

"We might send another team by later to do a search for prints," Paul mentioned to allay the landlord's suspicion when the local police finally arrived.

While the landlord was busy watching Jack, Paul slipped his stash of papers and the I.D. badge into a plastic bag and slid it into his briefcase. When they were satisfied that they had gathered all the clues they could, they asked the landlord if he would introduce them to the other tenants on the floor. He was less than gracious about complying, but he took them around, more to keep an eye on them than to be helpful. Paul and Jack took turns asking questions, but no one reported having seen anything suspicious in or around the building. None of the tenants seemed to have taken any interest in Ms. Duncan other than the women noticing that she tended to wear tight fitting clothes and too much perfume, and the men noticing that she had a fine pair of legs.

"Let's ship these papers up to Ian in London to get them processed for prints," Paul suggested as he and Jack returned to their car. Ian McBriad was one of Brad's contacts at New Scotland Yard. He was thoroughly professional and could be trusted to assist with an investigation without interfering. He had worked with the team often enough to know that when they had pieced together a trail of evidence, the data would be given to him in strict confidence for follow-up by the Yard. "See about getting Ms. Duncan's phone records," Paul continued. "They might give us a lead."

"O.K. and I'll see if I can track down her company."

"Good. And see if you can figure out what this is all about," Paul said handing Jack what appeared to be a miniature video camera.

Jack took the camera and fiddled with it for a moment before shaking his head in admiration.

"She's either a clever girl or has some technical backup. This little gadget's rigged with a timer set to start recording at 7:45 a.m. and run until 8:30. It's designed to be held in place with this magnet. Want to bet that Stanley's desk lamp has a metal shade?"

"What would . . . shit! Keystrokes for Stanley's pass code. She's not some amateur, Jack. It would take a professional set up to interpret the results of that kind of recording."

"She obviously had some help duplicating Stanley's key card too. He may not have been trying to help her, but he was a weak link in the system."

"She must have found a better source. She got some classified information after she ditched him."

"That's for sure. Are you going to tell the Plymouth police about Christine's second flat?"

"Not just yet. They'll find it if they ask the right questions. If not . . . well, maybe I'll give them a clue in a day or so."

It was an anxious wait for the team, but three days later a messenger arrived with a package from Doris, their contact at British Telecom. The packet contained a record of every name and number Elizabeth had called from her Saltash flat, listing date and time of day. It didn't take much analysis to conclude that Elizabeth made more calls to someone named Bennett Wildridge than to anyone else. As Doris commented, it was obvious that Elizabeth was either dating Bennett, or he owed her money.

A quick check of Marcolm and Blake employee records indicated that Bennett was Elizabeth's contact. The puzzling snag was that Ian McBriad reported that the prints from Bennett's security clearance file did not match those found on the papers in Elizabeth's flat. Brad felt that in one confidential interview with Bennett he could link him to Marcolm and Blake security problems and settle the matter quietly. Once the team pulled out, the police could take over determining what had happened between Bennett and Elizabeth.

It didn't turn out to be that simple, however, for when Brad went to interview Bennett, he was nowhere to be found. Co-workers reported that he hadn't been seen at his work area for over a week. After more questioning someone remembered Bennett saying something about having to leave town on personal business. Brad decided that it would not be out of place of him to pay a visit to Mrs. Bennett Wildridge in his role as Doctor Chillingsworth.

Brad drove out to the house in Trematon alone. It was a fairly impressive place with a red brick exterior and well-kept grounds—altogether much more costly-looking than one would expect for someone in Bennett's position. Brad was not surprised, however, for Lilla had filled him in that Mrs. Wildridge was the one who had the money in the family. She was the third Mrs. Wildridge and it was rumored that Bennett had traded up each time.

An older woman with a bulldog frown opened the door in answer to Brad's ring. She listened to his explanation of being from Marcolm and Blake Ltd. with no expressed interest, took his card, and left him standing on the doorstep. She reappeared after five minutes and ushered him into a small study off the entrance hall. The room had dark cherry paneling enlivened only by the light reflecting from several crystal candleholders and the small brass door handles on the cupboards built into one entire wall. Brad stood eyeing the room critically for clues about its owners until the door opened and a woman who looked as though she might have stepped off the pages of a fitness magazine slid into the room. She appeared to be in her early thirties and her dark, shoulder-length hair was held away from her perfectly tanned face by an elastic sweatband. She was wearing pink stretch pants and a pink and white sweater. Her puffy eyes and tight-lipped expression did not match her gay plumage.

"Good afternoon, Doctor Chillingsworth. Sorry to keep you waiting, but I was in the shower after my workout. To what do I owe the pleasure of a visit from a representative of Marcolm and Blake?" she asked, stepping toward Brad. She had a glass of dark liquid in her hand, and from the smell of it, Brad knew it wasn't iced tea.

"I'm sorry to bother you, Mrs. Wildridge," Brad began politely, "but I need to talk to your husband. He hasn't been seen at his office for over a week and no one seems to know for certain where he is. I thought perhaps you might be able to help me."

"Have we met before?" she asked cagily. "I don't remember Bennett mentioning your name."

"I'm new at Marcolm and Blake actually, and no, we haven't met before."

"I didn't think so," she said slowly. "Did Roger Dremann send you to check up on Bennett?"

"I work for Roger, but he didn't send me. I have my own reasons for wanting to speak to your husband."

"I see," she said as she turned and walked to a cupboard to the right of the door. "Would you like a drink?" she asked pulling open a cherry wood door.

"No, thank you," Brad responded.

"Is it against Marcolm and Blake rules to drink during working hours?"

"I don't know. I haven't inquired yet. Do they have a reputation for having strict rules?"

"I wouldn't know. Bennett is not one for living by rules, any rules." She poured whiskey into her glass, closed the cupboard door, and settled onto one of the high back chairs.

Brad watched her for a moment and then sat in the chair across from her. "Is Bennett in the habit of going off without telling anyone?" he asked.

"Habit? My dear Doctor Chillingsworth, Bennett doesn't seem to live by habits. He does whatever he pleases."

Brad did not respond and she sipped her drink before continuing. "Bennett is careless about telling me where he is going. Occasionally he calls to tell me he has to stay late for a business meeting or some such thing. I've learned not to question him. I don't believe him, of course, but I no longer question him. Are you sure you wouldn't like a drink? I feel so dissipated when I drink alone."

"I didn't mean to make you feel uncomfortable. I'll have whatever you're drinking."

"Good," she said quickly putting her glass down on the side table and going to the cupboard. "Would you like ice? I've not forgotten how to do it right, you know. I just don't bother when I'm alone."

"Ice would be fine," Brad said and then paused before plunging on. "It must be hard to be in this big house all by yourself. Does Bennett go away often?"

She had her back to him, but Brad heard ice clink in a glass and then the cupboard door snapped shut. "Bennett is never home, Doctor Chillingsworth," she said coming back to Brad and handing him a glass. She settled into her chair again, drew her knees up to her chest and took up her glass. "Cheers!" she said, giving her drink a half-hearted wave in Brad's direction.

"Cheers," Brad responded. He took barely a taste of his drink and settled back in his chair. "When was the last time you saw your husband?" he asked casually.

She took a sip of her drink and paused as if deciding if she wanted to talk or not.

"Ten days ago. He came home in the middle of the afternoon and said he had to go out of town for a few days on business. That's what he always says, but it isn't true—none of it." She put her drink down and circled her knees with her arms. "The truth is, Doctor Chillingsworth, my husband chases other women. Heaven knows why. I give him anything he wants. I guess the grass is always greener . . ."

"How long have you been married?" Brad asked in a friendly manner.

"Four years—four long, lonely years. My father tried to warn me about Bennett, but I wouldn't listen. I met him just after my first husband died. Terence was keen for fast cars and his blasted AC Cobra did him in. Bennett is much older than I and I thought he would be more settled. He has a brilliant mind and had developed his career. I was wrong. I was terribly wrong. I know now. He married me for my money. I've become the butt of crude jokes at the club and the laughing stock of my social set."

"I am sorry to hear that. Surely your friends would not fault you for your husband's indiscretions."

Ms. Wildridge got up from her chair, went to the cupboard, and poured herself another drink. "I shouldn't drink this stuff," she mumbled almost to herself. "It dehydrates one something terrible, you know." She came back to her chair and sat before continuing "You don't know the half of it, Doctor Chillingsworth. Bennett has insulted and alienated all of my former friends. I don't even go to the club to work out anymore. I had a complete weight room installed right here. Not very social, but one hates to exercise when people are whispering behind your back. This house was a wedding present for Terence and me from my father. I used to love it when Terence was alive, but I've grown to loathe it. You're the first visitor I've had in weeks."

"That's very sad," Brad murmured sympathetically. "And you have no idea where your husband is now."

"No, but I suspect the bastard's run off with the woman he's been seeing."

"Do you know her name?"

"Does it really matter now that he's gone?"

"Perhaps not. I just thought the police might be able to trace her if you had a name."

"The police? Who wants the bloody police to get involved? The scandal is bad enough as is. As for names, I've given up trying to learn their names. No one tells me anything. I just get rumors, you see. Well, maybe that's best. If I knew their names, you can be sure they would regret having made a fool of me," she said bitterly.

Brad finished his drink quickly. "If you hear from Bennett, would you call me? I really need to talk to him."

Mrs. Wildridge seemed to be feeling the effects of all the alcohol or was lost in thought, for she didn't answer. She sat silently with her feet tucked up, as if protecting herself from the world. Her lips had tightened again.

Chapter Five

After leaving Mrs. Wildridge, Brad decided to pay a visit to Inspector Tomlin at police headquarters. To date the police had no idea that anyone had been stealing secrets from Marcolm and Blake and Brad was struggling to keep it that way. The police had confirmed that the dents on Stanley's car were the result of a minor traffic accident which he had reported to his insurance company, and Langston Crist had arranged for him to be released on bail. He had not returned to work, however.

Inspector Tomlin was just finishing an interview when Brad arrived and he greeted him warmly. "Well, if it isn't Chillingsworth from Marcolm and Blake. Come in! Come in! I never have had time to tell you how impressed I was with your assessment of Stanley Pommer."

"It was something of a lucky guess," Brad replied modestly.

"However you managed it, it was a good piece of work. What brings you here today?"

"I was just passing and I was curious as to whether there have been any new developments on the case."

"Not much really. That barrister Stanley hired talked him into admitting that he knew where Christine Saunders lived and I sent a man to have a look around."

"Really," Brad said, feigning surprise. "Did you find anything?"

"No. She moved out three months ago. We're trying to track her down through the removal companies, but it's slow going—takes a lot of leg work."

"Oh, Christ," Brad said apologetically. "I'm a bloody idiot! I was supposed to tell you a bit of news I had from Langston Crist. He went to check out Stanley's story about where Christine lived. She has moved, but Crist said he talked to a neighbor who remembered seeing the company van. They were from Watson's Limited."

"Well that's a bit of luck. I'll send someone right over."

"I'm sorry I didn't mention it before, but with Stanley off work, everyone at Marcolm and Blake is in a dither and I've been quite busy."

"That's understandable," Inspector Tomlin answered. He seemed glad to have a new tidbit of information to chew on.

After Brad left the police station, he decided that it was time to investigate the second lead the team had received from Doris at British Telecom. In addition to showing that Elizabeth Duncan had made frequent calls to Bennett Wildridge, her phone records indicated that she also called someone named Mysie Platt with singular regularity. Brad traced Mysie's address through Doris, but reasoned that she might open up more to a woman. Consequently, he decided to send Geilla, Kon's wife.

In order to give Geilla an opening, Brad set Jack to work to produce a link to Elizabeth Duncan. Using the equipment at Marcolm and Blake, Jack was able to enhance the rather poor photo on Elizabeth Duncan's fake I.D. badge. He then combined it with the name he had found for Elizabeth's business. Instead of using the post office box, however, Jack used Mysie Platt's address. By adding a splash of red, some bold lettering and printing the result on glossy paper, he produced a professional looking sales brochure that would do credit to any legitimate business. Jack was so pleased with his work, he printed several business cards to match the brochure.

Armed with the fake sales brochure, Geilla drove to Mysie's flat on Friday. It was her first assignment with the team since she had become pregnant with Edgar Paul. Although E.P., as little Edgar Paul was affectionately called, had been tiny at birth, Geilla had breast fed him for six months and he had grown strong and healthy. After being away from the team for so long, she felt a renewed sense of excitement tempered with guilt. She loved her son deeply, but felt he would be safe and well cared for by Brad's wife Mary. Mary was delighted to have the opportunity to have E. P. all to herself for a while. She longed for a baby of her own, and sometimes regretted the bargain she had made with Brad when they married, not to have children because of the dangerous nature of his work. She had tried to get Brad to change his mind on occasion, but so far he had been adamant.

Unfortunately, Charlotte Marné had not been happy about Geilla's decision to rejoin the team. Geilla still felt that her relationship with Charlotte was rather tenuous. She wasn't officially Charlotte's daughter-in-law, since Charlotte was not actually Kon's mother, although over the years she had fulfilled all the duties and obligations of that role. Kon felt unwavering loyalty to Charlotte and her husband, Edgar, and was eternally grateful that they had taken him from virtual slavery at a hotel in Milan and disciplined and nurtured him along with their own two sons. Under their strict tutelage, Kon had risen to a position of prominence in the banking world of Geneva and Paris.

Geilla was aware that it had cost Kon a great deal of emotional pain to go against their wishes in order to marry her. She did everything she could to win Charlotte's approval, and E.P.'s birth had done a lot to establish a bond between them.

Initially Geilla had joined the team in order to work close to Kon, but over the years, she had begun to play a larger and larger role in investigations. Why should she stay home to cook and clean and play housewife? When it came to producing a meal, Kon out shone her in the kitchen. He could make pastry so delicate you could read the morning paper through it, and he could command bread dough to raise by the sheer force of his personality. She had never seen him use a recipe or seem to be working. He just moved around the kitchen with calm certainty. She laughed that he could cook in his sleep, and he admitted that all the while he had worked at the hotel in Milan that was precisely what he had been forced to do in order to stay alive.

Actually, Geilla felt that Kon needed more careful watching than E.P. He had often been injured and even now was not fully recovered from his last ordeal. Oh, he pretended that his memory was back to normal, but she had lingering doubts. He was not about to discuss his difficulties with her, however. He was too private a person for that. No amount of beating or torture would ever change Kon's secretive nature. All those years of never admitting who his parents were or where he came from had put a mark on him.

Geilla arrived at Mysie's flat, rang the bell boldly, and asked for Elizabeth Duncan. When a woman's voice answered that no one by that name lived there, Geilla persisted.

"But Elizabeth *must* live here. She gave me a card with this address. It's listed on her sales brochure too."

"Sales brochure? What sales brochure? I have no idea what you're talking about. There must be some mistake."

"There can't be!" Geilla said, feigning distress. "Elizabeth is selling my house and helping me move to Plymouth."

"Did you say, selling your house?"

"Yes. Oh, please, you must help me find her," Geilla pleaded. "I don't understand what has happened, but my husband will kill me if he finds out I've messed things up again. I am supposed to be handling the move. Please, won't you at least take a look at the brochure? Please!"

There was a long silence before the woman responded, "Well, I don't know what good it will do, but I guess I can look. Come on up."

"Thank you. Thank you so much. I don't know where to turn and my husband will have a fit if I've lost our money."

A moment later Geilla heard the door buzz and she hurried in. She took the stairs to the second floor and saw a young woman waiting in the doorway of a flat at the far end of the hall. The woman gestured hesitantly and Geilla hurried forward waving the brochure and babbling excitedly, "Thank you. My name is Audrey—Audrey Weeks. It is very kind of you to help me. I'm not very good at business matters, I'm afraid, and I just don't know what my husband, Patrick, will do if I've done something stupid."

"Yeah, I know the deal. I've been there a few times myself," the young woman answered. "Let's have a look at that brochure. I can't imagine why it has my add . . . bloody hell! Where did you get this?"

"I told you, Elizabeth Duncan gave . . ."

"When? When did you see her?" the young woman demanded.

"It was over a week ago. We had a business deal, or at least I thought we did. What's wrong?"

"Look, you better come in. I don't understand what she's up to either, but it's very like her. She never tells me anything."

"Oh, dear," Geilla responded in mock alarm and stepped into the flat. As the young woman closed the door behind Geilla, a little girl ran into the hall calling, "Mummy? Mummy?"

From the quick glimpse Geilla had of the child before the young woman scooped her into her arms, she judged her to be about two years old. The woman held the girl protectively and crooned a promise that Geilla sensed had been made many times recently. "No, sweetheart, it's not mummy. Mummy will be back soon. I promise. You know she's real busy, luv, but she'll come. She'll come."

Without looking at Geilla, the young woman carried the child into the sitting room. Geilla followed. When the woman sat down, Geilla followed suit without waiting for an invitation. She sat quietly for a few minutes, watching the young woman hug the child with obvious affection.

"I'll get you some lunch, Lonie. Are you hungry?" the woman questioned and the child nodded her head vigorously.

Ignoring Geilla, the woman set the child down, took her by the hand, and walked her out of the room. Geilla waited a few moments during which she heard cupboard doors being opened and closed rapidly, then she went to look for the woman. She found her in the small kitchenette. The child was seated at a miniature table in the corner. She looked the picture of contentment as she took a bite of her single slice of bread, then smiled and waved it at Geilla. Geilla noticed an empty jar of Marmite and an empty bread wrapper on the counter. The woman opened and closed a few more cupboard doors and frowned. "That's the end of it. What am I going to do when she gets hungry again?" she asked Geilla, shaking her head hopelessly and biting her lip.

"What's happened?" Geilla asked sympathetically. "Do you know where Elizabeth is?"

The woman looked at Geilla and shook her head. "Not in front of her," she whispered. "Let's go in the other room."

Geilla nodded. As she backed out of the room, she heard the woman telling the child to be a good girl and eat her lunch. When the young woman was seated across from her, holding her head in her hands, she inquired again, "Do you know where Elizabeth is?"

The woman looked up in frustration. "I don't even know any Elizabeth. I know she uses different names, but that picture . . . that's Elaina."

"Elaina? Elaina what? I really have to find her."

"Elaina Spengler. At least that's what she told me, and I just don't know what's happening. Elaina left over a week ago. She said she had a job, but it's not like to her stay away like this. She always calls to check on Lonie. I'm worried sick."

"Did she tell you anything else about what she was going to do?" Geilla asked gently.

"No. I think she's working as an estate agent, but I never saw that brochure. She has a lot of different jobs. I never know what she's doing. She keeps it that way on purpose. But she's never been away this long. I've run out of money! I've run out of food! The rent's due next week! What am I going to do? I could manage on the street, but what about the baby?"

"She's Elaina's baby isn't she?" Geilla said softly.

"Yes. I just take care of her, but I love her like she was mine."

"I can see that," Geilla said sympathetically. "She's a beautiful child."

"She's so good, too. Elaina loves her, but she's never here. She says she don't want anybody to know Alona is her kid, so I pretend to the neighbors that I'm her mum."

"What's your name?" Geilla asked although she knew the answer.

"My name's Mysie, Mysie Platt."

"How did you come to meet Elaina?"

"We met in Milton Keynes," Mysie said with a dry laugh. "We were on the same maternity ward. She had Alona, and me . . . I had a little boy. He only lived one day—poor little tike. He was so sweet, so beautiful. I never even got to hold him until it was all over. He was so tiny . . ." she sighed deeply with remembering. "He was too early, ya see. He didn't have time to get all grown and he couldn't breathe right."

"I'm terribly sorry," Geilla said. "I know how it feels to lose a baby. My first little boy drowned when he was only three years old."

"It's hard. It's so hard," Mysie said slowly. "It was a shame, ya know. If he'd had just a little more time . . . but Mark . . . he didn't really want a baby. Hell, I didn't think I wanted one when I first found out I was pregnant. But then, as I started gettin' bigger and I could feel him jumpin' around, I started to look forward to seeing

41

him. Co's I didn't know it was going to be a boy. Toward the end I started buying clothes and things . . . just bits and pieces here and there. I even thought of calling my mum to let her know. But I didn't. Mark was against it. He said she took sides against him when she kicked me out for taking up with him. I wish I'd had called her.

"She was right about Mark. He wasn't good to me. He'd slap me around over some little thing. Something he didn't like about my clothes or my hair. Oh, he'd buy me a little bracelet, now and then, just some cheap trinket and I'd think he really wanted to make it up to me. Then we'd just go on for a while. Maybe we'd go to a dance or something. He never took me anywhere nice. We'd just hang out with his friends and drink and maybe he'd smoke a joint or two. I used to, but I stopped once I knew about the baby.

"Anyway, he started getting meaner right about the time I was getting bigger and everybody knew I was pregnant. I thought maybe if we could get married he would settle down and everything would work out all right. But he didn't want that. I guess he never wanted me either, but I was too dumb to see it. I was just a kid when I started hanging out with him. I was 15. He was 22. It seemed like he just came struttin' by one day with them killer good looks and the next thing I know I'm in his flat with my knickers off. Oh he was good, no doubt about that, but it didn't last."

"That's a shame," Geilla said. "I met the man I'm married to now when I was 12, but I didn't like him very much. We had a lot of problems before we finally got together. Did you ever think of leaving Mark?"

"I don't think I ever thought about it serious like. I would get mad from time to time, but I never did anything about it. I never planned nothing. I was afraid of him, but I was even more afraid to be without him—without nobody. Does that sound crazy?"

"No . . . I think I can understand. I once married a man I didn't love because I couldn't figure out anything else to do. I felt very alone and helpless at that time."

"You did that?"

"Yes. I was 17. My father was sick, and I had hurt my hand and couldn't work."

"Well at least he married you. Mark didn't want that. He started slapping me around more and more often and then one night he got drunk and really took after me. He kept punching my stomach and calling me a whore. I must have started screaming 'cause the neighbors called the coppers. I was bleeding pretty bad and was really afraid for the baby. I don't know what happened to Mark. I don't even remember how I got to hospital. I was hurting so bad and I was scared. I didn't have nobody to talk to and I didn't know what I was supposed to do. Somehow I got through it all and they was telling me I had a little boy. I kept askin' to see him, but they told me he was too small and they had to keep him in a machine. Later they let me go down to see him."

Mysie stopped talking and Geilla put her hand over hers. "That must have been very hard for you. My second little boy was very tiny, but at least they let me hold him. His father was scared to death that he was going to die. He never told me he was worried, but he wouldn't let the baby out of his sight for almost two months. I think he would have gone crazy if anything had gone wrong."

"It was hard, but . . . you know . . . I think Mark had convinced me that nothing good was ever going to happen to me. It just didn't seem like that beautiful little baby was really mine."

"But then you met Elaina and got the chance to look after another beautiful baby."

"Yeah. As soon as she saw my bruises she knew what had happened. She told me she had been slapped around a few times herself. She wasn't living with anyone at the time. She had come to Milton Keynes to have her baby so that no one would find out about it. She said she'd had a couple of abortions, but she wanted this baby. She was tickled pink it was a girl."

"So you've been with Elaina ever since hospital?"

"Yeah. She needed someone to take care of Alona, and I didn't have nowhere else to go. I didn't want to go back with Mark."

"Don't you have any money you could use for food?"

"No. Elaina don't pay me to watch Alona. She just lets me stay here. She pays the rent and gives me money for food. I don't usually complain. She's been real good about havin' me here. It's the nicest place I've ever lived. Elaina's used to nice things. She's always telling me about all the parties she used to go to on people's yachts and the times she flew to Switzerland just to ski. She has beautiful clothes and jewelry, and she wants it to be nice for Alona. She said she don't want her baby to want for nothing."

Geilla took a quick look around the flat. Yes, Christine or Elaina or whatever your real name is, you have accomplished that. It's all very nice, but what now? Didn't you realize what you were getting into when you started stealing secrets from Marcolm and Blake? Didn't you stop to think about your baby? Look who's talking! Geilla thought with a twinge of guilt.

"Well, maybe I could help you," Geilla offered. "Most of my money is tied up in the move, but I have some cash we could use for groceries."

"But that don't seem right," Mysie objected half-heartedly.

"Well, we can't let the baby starve. It would only be until her mother comes back."

"Oh, I just don't know what to do. Elaina's sort of crazy sometimes, but she's never done nothing like this."

"Maybe we could help each other. I need to find out if Elaina has a check for me. She was supposed to get a deposit from whomever she lined up to buy my house. Did she say anything to you about it?"

Mysie shook her head. "No. She don't tell me nothing."

"Oh dear. Patrick is going to be very angry with me. He's a good man and I love him, but he does have a temper."

"Can't you just tell him you don't know where the money is?"

"Oh, I couldn't possibly do that. You don't know Patrick. And it's not the first time I've messed things up. I know I'm not good with money, but Elizabeth seemed so nice and she was very helpful. She said she would take care of everything for me. Her brochure looked so impressive—I even showed it to Patrick. Can you think of any place that Elizabeth might have gone? Did she have other clients we could call?"

"I really don't know nothing about her business."

"Oh God! Patrick is going to kill me," Geilla wailed, picking up the brochure again. "Do you suppose she really does have a post box somewhere? It's listed on the brochure."

Mysie brightened a bit. "She does have a post box. I was with her one day when she picked up her mail."

"Then at least that part may be true about her business. I don't suppose you know where the key is?" Geilla inquired hopefully.

"Yes I do!" Mysie said, as if she suddenly remembered it. "Elaina said she kept the key here for safe keeping. She said she might have to call and have me pick up her mail sometime. I never did, but I know where she keeps the key."

"Wonderful! Do you suppose you could check the box to see if she got a deposit for my house? I really would like to tell Patrick that the money is coming. It would make it so much easier to tell him I don't know where Elizabeth is."

"That's not so easy to do. The box is over at Estover. I have no way to get there."

"That's not a problem. I have a car. We could get some groceries and then go check the box."

"I don't know," Mysie said hesitantly. "Elaina might not like it."

"But we don't know where she is or when she's coming back. You can't let Alona go hungry and I need to know if anyone's made a deposit on my house. You don't have to give me the check. I just need to have something to tell Patrick. Oh please. I think you can understand how angry he's going to be that the deal is being delayed."

"Oh I understand that part of it," Mysie agreed.

"Then please, help me to find out if there's a deposit from whomever is buying my house. At least then I can tell Patrick the deal is moving forward."

"If I open the box, you promise you won't take anything?"

"Certainly! If there is a deposit check it will be made out to Elizabeth or her business. There's nothing I can do with it."

"And you'll give me money for groceries?"

"Yes. I brought some cash with me. For all his faults, Patrick will understand that I couldn't let a little girl go hungry."

Mysie sighed. "I don't know what else I can do."

"I'm sure Elaina would understand that you have to take care of Alona."

"Yes, she makes sure Alona has everything she ever wanted. All right. I'll get the key."

"Oh, thank you. I'm sure things will work out all right," Geilla said and hated herself for lying. *Well, I can't bring Elaina back, but I will do all I can to see that Mysie and Alona are taken care of.*

After a short wait, Mysie appeared wearing a cloth coat and carrying a light blue jacket and matching bonnet for Alona. The girl seemed excited about going out and Geilla guessed she didn't often get the chance.

Geilla felt another pang of guilt, or was it a mother's longing, when she saw Alona's blonde hair curling out from underneath her pom-pom-topped bonnet. *Am I being a bad mother by leaving Edgar Paul? I thought I was helping in the search for a murderer, but now I am helping a young woman and a baby. Would Edgar Paul understand? I know Kon would. He loves his family fiercely, but he works tirelessly to fight injustice.*

It was a short drive to the market and Alona seemed to enjoy the ride. She sang and laughed all the while. Geilla encouraged Mysie to stock up on whatever her heart desired, but Mysie was not accustomed to being frivolous. Aside from two loaves of bread, four bottles of fresh milk, and two dozen eggs, she chose only potatoes, carrots, apples, two pounds of ground mince, and a jar of Marmite. Geilla added some bottled fruit juice and a small green cabbage to the cart. Then when Mysie wasn't looking, she slipped in a tin of biscuits.

Mysie looked sad as the checker rang up the bill. Geilla paid in cash and pretended not to notice. "I feel so much better knowing you'll have something to feed the baby when I leave," she said as they carried the bags out to the car. "You know, my husband is an excellent cook, but when he's by himself, he quite often forgets to eat."

Geilla drove back to Elaina's flat and helped Mysie put away the groceries. She was pleased that Mysie had shown such good sense in choosing what she fed Alona. She wondered how often Alona saw her real mother. She hoped for Alona's sake that it hadn't been often.

It was a longer drive to the post office, but Alona was still eager and happy as she sat in Mysie's lap and peeped out the window. When they got to the post office, Geilla pushed open the door, and

Mysie carried little Alona into the building. Mysie had the key ready, but they had to search for the number. Alona started squirming as Mysie put the key in the door and Geilla offered to hold her so that Mysie could use both hands to sort the papers in the box. There actually was very little mail, but Geilla noted that one business envelope was addressed to *Select Estate Agents*.

"That could be the deposit check," she told Mysie excitedly.

"I suppose so," Mysie conceded, "but there's no way to be sure."

Geilla bounced Alona in her arms and turned her back to Mysie as if engrossed in entertaining the baby before adding casually, "Couldn't you open it and just take a peek? After all, I am a customer."

"Well . . . it don't seem right to go looking through Elaina's mail, but what the hell—she's pissed me off disappearing and leaving Lonie without no food." Mysie slid her finger under the flap of the envelope and tore it open. "Besides, it can't do no harm to look, can it?"

"Of course not!" Geilla agreed readily. "It's just business stuff. It wasn't marked personal or anything like that."

"It is business," Mysie confirmed. "It's a check to *Select Estate Agents*. Could that be the deposit you're looking for?"

"It might be. How much is it for?"

"Five hundred pounds. Does that sound right?"

"A bit small, but it could be," Geilla said, still keeping her back to the open box. "Who's it from? I can't remember the name Elizabeth told me. I should have written it down somewhere."

"It's from Kenneth Wobel."

"Wobel . . . Wobel—that does sound familiar. Does it show an address?" Geilla asked turning as if she was only mildly curious.

"It's from Cornwood."

"Cornwood? No that couldn't be for my house. Elizabeth said the man was from Plymouth. Damn! Are there any other checks?"

"No, I'm afraid that's it."

"Oh dear. Patrick is going to have a fit," Geilla moaned.

"I'm sorry," Mysie signed. "Is there anything else I can do?"

"I don't think so," Geilla replied and then as an afterthought added, "When did you say you last saw Elaina?"

Mysie thought for a moment before replying, "It was about ten days ago. I can't imagine what she's up to."

Mysie closed the box and relocked it. Geilla handed her the baby before suggesting quietly, "Maybe you should check with the police. Something could have happened to her."

"I don't know," Mysie sighed. "I'm not sure Elaina would approve. She never told me much, but I got a feeling Elaina would just as soon the police didn't know about some of the things she does."

"Oh," Geilla said, feigning surprise. "But still . . . ten days is a long time. What if something has happened to her?"

"I don't know."

"You could report that she's missing. You wouldn't have to give a lot of details. After all, you can't tell anyone what you don't know."

"Maybe you're right," Mysie conceded. "It really ain't like her not to call about Alona, but I don't know . . ."

"Of course she would call. I know I do when I have to be away from my baby. That's what has me concerned, Mysie. I really think you should talk to the police. I could drive you there."

Mysie bounced Alona up and down a few times and kissed her on the nose which made her laugh. "Where do you suppose your mum has got to, Lonie?" she said lightly before turning to Geilla and adding more seriously, "I just don't like talkin' to cops, Audrey, and I don't want to have Elaina get all upset with me."

"It can't do any harm to report her missing. You don't have to tell her you did it if she turns up tomorrow."

"Yeah, I know, but then I'd have to call up and say she's back and they might have questions. What if she don't come back and they find out Alona's not my kid?"

Geilla would have said more, but just then Alona who seemed worn out from the excitement of going out started to squirm and fuss.

"Lonie's tired," Mysie said quickly. "Let's just go home. Elaina's got to come back. She's just got to."

"Well, all right if that's how you feel," Geilla agreed.

Mysie was very quiet during the drive back and didn't object when Geilla followed her up to the flat. As they came by the kitchen, Mysie tossed her keys and handbag onto the counter and carried Alona into the sitting room. Geilla carefully set her bag next to

Mysie's. Mysie seemed detached, and Geilla suspected she was becoming despondent about her situation. She sat, hardly aware of Geilla and barely paying attention to Alona who sat beside her pulling on her sleeve. Finally Geilla went into the kitchen and poked around in the cupboards. It was a modern kitchen and Geilla guessed Mysie was worrying how she would manage to keep the flat if Elaina didn't turn up. She put the kettle on the stove, then quietly pressed each of Mysie's keys against the Plasticine she carried in containers made to resemble makeup compacts. She wasn't positive which of the keys opened the front door, but she guessed it was the one with the bit of red yarn tied around it.

Mysie looked up in surprise when Geilla carried a tray out to the sitting room. "Oh thanks, Audrey," she muttered. "You're a luv for doing this. Poor Lonie must be starved." She quickly took up a plate of scrambled eggs and started to spoon them into the child. Geilla poured tea for Mysie and herself and nibbled on a piece of toast.

"Did you finish school before you took up with Mark?" she asked trying to assess the extent of Mysie's difficulty.

"No," Mysie said softly, shaking her head. "I just kind of . . . stopped, you know. Being with Mark seemed much more exciting. My mum was fit to be tied. She kept saying 'you've only got another year,' but a year seemed so long . . . I should have stuck it out."

"Have you ever had a job?"

"Not a real one . . . I mean with regular hours and stuff. When I found out about the baby, somebody at the clinic gave me the name of a lady who ran a beauty shop. She showed me how to wash the customers' hair and clean up the shop. It wasn't much, but she was real nice to me. She made sure I drank lots of milk and . . . he would have been a healthy little tike if he'd had the chance to finish growing."

Geilla noticed that Alona's head was starting to droop and she waited, sipping her tea, while Mysie carried her into the bedroom and put her to bed. When Mysie came back she poured herself another cup of tea, but sat without drinking it.

"Do you know if Elaina has any family?" Geilla asked.

"She never mentioned any. Alona was all I knew about. I don't know what to do, Audrey. If Elaina don't come back, there ain't no way I can keep the flat. I can't even afford to feed Alona."

Geilla wasn't sure what she was supposed to say. The situation had been bothering her all day. She had come here expecting to find a lead to Elaina's business, but instead she found herself in the middle of a dead woman's private life. After seeing Mysie and holding Alona, it wasn't a fact-finding mission anymore. Well, what was it? She wasn't from Social Services. She wasn't sure how Brad would view the situation, but she was sure that Kon would have a fit if Alona ended up being separated from Mysie. Having been orphaned at thirteen, Kon would go to great lengths to see that children were kept in a family situation. Well, maybe there was a way to continue her fact-finding and help Mysie.

"Does Elaina have anything valuable you could sell to raise some cash?" she asked hopefully.

"Valuable? Like what? I can't go selling her car even if I did know where it was?"

"What about her personal belongings? Any jewelry?"

A look of relief spread across Mysie's face. "Jewelry? Sure! Why didn't I think of that? Elaina 'as tons of stuff. I could pawn it to pay the rent and when Elaina comes home she could get it back again."

"That's very sensible, Mysie," Geilla answered. "What kind of stuff does Elaina have? Could I see it?"

"Why? You interested in buying?"

"No, not for myself, but I know something about jewelry. If it's really good, you would get more if you found an individual buyer. Say in London."

"London! You might as well tell me the Queen might want it. There ain't no way I'm gonna get to London, and I wouldn't know where to go if I got there."

"Maybe I could arrange something for you. I have a few contacts."

Mysie was suddenly suspicious. "What kind of business are you in, Audrey? Do you think I'm dumb enough to turn over Elaina's stuff to a stranger?"

"I'm not in the jewelry business. I just happen to know you could probably get more for nice pieces from a buyer in London than from a pawnshop in Plymouth. And I don't expect you to give me the jewelry. I could take pictures of it and see if I could arrange a sale. Maybe I could even find out where she bought it so we would know what it's worth."

"That sounds reasonable enough," Mysie said contritely. "I'm sorry I got smart. I'm just upset. Elaina's runnin' off leaves me in a bad way. I wasn't exactly prepared for it."

"I understand that. It's very worrisome, but you've got to think of Alona and how you are going to care for her."

"You're right. I love Lonie like she was my own. Elaina knows that. She never gets jealous. She wants Lonie to be taken care of."

"And I can see you do a wonderful job. Why don't we look at the jewelry to see what we have to work with? If nothing comes of it, at least you'll know we tried."

"All right. I've got to do something."

When Geilla saw Elaina's collections she knew it would be easy to trace the pieces. Each one was still in its original box with the name of the store emblazoned on the top. There were seven boxes in all. Four showed signs of wear indicating Elaina had owned them for a while, and three were newer and were all from the same shop. One box was empty and Geilla guessed it held the necklace and matching earrings that Elaina was wearing when she was killed. Looking at the jewelry, Geilla knew that all of if had been gifts. Aside from one gold broach set with four emeralds, the diamond necklaces were meant to dazzle and impress. Geilla looked over the collection with admiration and went to get her camera from the car. She took shots of all the pieces, being careful to get close-ups of any markings on the clasps. She knew Mappin and Webb would have purchase records of the expensive items that made up Elaina's collection.

"What are you goin' to do about your house?" Mysie asked after they had carefully packed the jewelry back in Elaina's dresser drawer.

"I don't know," Geilla sighed. "I suppose I'll have to tell Patrick what happened and listen to him rant and rave. I'll probably end up looking for another agent. I've got to sell my house."

Chapter Six

Kon sat across from Brad in Brad's room at the Duke of Cornwall Hotel. He had only recently been allowed to take a field assignment with the team. For months he had been restricted to translating, and verifying documents and sorting through bank records. Almost a year had passed since he had been kidnapped by the Direct Action terrorists while working to help Etienne Rubard. He was still suffering the effects of the vicious beatings he had endured. His fractured wrist and cracked ribs had healed well, but his violent, recurring nightmares had finally driven him to seek counseling. It was not in his nature to trust, and discussing his feelings had been almost physically painful for him.

Although most of his memory had slowly returned, he still could not recall the details of what the terrorists had done to him. Their cruelty was somehow linked with his step-father's brutality and it ran deep within his consciousness. He knew he was impatient and had a hard time controlling his temper and had always feared that he would turn violent himself.

But the counselor had shown him that through all the brutality he had clung to the memories of his loving mother and the teaching of Father Demetrius. From the time at age eight when he had been brought before the old Greek priest to confess his sins, until he left home at age thirteen, he had spent many quiet hours talking and studying with the priest. It was from that gentle, saintly old man that he had absorbed the ideas of love and forgiveness. Those ideals were as much a part of him as his quick temper.

He was glad to be back with the team and had been on the phone all afternoon, following up on the name, Kenneth Wobel, that Geilla had unearthed from the check in Elaina's post box. Elaina had established an account under her business name and had told Stanley that she worked as an estate agent, but so far the team had not been able to confirm that she had any clients.

"So what did you dig up about Kenneth Wobel?" Brad asked,

pouring coffee into a cup and carefully placing it on the highly-polished wooden table between them.

"Quite a bit actually. Unlike our Ms. Spengler, he doesn't have a string of aliases to sift through. He's from London originally and worked for the Department of Trade and Industry until about two years ago. Then there was a shake up in the department and he was booted out—no scandal involved, just a political thing. He must have some contacts in this area, because he's now working as a consultant for a computer firm in Plymouth. He's probably cashing in on his connections with the Department of Trade. He's managed to buy a sizeable place near Cornwood, but it's mortgaged to the hilt."

"With those connections, he could be the conduit Elaina was using to sell Marcolm and Blake trade secrets," Brad responded.

"It certainly looks suspicious," Kon said, taking up his coffee. "According to Wobel's bank records, he's been making payments to *Select Estate Agents* regularly for the last six months."

Brad smiled. With Kon's connections in the banking industry, there was hardly any financial information he couldn't get his hands on. He probably knows the cost of my yearly upkeep on "Wavely Farm." Fortunately, Kon is too secretive to ever tell anyone anything. I admire him for his ability to keep a confidence, but that trait almost cost him his life on the Rubard case.

"How much has she got from Wobel so far?" Brad asked.

"A little over sixty thousand pounds."

"That's not much for the kind of information she's been stealing."

"It does seem low, but maybe she doesn't know what it's really worth."

"But surely Bennett would know and he's chronically short of cash."

"Well, I intend to visit Mr. Wobel this afternoon and find out what he thought he was paying for."

"Capital idea! But be careful, Kon. If Wobel was Elaina's contact, he might have some nasty friends."

Kon was about to remind Brad that he didn't need to be told how to do his job, but he checked his tongue. His record for getting into trouble was too long to defend with one sharp remark. He knew that it took a toll on Brad when anyone on the team got hurt and he had done more than his share to add to the distinguished gray in Brad's hair.

"Thanks for the coffee . . . and the advice," was all he said.

Kon drove to Cornwood alone. Geilla had taken the train to London to check on the source of Elaina's jewelry. Paul had offered to go, but she had insisted on going herself. She admitted to Kon when they said good-bye at the train station that she felt an overpowering need to check on E.P. She didn't want Brad to think that she doubted Mary's ability to care for her child, but it was Friday and she wanted to spend the weekend with him. Kon knew Geilla contributed a lot to the team, but she was a mother now, and he was glad she hadn't forgotten it. He was slowly getting over his irrational fear that his son was going to die suddenly of some terrible ailment, but he had wanted a child of his own for too long to take the responsibility lightly.

The Wobel's home was large and stately, with four brick chimneys, but Kon judged it a bit too formal for his taste. He liked to relax and be comfortable in his home and preferred investing his money for his son's education, rather than wasting it on display. He was grateful that Geilla seemed to feel the same. Kon had been surprised that Wobel agreed to see him at home when he had called to make an appointment. Kon had given his name as James Logan, and explained that he was doing an audit of Elizabeth Duncan's business, *Select Estate Agents,* for the Registrar of Companies.

In response to Kon's ring, an older man with a sparse fringe of hair and dark-rimmed glasses opened the door.

"Yes, yes, I am Kenneth Wobel," he said in answer to Kon's inquiry. "Come in. Come in."

"I'm sorry to bother you at home, but it is a rather private matter," Kon apologized.

"Yes quite. Frankly, I'm anxious to get it out of the way before my wife gets home. She's at one of her infernal bridge tournaments. She's absolutely mad for bridge—goes all the time. I suppose I shouldn't fuss. Gives her something to do and she's actually rather good at it."

"I see. Well, perhaps her absence will allows us to talk more freely."

"Yes, perhaps so," Wobel mumbled nervously. He ushered Kon into a small study off the foyer. Touching the back of a chair as a signal as to where Kon should sit, he hurried around a large desk and sat facing Kon with his back to the window. Kon studied him for a few moments, noting that he was perspiring slightly and seemed very ill at ease. He sat away from the desk, as if wishing that the separation between himself and Kon were even greater.

At last Kon broke the silence. "How long have you been doing business with Elizabeth Duncan?"

Wobel started slightly at the name and put his hand to his head as if thinking. "I would say just a few months," he answered.

"Just a few months . . . ," Kon repeated slowly before adding, "Would that be two months or a bit longer?"

Wobel tried to look firm as he answered, "Two months," but Kon had sat across the desk from too many loan applicants to be fooled.

"I see," Kon said, seeming to accept Wobel's answer. Then he added quietly, "Does your accountant handle the transactions?"

Wobel cleared his throat before answering, "No I handle them myself."

"Then I think your sense of time is faulty, Mr. Wobel, because your bank records show that you've been making payments to *Select Estate Agents* for over six months."

A look of panic passed across Wobel's face, but it was quickly replaced by anger. "And just who has empowered you to check my confidential bank records?" he demanded.

"I have done some preliminary investigation, Mr. Wobel. The Registrar of Companies and the police have reason to believe that Ms. Duncan was running a massive real estate scam that has cheated hundreds of potential home buyers."

Wobel looked even more panicked. "Surely you don't think I am involved! I know nothing about her blasted business!"

Kon dropped the calm inquiry tone and went on the attack, purposely making his question sound like an accusation. "Then why have you been paying her all this time? As far as I can tell, there hasn't been any transfer of property or goods."

Kon knew he had hit home when Wobel stood abruptly and turned his back to him. Kon probed again, warning, "If you're running this scam with her, it will only be a matter of time before the Registrar tracks you down."

Wobel seemed preoccupied with looking out the window. Finally Kon continued softly, "If she pulled you into this, there's still time to give evidence and pull out quietly. I'm sure the Registrar would be grateful for your cooperation. They might even . . ."

"I can't cooperate!" Wobel suddenly shouted, turning to face Kon. His face was a study of fear and confusion. "I told you I don't know anything about her business!"

"Then why were you paying her?" Kon demanded.

"Oh God! After all this time . . . she's blackmailing me! The bitch is blackmailing me!"

Kon was only mildly surprised. "Blackmail . . . About what?"

"Does it matter?" Wobel almost pleaded.

"I'm afraid it does?"

"Oh Christ! What a bloody mess!" Wobel said and fairly collapsed into his chair.

"Start at the beginning," Kon said quietly.

Wobel sighed before starting. "I met Elizabeth about three years ago at a party in London. I was there alone and . . . if you've seen her you know what I mean . . . I couldn't take my eyes off her. She must have been on the prowl because even then I couldn't believe how quickly one thing led to another. Before I knew it, I'd rented an apartment for her and started giving her presents. My poor wife never suspected anything. She didn't know anything about my business affairs—still doesn't. It was easy to hide the expense in my business accounts. I don't know how long the affair would have gone on, but one night Elizabeth told me she was pregnant. She said it was my child and it seemed more than a possibility. I was appalled. I thought she knew better than to let it happen. She was no innocent—I knew it even then, when I was blind to everything else.

"I told her I had no intention of starting another family. I have two sons in school and that is quite enough. I told her I would give her money to have an abortion. She agreed and left London to have it done. I don't know where she went. I waited for her to come back, but she never did. Right about that time there was a change in the department and I became redundant.

"My wife and I came back here. All her people live in Plymouth. She knows everyone and we thought that might help. Some cousin or other of hers got me a position as a consultant to a computer firm. I still have some contacts in London which helps. I bought this big house for her . . . from guilt, I suppose. It's mortgaged to the hilt, as you've probably found out. I was starting to pull things together when all of a sudden, Elizabeth showed up with a baby she claimed was mine. I was crushed. I tried denying the baby part, but she had canceled checks and jewelry and furs from the affair. I was sunk, so I paid, and I paid, and I paid! Christ will it never end? And now you want to drag me into her real estate scam. Well, she's capable of gulling people into anything, but I'm not involved in her latest scam. So investigate all you will. You won't find a shred of evidence. Ask her why I was paying!"

"That's not so easy, Mr. Wobel. She's dead," Kon replied.

"Dead?" Wobel sounded surprised, but Kon wasn't sure if he believed Wobel or not.

"What happened? Did one of her former lovers strangle her?"

"Why do you suggest murder?" Kon asked immediately.

"I don't know. Perhaps because that's what I wanted to do when she told me she was pregnant. Or maybe because that's what she's done to my life. I don't care how she died."

"Well, I will tell you anyway. Her body was found along the road near here and she had been murdered."

Wobel considered this information thoughtfully for a moment before replying, "Oh bloody hell! After what I just told you I suppose I'm a suspect."

"I'm afraid so, Mr. Wobel."

"Why didn't the police come instead of sending you?"

"Oh, they'll be here. I just had to gather a few details for my department."

"Well, you won't be able to find any more evidence tying me to her murder than to her real estate scams."

"I hope not, Mr. Wobel, but what about your wife?"

"Frances? What about her?"

"Are you sure she never knew about your affair with Elizabeth?"

"Absolutely!"

"What time will she be home?"

"Why?"

"Perhaps you'd better have a talk with her before the police arrive."

Geilla had satisfied herself that little E.P. was fine. She had known it all along, but still, it was a comfort to hold him again. She questioned the wisdom of going back to the team. After all, she and Kon didn't need the money. But she wasn't doing it for the money—neither was Kon. They were both on the team to gain the personal satisfaction of seeing that criminals were found and punished and that innocent people were given a chance to straighten out their lives. She and Kon both felt immensely pleased that Etienne Rubard and Edouard Sabasté had been rescued from the Direct Action terrorist group and given the opportunity to do something productive with their lives. She had a hard time explaining her feelings to Charlotte Marné, however.

Charlotte had brought up the subject of Geilla's working more than once. She had made the mistake of bringing it up in front of Kon, however, and he quickly reminded her that although she had not pursued a career outside her home, she had left her sons in the care of a series of nannies, au pair girls, and even Kon himself, while she went about her volunteer work for numerous charities. Kon reminded her that Albert and Charles had not suffered because she was not always with them. Although Charlotte would not admit that Kon had a point, no more was said about Geilla's return to work.

Geilla had spent the weekend at Mary's, holding E.P. and just watching him sleep. She felt a renewed sense of gratitude that despite her difficult pregnancy and his premature birth, he had turned out very healthy and very beautiful. On Monday morning, however, she disciplined herself to get up early and catch the train to London. She caught the Bakerloo line up to Oxford Circus and struggled through the throngs of shoppers on her way along Regent Street. As she passed Liberty's she determined that on her way back from the jewelry store, she would stop and browse. As soon as she got to Mappin and Webb she knew that whoever had given Elaina her jewelry had been concerned with quality, not price. The shop boasted not only "By Appointment to the Queen," but also "By Appointment to the Prince of Wales."

Using the identification that Brad had supplied, she was able to pass herself off as Nicole Trindor, insurance investigator. From a search of the store's records she learned that most of the jewelry had been purchased by a man named Steven Compton. However, after looking at the photos, the staff agreed that one of the necklaces had come from a company in France. The manager assured Geilla that no one in the U.K. carried such at item. After thanking the staff for their information, she called Compton to make an appointment. Fortunately, he agreed to see her that very afternoon. Geilla checked her watch and hurried back to the underground station. So much for my leisurely stroll through Liberty's. Thank God for the day-pass, she thought as she slipped her ticket into the slot on the metal gates. It saves one from infernal queues. She followed the crowd down to the Victoria Line, got off at Victoria Station and transferred to the Circle Line, to bring herself close to where Compton's office was located.

She strode through the glass doors of the Ministry of Transport at 1 Victoria Street with her briefcase in hand and was directed to the upper floor of the ultramodern tower. She gave her name to the young woman behind the desk and had barely sat down when the woman approached again. "Mr. Compton will see you now. His office is right this way," she said waving Geilla toward an office close behind the reception area.

As Geilla entered, a well-built man in his early thirties came forward to meet her. His handshake was firm, but the overstated wave in his carefully trimmed blonde hair and his wide curly moustache gave him the fastidious air of a man overly full of himself. He remained silent as if assessing both Geilla's physical appearance

59

and her financial worth.

"Good afternoon, Mr. Compton. It's very good of you to see me," Geilla began, withdrawing her hand. "I promise not to take too much of your time."

"I will be happy to answer your questions, Ms. Trindor, but I really don't know how I can be of any help."

"As I mentioned on the phone, I am with Stocks Ltd. I'm investigating a claim for some jewelry that has been reported missing. I've traced most of it to the point of purchase and then to you. I was hoping that perhaps you could provide me some answers."

"I see," Compton said rather noncommittally.

Geilla sighed before starting again. "I feel rather embarrassed to be asking personal questions, but you must understand that my entire investigation is completely confidential. Well, to get to the meat of it, did you ever make a gift of jewelry to Ms. Elizabeth Duncan?"

Compton looked a little taken aback for a moment before admitting, "Yes . . . but that was a long time ago."

"Oh I can see that by the dates on the receipts. I was just wondering . . . did you by any chance take the jewelry back?"

"You mean, did I steal it? Certainly not!"

"Oh no . . . I didn't mean to imply . . . oh this *is* awkward. Did Miss Duncan perchance give the jewelry back?"

"No! It was a gift—all of it!"

"I am sorry . . . you don't happen to know if she might have given it to someone else, or perhaps sold it?"

"I have no idea what she does with any of her things, Miss Trindor. I haven't seen Ms. Duncan for almost a year."

"I see. Well, you must have known her quite well at one time if . . ."

"She knew a lot of men, Miss Trindor. She was a tramp—a very beautiful, clever one, but nevertheless a professional tramp. We had an affair, but she broke it off when she found someone else. End of story!" he concluded forcefully.

Geilla studied her hands and tried to show the proper mix of professional detachment and embarrassment. "I don't mean to pry, Mr. Compton, but this particular investigation has been somewhat complicated. You see, Miss Duncan reported that some jewelry and furs were missing and then she herself disappeared. So while I am looking for Miss Duncan's belongings, the police are looking for Miss Duncan. It's beginning to look as though Miss Duncan is trying to defraud my company."

"Are you suggesting that I might be involved in insurance fraud?"

"No. I'm just trying to track down Miss Duncan and I thought perhaps you might still be in contact with her. Did you know she was involved with a real estate business?" Geilla continued, quickly handing him a copy of one of the fake brochures for *Select Estate Agents*.

Compton took the brochure and studied it for a moment before shoving it back at Geilla.

"As I've said, I have no idea what she's doing or where she might be. I haven't seen her in over a year."

"I'm sorry to hear that. It makes my job much more difficult," Geilla said, putting the brochure back into her briefcase.

"There's nothing I can do about that and I really do not want to waste any more time over this matter."

"Yes. I certainly agree, but before I leave, could you possibly give me the names of any of Miss Duncan's other . . . ah . . . friends?"

"You mean lovers, don't you? Women like her don't usually have platonic relationships."

"Well, any leads would be helpful."

"Well, I have no idea where she's gone off to, but wherever she is, you can be sure some man is involved. She doesn't remain unattached for long! But who am I to talk. I must reek of sour grapes, but . . . Elizabeth was very special. Not someone you would marry, of course. I could never picture her being domestic and proper. She was a man's fantasy in the flesh. Does that make me sound lewd?"

Geilla shrugged. "I didn't come here to judge you, Mr. Compton. I'm just investigating the loss of her jewelry."

Geilla felt tired after the interview with Steven Compton, or perhaps she was just depressed from sorting through the sordid details of Elizabeth's life. With her penchant for affairs and intrigue, she was not a good candidate for motherhood. Geilla felt that poor Alona was

61

likely to have been orphaned early in her life and perhaps it was best that it happened while she was too young to remember. Geilla shook off her depression and replaced it with determination to see that Alona and Mysie could remain together.

From the phone in the lobby, she called Ian McBriad and arranged to drop off the brochure that Compton had handled. The team was still trying to find a match for the prints they had found in Elizabeth Duncan's flat in Saltash. After making the short walk from Compton's office to New Scotland Yard, she took the Circle Line one stop, transferred to the Bakerloo Line and got off at Waterloo. She bought a newspaper to read on the train to Dorkin.

Chapter Seven

Brad was in his office at Marcolm and Blake on Monday when Roger came in to report that Inspector Tomlin had located Bennett Wildridge. His body had been found tangled in the lines of a yacht moored in the Tamar River. Positive identification had been made through dental records and a fingerprint check of Marcolm and Blake employees who had high security clearance. The medical examiner's report concluded that his skull had been fractured before he was placed in the river. Tomlin reported that Mrs. Wildridge's emotional display at the news had been restrained to say the least. Brad wanted to interview Mrs. Wildridge himself and Roger concurred that it would be appropriate for a representative of Marcolm and Blake to convey corporate condolences to the widow.

The bulldog housekeeper was still guarding the door when he reached the Wildridge estate, but this time she let Brad wait in the large entry hall while she went to find the mistress of the house. When she returned she announced grudgingly that Mrs. Wildridge was in the midst of her exercise routine, but she would allow him to come in if he wished. Brad accepted the offer to visit one of the private rooms in the huge house. Perhaps the invitation meant that Mrs. Wildridge was even more in need of company since her husband's death. He followed the housekeeper along the wood-paneled corridors to the west wing of the house until she opened a door and waved him inside.

The room seemed glaringly bright after the dark corridors, and he blinked to adjust to the light. It took him a moment to realize that the room appeared more spacious because of the wall-size mirrors hung opposite the windows. Loud music with little melody, but a strong rhythm blared from hidden speakers positioned around the room. At the far end of the room in the open space between a tread mill and a rack of gleaming chrome-plated weights, Mrs. Wildridge was pedaling an exercise bike so vigorously she looked as though she was trying to generate electric power for her entire house. Her physical development was apparent in the way her clothing clung to her limbs. Brad had no doubt that she had more strength than Bennett who sat in front of his computer all day unless he was lucky enough to get the opportunity to activate the one small part of his anatomy that wasn't controlled by scientific reasoning.

Kathryn Wildridge was still uniformly tanned, but she looked tired. She greeted Brad without enthusiasm, shouting over the loud music, "Ah, Doctor Chillingsworth, how nice to see a familiar face. Turn that music off, will you—over there on the wall." Without slowing her pace, she extended a sinewy arm and pointed to the wall on her right. Brad found the controls and silenced the deep base tones.

"Come to comfort the grieving widow, have you?" Mrs. Wildridge said sharply as he approached. "I hope you're not disappointed that I'm not draped in black and collapsed in a corner."

"I would not expect such behavior from a woman as active as yourself. And exercise is good for reducing stress."

"Stress . . . yes, one does get stressed from having the police parading in and out—not to mention being ferried down to identify Bennett's body."

"I can imagine that was very unpleasant for you, but it is necessary in these cases," Brad said soothingly.

Mrs. Wildridge suddenly stopped pedaling. "Oh, hang it all, I've lost track of the time! Surely that must be long enough." She jumped off the bike, grabbed a towel from a rack, and dabbed at the sweat that was running down her face. "Can you really imagine what it's like, Doctor? Have you ever seen the dead body of a person you loved all distorted like that? It was horrible!"

Brad hesitated then chose an answer half way between telling the truth and keeping his cover. "I have, and I'm terribly sorry you had to go through it."

"I suppose for you it is all scientifically interesting, but for a wife . . . I shall never forget it. But I told myself I would not dwell on it and I won't. I must have a shower," she said abruptly. "Would you care to wait and have a drink with me?"

"I would like that very much, but wouldn't that negate the benefits of all your exercise?"

"Don't be so blasted scientific, Doctor. Doesn't the grieving widow deserve a little pleasure?"

Brad smiled. "I'm sorry. Of course you do and please call me Randolph."

"As you wish, Randolph. Why don't you wait for me in the study? Can you find your way?"

"I think I can manage, Kathryn."

She smiled coyly and Brad surmised that the image of Bennett's bloated body might be fading as they spoke.

After Kathryn disappeared, Brad took his time wending his way down the stairs to the study. He had barely seated himself when he heard her talking to the housekeeper in the hall. A moment later she opened the door and stuck her head in.

"I've asked Elma to bring us a bit of lunch. I do hope you won't disappoint me and dash off."

Brad smiled. "How could I possibly disappoint a lady in need of consoling." When he dug into his lobster salad a short time later, he was prepared to forgive Elma's bulldog attitude. Perhaps the woman can't manage a smile, but she certainly can cook.

After a suitable interlude of nibbling lobster and sipping white wine, Brad began to steer the conversation back to business. "I did want to ask you some questions relative to Bennett's unfortunate end. Not to satisfy my personal curiosity, you understand, but Roger has appointed me to act as liaison with the police. You can't imagine the number of tedious details that have to be cleared up."

"I understand. The police have already been here, poking about the house and the garage and asking me scores of personal questions about Bennett and our marriage. Do they seriously think I killed Bennett and threw him in the river?"

"Oh, I doubt that's the case. I'm sure it's only the usual suspicious mentality of the police that drives them to ask the most outrageous questions. Please don't let it bother you. You mustn't take it personally, Kathryn. It's all part of their job."

"Well, I shall try to follow your counsel. I'm sure you know more about these kinds of things than I do. How terribly tedious it must be for you to have to be involved. Why did Roger pick you to handle the matter? Why didn't he do it himself?"

"I suspect he has more important things to do, and as I'm rather new to Marcolm and Blake, I don't have as many projects on my plate. It is tedious though. Shall I just get on with the questions so we can make an end to them? I would prefer to enjoy your company without this official duty hanging over my head."

She drew in a large breath raising her shoulders and let in out with a huge sigh. "Oh if we must I suppose we must. But let me call for more wine before we begin. I am very unsettled by the whole matter." She got up quickly before Brad could respond and hurried out the door. After a moment, Brad heard a commotion in the hall and he went to the door. He opened it far enough to see that Mrs. Wildridge and her housekeeper were in the midst of an argument. He tried to make out the words, but all he caught was the housekeeper's admonition, "No! You'll make yourself sick. I won't let anyone in if you're going to behave like this. Let me make some tea. It will keep you calm without . . ."

"I don't want tea!" Mrs. Wildridge shouted. "If you won't get the wine, I will! And if you're going to interfere in my life, you can bloody well pack your bags and clear out!"

The housekeeper put her hand to her lips and shook her head. Then she turned her back and walked away. She called something over her shoulder, but Brad couldn't make it out. He saw Kathryn stalk away before he closed the door.

A short time later Kathryn came in carrying two bottles of wine. "I couldn't find Elma, but this should hold us." She set the bottles on the cart with the remains of their lunch and began to search though the cupboards.

"Can I help you, Kathryn?"

"Ah, no, I've found it," she answered, coming back with a large brass corkscrew fashioned in the shape of a fish. Without asking for assistance she opened both bottles with a twist of her wrist and poured a goodly measure of wine for Brad and then for herself. This could be a long afternoon, Brad mused, taking up his glass.

Kathryn picked up her glass, settled back into her chair, and took several long swallows. "Now we can begin. Ask what you will."

"It's just an odd detail really, but I thought you might be able to straighten it out for me."

She took another sip of wine and nodded for him to continue.

"None of Bennett's personal belongings have been found, but after the police identified the body, the clerk at the station's Lost Property desk called Inspector Tomlin about a wedding ring that had been turned in. The inscription read, "BSW and KE forever." Was that Bennett's ring?"

"It was," she said evenly. "I told the police that when they were here."

"Why do you think the murderer would discard Bennett's wedding ring when he or she kept everything else that could identify him?"

Kathryn raised her glass to her lips then clutched the stem so tightly Brad thought it might break in her hand. "Because Bennett wasn't wearing it," she said so softly Brad almost did not hear her.

"What? When did he take it off?"

Mrs. Wildridge looked at Brad, then quickly turned away before she blurted, "Oh God! I'd hoped it wouldn't come out. I wanted to have him buried with some semblance of dignity."

Brad moved closer and took hold of her empty hand. "What are you talking about, Kathryn? What happened?"

She gripped his hand for a moment then pulled away. "No. I can't tell you. I'm so ashamed. How could I have stooped so low?"

"I know he hurt you. Tell me what happened."

"Can you believe that after all the times he was unfaithful, I still loved him? It doesn't make sense does it?"

"Love often doesn't follow logic. Tell me what happened . . . please."

She drained her glass and then suddenly stood up and went to the liquor cabinet. Brad went after her. "Don't do this to yourself, Kathryn." He took the bottle she was holding. "Whatever it is, you can tell me. Come sit down."

She hesitated, then reached for the bottle. He took her hand. "You don't need it, Kathryn. Come, have some wine and tell me what happened."

He put his arm around her and she let him lead her back to her chair. He held both of her hands for a few minutes, then refilled her glass and went back to his chair. He waited silently, focusing all his attention on her face and not taking up his glass. After several minutes his patience was rewarded.

She picked up her glass, took a sip of wine and began in a voice just above a whisper. "I knew Bennett was seeing other women. He always made some excuse that he had a business meeting or had to go out of town for the company, but I knew he was lying. Sometimes the woman was brazen enough to call here. He got one of those calls shortly before he disappeared. He had come home early in the afternoon and announced that he had to go out of town for a few days. It was the usual story and I paid little attention to it. But then that evening Bennett was in the office with the door open, and I happened to overhear him frantically whispering into the phone. I knew he was planning something and I was curious. I hurried into the hall and picked up the receiver. I could tell it was the end of the conversation and all I heard was Bennett promising to meet someone at 2 a.m. at the railroad station in Plymouth.

"I was furious. Who would he be meeting at that hour? It had to be a woman. I hurried into the sitting room, thinking that Bennett might come out and tell me some story about having to go back to the plant, but he didn't. He stayed in the office until I went to bed about eleven. I don't know what time Bennett came in, but I pretended I was asleep. He stood by the bed for a few minutes and then he left.

"As I was lying there wondering who he was going to meet and what I was going to do about it, I grew more and more upset. I was almost disappointed that he hadn't offered any excuse for going off in the middle of the night. Then I got the idea to follow him. I wanted to catch him red handed and prove him a liar once and for all.

"I jumped out of bed, got dressed, and drove to the railroad station. I got there about twenty till two. It was very quiet, but it didn't take me long to find Bennett. He was pacing back and forth next to his car as if he couldn't wait for his lover to arrive. I pulled in beside his car and . . . and . . . we had the most violent quarrel we'd ever had. I can't begin to remember half of what I said, but I accused him of all sorts of vile things. He didn't even try to lie to me.

He said he wanted a divorce. He said he had intended to ask for one so he could marry someone else. He wanted to go into business with her, but now she was dead. I had never seen him so upset.

"He was ranting so, I could hardly follow what he was saying. We were standing there, screaming at each other, when suddenly he pulled off his wedding ring and flung it away. I never expected him to do a thing like that and I became hysterical. I lunged at him and scratched his face with my nails. He pushed me away and told me it was over. He didn't want me or my money any longer. I had thought for a long time that he had married me for my money, but it cut my heart out to hear him say it. I pleaded with him to come back, but he wouldn't answer. I finally went back to my car and somehow I managed to drive home. I never saw Bennett again."

Brad went to her chair, and kneeling beside it, he took her hand. "Oh, Kathryn, I'm so sorry. And you never called the police to report that he was missing?"

"No. I didn't think he was *missing*. I thought he had run off with some other woman. How was I to know? If only I had reported it, he might still be alive."

"You mustn't torture yourself, Kathryn. He was alive when you last saw him. Look, I think you should lie down for a while. I don't have any more questions right now, but I need to get back to the plant. Will you promise not to drink yourself to death after I leave."

"I won't promise, but I will try."

"Good. Would you like me to get Elma and have her help you to your room?"

"Elma? Good heavens no! She's trying to take over my life. Why don't you just go. I'll be all right."

"Very good then. I will come again if you call me, Kathryn. You don't need to be alone."

"Thank you, Randolph. I may just do that."

Brad drove back to Marcolm and Blake pondering whether it was grief or guilt that was driving Mrs. Wildridge to drown her memories in alcohol.

♦♦♦

Mysie switched off the television and sat with her head in her hands. She didn't usually watch news programs. All the talk of politics and parties confused and bored her. But on Sunday night she had fallen asleep while watching a comedy program and had awoken in time to hear the end of an announcement that the police were asking help to identify the body of a woman they had found on Cornwood Road. Mysie had only half-heard the description, but she had immediately thought of Elaina. She had made a point to catch the news on Monday morning and once again, the description fit Elaina to a tee.

Now Mysie was having trouble deciding what she was going to do. She didn't really want to talk to the police, but Elaina still hadn't shown up and she was worried sick. She hadn't heard from Audrey Weeks and she was almost out of the money Audrey had left her.

It would be a long bus trip to the Crown Hill police station, and she would probably have to transfer at least once. She wished she had a car, but Elaina had been against it. She had said they weren't going to be in Plymouth for long. Elaina had been good to her by providing her with clothes and a place to live, but sometimes she was very bossy and domineering. Mysie had never dared to ask a neighbor for a ride. Elaina had forbidden her to get too friendly with any of them. They might ask questions. They would certainly wonder if she came begging for a ride to the police station. It was safer to take the bus.

At least the weather is still nice, she mused as she got dressed. She checked her bus map and was pleased with herself that she could figure out the route. She puttered around the flat, putting things in order. She didn't know how long she would be gone and she wanted everything to be secure. Then she dressed Lonie and pulled the stroller out of the closet. Lonie preferred to walk rather than go in the stroller, but the trip was just too long and Mysie was anxious to get it over with. She had to report that Elaina was missing whether or not the body the police had found was hers.

Everyone at the police station was polite and nice to her, but she was not prepared for all the questions. She described Elaina as best she could, but she didn't have a picture to give them. When they started to show her pictures of Elaina's clothes and jewelry, her heart sank. Her tears started to well up and she could only nod her head in answer. She nodded when they asked her to view the body they had, but she didn't really want to. She wanted to believe that Elaina was alive, that she would walk in the door and take care of everything like she always did. Sure she was bossy, but . . . what now?

It was a short ride to Derringford Hospital. She sat in the back of the police car between two female police officers. She was trying not to be nervous and upset Alona, but Alona wasn't fooled. Mysie was holding her so tightly she could hardly breathe and she started to cry.

Alona's cries only made Mysie more nervous. She tried to soothe Alona, by rocking her back and forth, but she was too close to tears herself to calm Alona. She feared the police might think she was not a good mum if Alona kept crying, and she was relieved when the car finally stopped. She was grateful when the officer on her right got out and took Alona from her so she could crawl out.

The officers seemed kind as they led her into the building and escorted her to the lift. She thought to take Alona back, but since she had stopped crying, Mysie didn't want to disturb her. She was hardly aware that she herself was clinging to the arm of the other police-woman. As she was ushered into the viewing room, she made a feeble attempt to reach for Alona, but heard several voices mummer, "It's better if she waits here. You'll just be a minute."

Mysie felt as if her world was falling apart and prayed that it would not be Elaina behind the curtain. It just couldn't be. Elaina was always so beautiful and so active. The policewoman offered Mysie a chair, but she declined. She wanted to stand—to be able to move, to run. She kept her eyes lowered when they pulled the curtains and at first all she was aware of was the bouquet of flowers—carnations—the flower of death. Of course she couldn't smell them through the glass, but she almost imagined she could. She knew the pungent peppermint and spice odor well. There had been so much death in her family, the smell of rotting flowers seemed to hang in the air all during her childhood. She had forgotten about it while she had lived with Elaina. But now Elaina was bringing it back to her.

"Take your time," she heard someone say, but she didn't want to drag out the uncertainty. She could lie to herself at the flat, but not here. She raised her head suddenly and gasped. It was Elaina—no doubt about it. Somehow they had made her look peaceful, but that was a shock too, because she had never been one to sit still. Mysie stared for just a moment and then felt herself sway. Someone took her arm and led her to a chair. "What am I gonna do now?" she heard herself ask.

"So you are positive that is Elaina Spengler?" someone asked.

"Yes, that's her." Suddenly she was glad Alona was not with her. "Don't let the baby see her! Please don't let the baby see her!"

"It's all right. She doesn't need to come in," the policewoman answered. "Someone will drive you home when you're ready."

Mysie nodded. And then they asked where she had met Elaina and how long ago. What could she say? She had to protect Alona—so she lied. She told them she was the one who had given birth to a beautiful little girl. It was Elaina's baby who had died. Elaina took Mysie in so she wouldn't be so lonely.

It was easy enough to tell the story that way. She didn't have to make up dates or other facts. She just switched her name with Elaina's. She hoped the police wouldn't check the details, after all, Elaina was dead. She began to be afraid they wouldn't let her see Alona ever again, but after a while they stopped asking questions and brought Alona in. Then they drove her home.

As they pulled up in front of her block of flats, she noticed a police car parked outside her building. Now what? she wondered. Are they going to follow me in and search the flat? And then the truth hit her—they already had. So that's their game, sneaking around spying on me, she thought. She felt a stab of bitterness inside. And here I was thinking those policewomen looked so young and pretty, like they was real people. You're a fool, Mysie girl. She got out of the car silently and took Alona in her arms. She waited while the police removed the stroller from the trunk, but turned down their offer to help her up the stairs with a polite, "No thank you. I will be just fine."

She went up to her flat and closed the door firmly behind her. She unbuttoned Alona's coat, then ran to check Elaina's jewelry. It was all there, right where she had hidden it. Bloody buggers aren't as smart at they think! She smiled to herself and went to put the kettle on for tea.

Chapter Eight

On Tuesday Geilla talked Kon into going with her to visit Mysie. After all, she was playing the role of a married woman and it would add credibility to her story if she actually produced a husband. Besides, she knew that once Kon saw Alona, he would move heaven and earth to help Mysie keep her.

Kon had been on the phone to Geneva, discussing stock deals with Edgar Marné for so long they had been late in setting out to dinner, and it was almost ten o'clock by the time they pulled up in front of Mysie's flat. Geilla had wanted to call ahead to let Mysie know they were coming, but Kon advised against it. He much preferred catching people by surprise.

Mysie was so slow in answering when Geilla buzzed that she wondered if arriving unannounced had been a mistake. Where could Mysie have gone? She hadn't mentioned any family or friends in the area. Mysie sounded a bit flustered when she finally answered, and Geilla announced that Audrey Weeks and her husband Patrick were downstairs. Mysie seemed hesitant, but when Geilla mentioned that she had some important news about Elaina's jewels, she finally invited them to come up.

Mysie met them at the door looking rather disheveled. The facing of her blouse was sticking up in back and the top button was in the wrong buttonhole. She waved them into the sitting room. When they passed the kitchenette, Kon spotted a helmet and a pair of leather gloves on the counter and immediately linked them with the motor-bike parked in front of the building. He smiled to himself, thinking, ah yes, coming unannounced does yield interesting information.

"You said you had some news about Elaina's jewelry. Is it real? Did you find a buyer for it?" Mysie asked as they all sat down.

"Oh, it's real all right—and very pricey. I tracked it to the store where it was purchased."

"Did you find someone to buy it? I'm gonna have to sell it," Mysie said sadly. "I heard something on the news and I went to the police and . . . Elaina's dead . . . hit by a car."

"Oh dear," Geilla said softly, but Mysie didn't seem to have heard and rambled on.

"They found her near Cornwood. They kept askin' me what she was doin' out there. How do I know? She never told me nothin'! What am I gonna do now? What if they find out Lonie is really Elaina's baby? I'd go crazy if they took her away. She's all I got."

"Calm down, Mysie," Geilla said softly. "I suspected that something like this might have happened to Elaina. I'm terribly sorry, but we're here to help and we want you to be able to keep Alona. I'm sure I can find a buyer for the jewelry, but this might not be a good time. We heard the police announcement too and we think maybe Elaina's death was not an accident."

Mysie caught her breath. "I thought she was involved in something funny. She was always going off at odd hours and she never would leave me a phone number. Sometimes she would turn up here all bruised and have to spend the day in bed, but she'd get real upset if I asked her any questions."

Geilla was silent for a moment before she asked, "Did Elaina ever mention a man named Steven Compton?"

Mysie blinked at Geilla and shook her head. "Why? Was he the bloke what gave her the necklaces?"

"Yes," Geilla admitted, "as least some of them."

Mysie sighed, "Well, I told you Elaina never told me nothin'."

"And you didn't tell her a lot of things either, did you?" Kon put in.

"Me?" Mysie said, looking surprised and nervous. "What d'ya mean? I don't have anything to tell."

"Oh? So I guess you two never discussed the merits of your friend with the motorbike."

Mysie's eyes opened wide and her pale cheeks flushed for a brief moment before she lowered her eyes. Then she raised her head and declared boldly. "Weren't none of her business. I keep a good eye on Lonie. I never go nowhere without her. A body's got to have some company once in a while."

"I quite agree. Loneliness is a hard thing to bear," Kon answered calmly.

"It ain't none of your business either who I pick to be friendly with."

"I'm not accusing you of any wrongdoing, Mysie," Kon continued, "but things you discussed with Elaina or what you know about her background may be important to finding out who killed her."

"What are you saying? Davey had nothing to do with that!"

"Why don't you ask Davey to come out and talk with us?"

"Why? Who are you anyway?" Mysie asked becoming excited and defensive. "I thought you was interested in buying a house. Are you from the police?"

"We aren't from the police," Geilla assured her quickly, "but we are interested in finding out who killed Elaina."

"But Davey had nothing to do with that!"

"Perhaps not, but we would like to ask him some questions," Kon answered.

"I don't know why you're botherin' me like this. Davey didn't do nothin' wrong. You can talk to him all you want," Mysie answered almost defiantly. Getting up from the couch, she went to the bedroom door which was closed and called, "Davey! Davey, come on out here." She waited a minute, but when there was no response, she opened the door and walked in calling, "Davey? Where are you? Come on out!"

Kon noticed there was no light on in the room. He got up from the couch and followed after Mysie. The window was open and Mysie was looking out. "Now why'd he go and do a fool thing like that? He ain't got nothin' to hide. He never even met Elaina."

"Are you sure?" Kon asked striding to the window.

"'Course I am. He would 'ave told me if he did."

Kon leaned out the window and saw that it would be an easy reach from the window ledge to the drainpipe fastened to the front of the building. Then he noticed a figure astride the motor bike in the street below. Suddenly he whirled around and pushed past Mysie. He tore though the sitting room, threw open the door and dashed down the stairs to the street door. As he yanked it open he could hear that someone was trying to start the bike, but the engine wouldn't catch.

The young man on the bike looked up for a fleeting moment

before he jumped off and started to run. Kon was only a few yards behind as the young man crossed the street and disappeared into an alley. The alley was dark, and Kon slowed slightly. He could hear the sound of someone running over the cobblestones and he followed. As he reached the end of the alley, Kon caught a glimpse of his prey and increased his speed. The young man was now fully visible straight in front of him and it was no longer a contest. Few people could outrun Kon's long, springy stride and in half a block, Kon had his hand on the collar of the man's jacket. He expected more resistance, but as soon as he twisted the man's arm behind his back he cried out, "O.K.! O.K.! I give. Watch the arm! Jesus! Let up! I didn't do nothin'!"

"Then you won't mind coming back to talk with us," Kon said, prodding the young man from behind.

"O.K. I'll come. Just don't break my arm."

Kon relaxed his grip enough to let the young man straighten his arm, but he hung on to him as they walked back through the alley. When they reached the block of flats, the front door was still open. Kon pushed the young man inside and closed the door with his foot before he steered him up the stairs.

Mysie was waiting by her door when they reached the second floor. She didn't say anything, but put her hand on the young man's arm as Kon pushed him into the flat and forced him onto the couch.

"Now, Davey—if that's your real name—didn't anyone ever tell you it's impolite to run out on a lady?"

"I don't have to answer your questions. I ain't done nothin'."

"So you're telling me you always leave by the second story window. That looks strange, Davey, very strange. Why did you run away if you didn't do anything?"

"He musta got scared, that's all," Mysie interrupted as she came in from the kitchen. "You came barging in kinda sudden and all. Tell 'im, Davey. That's all it was, wasn't it?"

"Yeah, I got scared that was all!" Davey agreed quickly.

"See! What'd I tell ya," Mysie said defiantly.

"Why would you be scared of having visitors?" Kon persisted.

Davey put his head down and kept silent, and a moment passed before Mysie answered for him. "Davey musta been scared 'cause he ain't never been up here before. I didn't think Elaina would like it, but . . . hell I don't like being here all alone. I ain't a kid no more, but Elaina couldn't see that. I don't think she really liked men. I know she went out a lot, but she never talked nice about anyone."

"How long have you known Davey here?" Kon asked in a tone so laden with disapproval Geilla guessed he had learned it from Charlotte Marné. Kon's tone of voice must have reminded Mysie of someone also, for she bowed her head before answering, "Almost three months, but he's never been up here before."

"Have you been sneaking out to see him? Is that it?"

"No! I couldn't leave Lonie alone. Davey just comes by and I kinda go out to talk to him."

"And Elaina never knew about him?"

"No. She would 'ave lectured me for sure. She was worse than my mum sometimes," Mysie said meekly.

"How did you manage to keep Davey a secret? Are you sure Elaina never saw him sitting out there on his bike?"

"What's it to you anyway?" Davey suddenly asked. "You're not her bloody father. You talk like I'm dumb or something. I didn't just ride up here and hoot the frigin' horn. I never actually met Elaina, but I knew what she looked like and what kind of car she drove, so I'd wait in the alley across the street until Mysie signaled me or until I saw her leave."

"So you waited in the alley, did you? Every night?"

"No—not every night—just . . . just a lot."

"Did you ever see anyone with her?"

"No. She was always by herself. I would just wait until I saw her get in her car and drive away."

"She always drove herself? You never saw anyone come to pick her up?"

"No. I never saw nobody come for her. She always drove or took a cab."

"A cab? Did she do that often?"

"Yeah. Couple a times a month."

"Do you remember when that was?"

"You mean what day?"

"Yes."

"I don't know the date, but it was always a Friday. Yeah, always on Friday. I remember 'cause I have to work late on Fridays and then I come by."

"Do you remember what company it was?"

"I think it was different ones, but last time it was Red and White. I remember 'cause one of my friends got a job with them and I was kinda wonderin' if it was him."

"So the last time you saw Elaina she was getting into a cab."

"Yeah. That's what I said," Davey said trying to reestablish his image as a tough guy.

"And that was the last time you saw her, Mysie?"

"Yes. She was wearing that strapless dress the police showed me. I forgot about that dress until I seen it again. But, you know, that dress was all torn up and frayed. That weren't like Elaina not to keep her things nice."

"Well, that gives us something new to go on," Kon said thoughtfully.

"Did the police ask to talk to you again, Mysie?" Geilla asked.

"They didn't say nothin' about it," Mysie answered shaking her head.

"Well, if they do ask to talk to you again, I would rather you didn't mention that we were here."

"Why? What's the big secret?"

Geilla paused for effect before answering, "Elaina was mixed up in some pretty nasty stuff, Mysie. We think that's why she was killed. We want to find out who killed her, but there's no point in dragging you through it all. At this point the less the police know about Elaina and her baby the better."

"Well, I'm not about to go blabbin' to the coppers about Lonie."

"Good! At least we all agree on that. Do you still have Elaina's jewelry—just in case?"

"Yeah, I got it stashed nice an' safe. Those dirty coppers went through the flat while I was at hospital lookin' at Elaina all laid out. They got no respect."

"Just hang on to the jewelry, Mysie. How are you fixed for money?"

"Strange you should ask. I called the letting agent yesterday to beg off payin' for a while and they told me the rent's been paid. They said they was sending me a receipt since it was paid in cash. Was that something you two cooked up?"

Geilla looked at Kon quickly before answering, "Yes. I told you we want to see that you get to keep Alona."

"I ain't some charity case, you know," Mysie objected.

"Think of it as a loan. And you didn't answer my question. How are you fixed for cash?"

Mysie looked at Davey and then lowered her head. "Davey gave me a bit, but it's gone for food."

"Then take this," Geilla said, opening her bag and handing out a stack of notes without counting them. "Get some more groceries."

Mysie nodded and took the money, so Geilla guessed the cupboards must be bare again. Most young girls with a baby would be on the phone to Social Services, but Mysie didn't dare risk an investigation into Alona's parentage.

Geilla stood up abruptly and Kon followed suit, adding, "It's late. We'd better get going. Since your bike seems to have mechanical problems, Davey, we'll be glad to drop you off wherever you want."

Davey shot a glance at Mysie before objecting, "I ain't leaving just yet."

Kon turned and fixed Davey in a hard stare before remarking politely, "Have you forgotten your manners again, Davey? It's well past the time to end a social visit and I think you need to rest your arm before it starts to hurt again."

Davey was used to being hassled and he quickly recognized the veiled threat in Kon's remark. He already knew that Kon was much stronger than he looked.

When Kon urged, "Say goodnight, Davey," he grunted, "See ya, Mysie."

Davey sulked all the way to the car with Kon and Geilla. He did not respond when asked where he lived, but when Kon threatened to drop him off at the police station, he came up with an address in Saint

Budeaux. It wasn't a good neighborhood.

"Where did you meet Mysie?" Kon demanded as he pulled up in front of the two-story building.

"I work at a food store," Davey answered slowly. "She came in a few times with Lonie and we got to talking."

"How come you work so far from home?"

"Ain't none of your business where I work," Davey growled as he opened the car door and got out.

He started toward the front gate, but suddenly his feet left the ground and he found himself pinned against the side of the car. He didn't see Kon, only the glint of steel on the blade that flashed before his face. "Listen, Davey, you need to learn better manners and I don't have time to give you lessons in deportment. You'd better be on your best behavior with Mysie, because if you hurt her or get her pregnant, I'll see that you take a dive off the Tamar Bridge. Do you understand?"

"O.K. I get the picture. She invited me in. What was I supposed to do?"

"Either keep your pants zipped or take precautions! Mysie's got enough with Alona."

"All right! I'll be careful," Davey promised.

"Good. I'm holding you responsible." Kon said, putting his knife away. "What are you going to do about your bike?"

Davey shrugged. "It'll have to sit until I can get some cash together to get it fixed. I been holding off—guess I waited too long."

Davey hung his head and even in the dark Kon could tell he felt defeated. Kon had never viewed his own youth as anything other than a nightmare he'd just as soon forget, but looking at Davey, he suddenly felt sorry for him. He thought of all the time Geilla's brother, Alonzo, had spent with him, teaching him how to fix his motor bike and even letting him ride with him. He had known Alonzo only a little while before he was killed, but having someone take an interest in him saved him from giving up on life at fourteen.

"Go to bed, Davey. I'll think of something," Kon said and stepped aside.

"You wouldn't really throw him off the bridge, would you?"

Geilla asked after Kon had started the car again.

"Probably not, but Davey doesn't need to know that."

"What's he going to do about his bike?"

"He doesn't have any plans. I'll have it hauled somewhere in the morning. My guess is the electrical system is shot."

"I'll go with you when you pick it up," Geilla offered quietly and put her hand over Kon's.

He grinned, knowing that with Geilla along, a simple delivery would turn into an adventure. Geilla could do tricks on a motorbike that would make a stuntman gasp. "Why don't I just buy you your own bike?" he said aloud.

"Heaven's no! Charlotte would have a fit. What would her friends think?"

"What do you care?" Kon asked casually, but he was pleased that Geilla was so sensitive to Charlotte's feelings. Even though he was grown and married, Kon still tried never to do anything that Charlotte and Edgar would not approve of. Well, at least not publicly, and above all, not in Geneva.

Chapter Nine

Borrowing the identity of a Scotland Yard inspector for a few days was one thing, but impersonating a police officer in Plymouth involved a much greater risk. Paul just smirked, however, when Kon gave him the lead on the Red and White Cab Company. After playing the role of Inspector Starks, he had anticipated that he might be called upon to play the role of a local officer and had secured some suitable I.D. Before he went to the company offices on Wednesday morning, he also took the precaution of carefully working out his disguise.

He applied theatrical makeup to his hair to make himself appear considerably older and padded his waist to give himself added weight. Then to draw attention away from his face, he used makeup to create a long, ugly scar on the back of his right hand, running from the tip of his middle finger half way up his forearm. Whenever he moved his hand the scar was visible. No matter how polite people were trying to be, they would focus on his cuff, wondering how long the scar actually was.

The cab company kept good records and in no time produced a record of Elaina's destination on the night she was last seen alive. The driver who had let her off was not in when Paul stopped by, so Paul drove directly to the address listed. It was a pub called The Three Crowns in the Barbican. Paul was surprised that Elaina had been bold enough to venture into such a popular meeting place where she was likely to be recognized by someone from Marcolm and Blake.

None of the waitresses recognized Elaina from the picture Paul showed, but the young bartender recalled seeing her come in alone. He remembered that she had met a man at the bar, but he couldn't give Paul a description. No one remembered when Elaina had left or whom she was with, so Paul started making the rounds of the cab companies. After several hours he had turned up five leads of people being picked up at the pub that evening. Four of them were couples and the drop point was a bed and breakfast or a hotel.

Paul decided to check out the one lone passenger who was picked up that night. The address was a two-story house in a long row of similar structures. The buildings would have been monotonous except for the individuality shown in the color and design of the doors and the artistic variety in the treatment of the front gardens. The door of the house in question was a dark forest green and displayed a well-polished brass knocker which Paul used to announce his arrival.

No one answered Paul's knocking, but after several minutes, he caught a glimpse of a woman watching him from across the street. He gave one more try on the knocker before stepping across the street toward the woman. As he came up to the house, however, the woman disappeared inside. He rang the bell several times, but the only response was high pitched barking. Finally he gave up on the bell and rapped on the door. Immediately the barking became more frenzied and was suddenly augmented by a deep howl.

Paul was beginning to wonder if he would be forced to call out, "Open up! It's the police!" when the door suddenly opened to reveal the older woman he had seen in the yard. Two Yorkshire Terriers took turns cowering behind her and darting their heads around her legs to bark at Paul, while a basset hound strained against his collar to sniff at Paul's pant leg. Paul stood his ground, but it flashed though his mind that the fake scar on his arm might become real at any moment.

"Now look what you've done!" the woman shouted above the high pitched barking as she pulled on the collar of the basset hound trying in vain to haul him away from the door. "He's too old to be upset like this. It's bad for his heart."

"I'm sorry to disturb you," Paul apologized quickly. "I'm with the police," he explained, waving his fake I.D. at the woman. "We're looking for someone who's disappeared and I thought your neighbors across the road might be able to help me."

"Be quiet, Tiny! Now sit! Sit!" the woman begged rather than commanded, but the dogs continued barking. "Well, even if they wanted to there's nobody there now," she shouted above the din.

"Yes, I see," Paul continued raising his voice. "Do you have any idea when they will be back?"

"Oh, get down, Tippy! Get down!" the woman screeched at the basset hound until he finally appeared to lose interest in Paul. "They won't be coming back. They've moved out."

"When?" Paul shouted.

"Almost a fortnight now. Oh do be quiet, Tiny and Bitsy! Hold on while I get them a biscuit, will you," the woman said, backing away from the door. "You'd best come in and close the door," she hollered.

Paul stepped inside and closed the door and the woman withdrew followed by the terriers. The basset hound stayed to keep a watch on Paul with his mournful eyes.

"You have a good alarm system," Paul commented when the woman reappeared and quiet was restored.

"Oh they make a row all right when anyone comes to the door, but I'm afraid the only damage old Tippy here would do a burglar would be to fall asleep on his foot."

Paul smiled. "What can you tell me about your neighbors. They were a couple you say."

"If by couple you mean a man and a woman, yes they were a couple. If you mean a man and wife, then my guess would be no."

"Why do you say that?"

"It was mostly her I saw. He only showed up at the weekend, once or twice a month. He drove, but she always came and went by taxi. And I never once saw her bring a bit of food into the place!"

"That does sound strange," Paul remarked. "Do you know their names?"

"No. I was never introduced."

"May I have your name for my report?"

"It's Mullins—Noreen Mullins."

"And that would be Mrs. Mullins, I presume?"

"Yes."

"Thank you, Mrs. Mullins. You said that the man always drove. Do you remember what make of car he had?"

"Oh, let me think. It was dark . . . blue, I think. Yes, a dark blue Bentley."

"Thank you, that's very helpful. Can you think of anything else you remember about them as a couple or individually?"

"Well, as I said, I didn't see him very often. I didn't even see them move out. I just figured it had happened when I looked out one morning and saw all the boxes by the curb. They were still there when I took Bitsy and Tiny for their walk. I couldn't help noticing that it seemed to be mostly her clothes—and beautiful things too. I hope it's not against the law, but . . . well, I sorted through the boxes and took most of it to give to Oxfam. It was just too nice to throw away."

"That was a generous idea. Do you remember what day you took it in?"

"Well, I haven't exactly taken it in yet. I just put it all in the bag with my other stuff."

"Oh. Say, do you suppose I could take a look at it?"

"I guess that would be all right, seeing that it's not really mine. Have a seat and I'll get the bag."

A few minutes later Mrs. Mullins returned lugging an enormous plastic bag. "I usually go by Oxfam once or twice a month, but I just didn't get there last week. It's all in here," she continued as she began to pull clothes out and show them to Paul. "Like I said, that lady was a dresser."

Paul took the garments from her and searched quickly for labels. They were all from quality manufacturers, but there were no clues to the identity of the owners.

"There was a lot of fancy underwear in the boxes, but I didn't bother with that. Oh yes—here's a few of his things too. They're a bit more worn."

Paul took the pair of suit pants she was holding and searched the pockets. "She certainly did have beautiful clothes," he said, palming a crumpled piece of paper that was clinging to the bottom of the pants pocket along with some lint. "I could drive you over to Oxfam if you would like. You've been a great help."

"Thank you, but I've got other things to do today."

"Right then. I'll be going," Paul said and began stuffing the clothes back into the plastic bags. He stopped when he noticed how wistfully Mrs. Mullins was looking at them. "Well I suppose you will need to sort them again before you take them in. If you find something you like you could always give them a donation—probably save them a lot of paperwork in the end."

Paul stood and pulled a card from his pocket. "If you remember anything else about your former neighbors, would you give me a call? I really need to locate them," he said and handed her the card.

"Certainly, but like I said, I never actually met them."

Paul waited until he returned to his car before he unfolded the crumpled paper. It was a credit card receipt for fuel purchased at one of the stops along the M5 from London. The signature at the bottom was faded, but Paul could read enough of the letters to make out the name Steven Compton. So much for his story about not having seen Elaina in years, Paul thought as he refolded the receipt. Since there was no sign on the property to indicate that it was a rental, Paul went back to the Duke of Cornwall and started phoning estate agents.

Pretending to be from Oxfam, Paul tracked the rental agent and convinced her that he needed the name of the former tenant in order to send a receipt and a personal thank you for the generous donation of clothing. The agent quickly succumbed to Paul's charm and gave him the name Clive Westbrook with a London address. A quick check with Doris at British Telecom confirmed that Clive Westbrook was a chartered accountant. Obviously Mr. Compton didn't want it known that he was renting a house in Plymouth. Paul felt he knew the answer, but he ran a check on Steven Compton's car registration and confirmed that he was indeed the owner of a dark blue Bentley.

When Paul reported his finding to Brad, Brad suggested that Kon should make contact with Steven Compton, but that Paul should go to London with him. They took the train on Wednesday evening and picked up their new identification papers. Kon didn't bother to call for an appointment. Instead, the following morning he strode boldly into Compton's office and terrified the receptionist by announcing that he was from Interpol and insisting that he speak to Steven Compton immediately. Compton was in a meeting, but he came out when the frightened girl slipped him a note.

"What is this about, Evelyn? Couldn't it wait? The meeting will be over at . . ."

"This is an investigation, Monsieur Compton," Kon interrupted, pointedly looking Compton up and down. "I assume you would like to discuss this privately," Kon continued without softening his tone.

Compton's mouth opened as if he planned to object, but suddenly thought the better of it. He sighed in apparent resignation. "Yes. Yes—my office." He turned to lead the way and then turned back to the receptionist who was standing at attention beside her desk. "Evelyn, would you please tell the committee that I will be delayed. I hope you realize what an inconvenience this is," Compton grumbled as he closed the door behind Kon.

"I hope you realize the seriousness of the difficulties you are in," Kon retorted.

"What difficulties? Would you mind telling me who you are and what this is all about?"

"My name is Griffin Bordet. I am part of the Interpol team investigating an international crime ring that's been involved in stealing technological secrets."

"Technological secrets? What has that got to do with me?"

"Frankly, Monsieur Compton your position with the Ministry of Trade and your association with Elaina Spengler, alias Elizabeth Duncan, make you a prime suspect."

"Elizabeth? What has she got to do with this? I heard she was missing, but . . . "

"Not just missing, Monsieur Compton. She's dead and we have reason to believe you were the last person to see her alive."

"Dead! Oh God! When? How . . .?"

"She was murdered and we think it has something to do with the industrial secrets she was stealing. I intend to prove that the two of you were funneling documents to France."

"Me? That's the most ridiculous load of rubbish I've ever heard! I have no idea what secrets you're talking about. And I haven't seen Elizabeth for over a year."

"Let's stop playing games, Monsieur Compton. I know all about your little hideout in Plymouth. You may have fooled your wife by calling your jaunts business trips, but you can't fool me. You should have been more careful of where you parked your car. We have witnesses, Monsieur Compton."

Compton appeared dumbstruck and Kon stepped up his verbal attack. "Why did you kill her—did she want more money for taking all the risks? Did she threaten to tell your wife about your affair? She was good at blackmail, wasn't she?"

"Stop it! I didn't kill her. I swear I didn't kill her."

"But you admit you were meeting her in Plymouth."

Compton got up from his chair and paced back and forth behind his desk twice before throwing himself onto the leather sofa with a groan.

"This is all so crazy. I can't believe Elizabeth is dead. You're twisting everything that happened."

"Then it's up to you to tell me what happened and straighten it out."

"Are you going to arrest me? I can't let you do that. If my wife finds out . . ."

Kon had remained standing, but now he went to the sofa and sat beside Compton. "What happens next depends on what you tell me now. I want the truth from you and I want it all."

Compton put his head in his hands and hid his face.

"When did you first meet Elizabeth?" Kon asked softly.

"Several years ago—at a party. She was on the prowl. I knew it even then, but I couldn't resist. She was dazzling. We started seeing each other and I began giving her presents—jewelry and furs. We'd meet in little out of the way pubs. I would tell my wife I had to stay in town on business and Elizabeth and I would go to Brighton. It was so exciting. She was like a drug."

"What happened then?"

"I guess I was so befuddled with Elizabeth that I forgot to pay attention to business. Anyway, I missed some important meetings and the next thing I knew I was reprimanded and I was passed over for promotion. Constance, my wife, was furious when she found out. She couldn't understand why I didn't get promoted when I was always working late or going to conferences at the weekend. I had to talk her out of bringing the issues to my boss. God! That would have been a disaster! Shortly after that Elizabeth met someone else at a party and she stopped seeing me."

"When was that?"

"About a year ago."

"What did you do then?"

"What could I do? I picked up the pieces of my job and went back to staying home with my wife. But after Elizabeth she seemed so boring, I felt as though my life was over."

"How did you get tangled up with Elizabeth again?"

"Elizabeth is unpredictable if nothing else. About five months ago she called me out of the blue. She said that she had taken a job in Plymouth and that she missed me terribly. She begged me to come see her, and like a fool I went. How can I explain it to you? You can't imagine what torture it is to be so besotted by a woman you become irrational."

Oh, but I do understand, Kon thought as he listened to Compton. I remember full well how I would put up with anything from Alyce just to be near her. I put myself in debt buying her expensive presents. And all for what? She walked out on me.

"Sometimes a woman can appear to be everything you ever dreamed of," Kon said with understanding. "Part of you knows it isn't true, but you want it to be real so fiercely that you're blind to reason. No one can help you as long as you are under her spell."

"God, how true that is! I knew I shouldn't go to see Elizabeth, but as soon as I went, I was lost."

"So you rented a house for her and started giving her presents again."

"Yes. I went down at weekends and it was so good. I think hiding it all from my wife made it even more exciting."

"Was it Elizabeth's idea to steal the secrets?" Kon asked quietly.

"No! You're all wrong about that!" Compton responded jumping up from the sofa. "I don't know a thing about trade secrets. I may have cheated on my wife, but I will not tolerate being accused of theft and murder!"

"Sit down, Monsieur Compton," Kon ordered icily. "We can either talk here or we can go across the street to Scotland Yard. I'm sure they would be very interested in your little tryst."

"You're bluffing about arresting me. What evidence do you have? I admit I was sleeping with Elizabeth, but I didn't kill her. I didn't even know she was dead."

"If you didn't know she was dead, why did you dispose of all her clothes and close out the house? You have to admit that looks suspicious."

"It was just a coincidence. I thought our affair was over and I was angry. I didn't want to see her ever again. I know the power she had over me. I knew I could never end it face-to-face."

"Why did you suddenly conclude the affair was over?"

"If you must know . . . I saw her with another man and it wasn't a business meeting. I was furious that she was cheating on me. And I was even more aggravated that she denied it."

"So she was cheating on you and you had a quarrel. I bet you felt like smacking her. But you controlled yourself. Maybe you just pushed her a little and she fell down. Of course you didn't really mean to kill her."

"No! No! That's not how it was! We quarreled, but I didn't hurt her! I didn't touch her."

"Why don't you tell me what happened that last time. I know you drove down to Plymouth on Friday night. What happened when you got there?"

"All right. I went down early on Friday. I was planning on taking Elizabeth to the country house of a friend. I didn't tell her before hand. I wanted to surprise her. I usually met her at the house, but when I got there I found a phone message from Elizabeth saying that she was going to be late. I was disappointed, but I viewed it as my own fault for not telling her. I sat in the house for a while, but then I got hungry and decided to go eat. We never dined together on Fridays. I always arrived too late. We usually just went for drinks or stayed in.

"Since I was alone, I didn't feel particularly cautious about being seen in Plymouth, so I went to The Three Crowns in the Barbicon. It was crowded and I had to wait at the bar until they had a free table. I was annoyed, but I settled in with a drink and then I saw Elizabeth at one of the tables. She was sitting very close to a man I had never seen. She was wearing a white dress. I remember it because I was with her when she picked it out. One more present the ungrateful bitch took from me." Compton paused then walked to his desk and pulled open a drawer. Kon was on his feet in a flash, but the only thing Compton took from the drawer was a hard pack of cigarettes.

"I'm trying to quit, but . . . Christ! This is all a bit hard to take."

"Go ahead," Kon said shrugging his shoulders. "Why don't you sit down."

Compton pulled a cigarette from the pack, lit it carefully, inhaled deeply, and slowly exhaled. When at last he sat, he chose the high-back chair behind his desk. Kon took the straight chair in front of Compton's desk, but he put his left elbow on the edge of desk and leaned toward Compton indicating that he was waiting for more information. "Pray continue," he added after a moment's pause.

Compton took another drag on his cigarette, as if realizing that he could not stall for much longer. "I was shocked to see her there with someone else. I watched her for a few minutes and as I said, it was not a business meeting. He had his hands all over her and she wasn't pushing him away. I was angry, but somehow I was embarrassed too. I wanted to charge up to her and accuse her of being unfaithful, but how could I? I kept thinking about all the lies I had told my wife. She thought I had gone to Paris for the weekend to get a start on some business. I was angry and confused, but I just turned and left.

"I walked along the waterfront for a while trying to get my thoughts together. It was the second time she had left me, but I couldn't bear the thought of never seeing her again. It probably sounds preposterous, but I still love her. I knew she could have anyone, but she kept coming back to me. I told myself she would do it again. I drove back to the house to wait, but all the while I sat there I was working on a plan to get Elizabeth to come back to London. I thought that if she was closer, we could meet more often and she wouldn't feel the need to see other men."

"Were you planning on leaving your wife for Elizabeth?"

"I was starting to think about it. Elizabeth had never seemed interested in marriage, but I thought if we were married she would stay put. You can see the lengths I was prepared to go to keep her."

"Did you ever mention your plans to Elizabeth?"

"Only once, that last night. I waited at the house for what seemed like hours. She finally showed up about eight-thirty, still wearing that white dress. As soon as I saw her, I began accusing her of seeing other men. She denied everything. She claimed it was part of her job

91

to entertain clients. She tried to get me to calm down, but I was furious. I told her about the weekend trip I had planned and to placate me, she agreed to go. She packed very quickly and said she was ready to go. I expected that she would change her clothes, but she said she liked her dress and would wear it for me.

"I calmed down a little after we were in the car and I started driving. I couldn't bear the thought of her with another man. I told her that I was going to leave my wife and asked her to marry me."

"What did she say?"

"She seemed surprised, but she agreed. I think now that she would have agreed to anything to keep me calm. She didn't like the idea of coming to London to wait for my divorce to go through, but said we could discuss it later. She sat close to me all the way to Cornwood and kept kissing my neck. I let my hands explore her and I became more and more eager to possess her as I drove. She kept telling me she loved me and that everything was going to be different for us once we were married.

"When we got to the house, I unlocked the door quickly and we went in. I was crazy to take her and started to unzip her dress, but she put me off. She said that we should celebrate and asked me to go down to the pub and get some champagne. I didn't want to leave her, but she coaxed me and I could never resist her. We kissed in the hall and she said she would run a bath and that I could join her.

"I drove into Cornwood like a madman intent on catering to her whim, as usual, but it was Friday night and the inn was crowded. It must have been forty-five minutes before I got back to the house. I got the bags from the car and walked up to the house. The door was locked, but that didn't surprise me. I assumed Elizabeth had locked it behind me. But when I went in, I noticed there were no lights on anywhere. I thought it was strange because the owners usually leave a light on when they are away. I called Elizabeth's name several times but she didn't respond. I turned on the lights and went upstairs. The second floor was dark also and absolutely quiet.

"Suddenly I became frantic for Elizabeth's safety. I turned on all the lights and searched the house from top to bottom. I kept hoping Elizabeth was playing a game and would pop up at any minute, and then I realized the truth. Elizabeth had been playing a game all along. She was very clever at manipulating people and she had agreed to everything I had said without meaning a word of it. She had no intention of coming to London or of marrying me. My concern for her turned to anger—at her for leaving and at myself for playing the fool once again. I closed up the house and drove back to Plymouth. "

"And you made no further attempt to find Elizabeth? "

"No! Believe me, that woman knows how to take care of herself. I figured she must have walked or hitched a ride into town and found a bed and breakfast. There's always someone who puts people up in these little towns. She would have no trouble convincing someone to give her a ride back to Plymouth. I thought of going home, but I had told my wife I would be in Paris until Monday night and she would wonder if I came home early. She has been very concerned about my job since I lost that promotion. So I went back to the house in Plymouth. It was so full of memories of Elizabeth that I knew I would go insane if I stayed there. I couldn't bear to look at the champagne, but the larder was stocked with gin and I started on that while I cleared out the house. I was upset and too drunk to sort anything and I just wanted to be rid of it all. I found some boxes from the stereo set I had bought her and I threw everything in them and put it all out to the street. "

"What about the furniture? "

"The place came fully furnished—the owners went to work in Saudi Arabia for a year. I left the stereo with them. I didn't want anything that reminded me of Elizabeth. "

"What did you do after everything was packed up? "

"I must have passed out because when I woke up it was four in the morning. I couldn't go home and I couldn't stay in that house, so I locked up and checked into the Grand Hotel. I stayed there until early Monday morning and then I drove to my office. "

"And you never saw Elizabeth again? "

"No. I thought I was over her, but your coming has opened the wound again. "

"Well, I can assure you, you won't ever hear from her again. Her body was found by the side of the road near Cornwood on the Saturday after you said she disappeared. "

93

"Oh bloody hell! Bloody hell! I suppose that makes my story look pretty thin."

"It does look bad. I will need the address of the house in Cornwood."

"Certainly. It's just Apbly Cottage—about three miles east of Cornwood. The sign's on the gate."

"Who owns it?"

"A friend here at the office, Jonathan Nash. He used to live there, but he was transferred up here. Now he uses it for weekends and throws a big do there every summer. My wife and I have gone down together twice."

"I see. And he gave you a key? You must know him quite well."

"We've worked together on several projects. I told him I wanted to take my wife on a getaway before the weather turned bad. I was supposed to check out the place and see that the man he hired to put in some brickwork had done the job. I was in such a panic I never even checked. I ended up telling him I had canceled the trip."

"Do you still have the key?"

"No. I gave it back as soon as I returned."

"Then I think you'd better tell him you're planning another holiday."

"I can't do that. I never want to see that place again!"

"Would you prefer to have me tell him that I'm investigating a homicide?"

"No! Oh God, what a bloody mess. What if he doesn't believe me?"

"Why wouldn't he believe you? He doesn't suspect about Elizabeth, does he?"

"Certainly not. All right! I'll ask him. He'll think it's strange I'm asking so long before the weekend."

Kon raised his shoulders in an exaggerated shrug. "Make up an excuse. You're good at lying."

"You cheeky bugger!" Compton spat in contempt. "Then what? Are you going to arrest me? Constance will have a fit. First the lost promotion and then this."

"Actually the homicide part is Scotland Yard's job. I'm more interested in the secrets that Elizabeth was stealing. Did she ever mention what she was working on?"

"No. She said something about being an estate agent, but I didn't pay any attention. She seemed to have a lot of different jobs."

"Can you give me any names of Elizabeth's friends or business associates?"

"As far as I know Elizabeth didn't have any friends. She just collected men. I think that was her real occupation."

"Can you think of anyone in particular?"

"I don't know their names. I never even got a good look at the last one. I guess I didn't want to learn the truth. She could make you believe you were the only one. She must have lied to all . . . wait a minute. I do remember one of them—the one she left me for the first time, Victor Rhodes."

"Any idea where I can find him?"

"Do you like flashy parties? That's where you'll find Rhodes. He's always cruising for women. That's how Elizabeth met him."

"Any idea what line of work he's in?"

"He runs an import/export business—somewhere over on Oxford Street. That's the real reason he goes to Ministry parties. Collecting women is just a side line."

"I think I'll pay Monsieur Rhodes a visit. As for you, Monsieur Compton, I would advise you not to leave London. Scotland Yard will want to talk with you."

Chapter Ten

As soon as the courier arrived with the key on Friday, Geilla drove out to Apbly Cottage. Luckily, the roads were dry and she had no trouble locating the sign on the rusty gatepost. She liked the house when she saw it. As she came up the drive, she fantasized about spending a tranquil weekend there with Kon. Tranquil! Now that would make Kon laugh. When did he ever want tranquil? Well, maybe just relaxing. But then again Kon was too high-strung to get completely relaxed for long. She often imagined Kon even slept with one eye open.

Geilla parked her car in front. Opening the glove box, she took out a miniature camera and checked that she had a full role of film. She pulled on a pair of fitted leather gloves, walked back from the house and shot a few pictures of the exterior before she went up to the front and unlocked the door. She tested the switch beside the door and found the hall light to be working. Compton had thought it had been on when he first came up to the house. The thin, faded rug by the door showed traces of gravel from the drive, but no discernable footprints. The hall floor was uneven, and the wide planks squeaked as Geilla stepped away from the door. She stood a moment, trying to feel what Elaina had been thinking when she stood in this hall. Was she excited about having received a proposal of marriage, or was she planning her escape?

Being careful not to disturb possible evidence, she walked toward the staircase across from the door. Suddenly she saw something white resting in the depression between the planks. She stooped for a closer look and discovered it was a single pearl. Strange, she thought, Elaina was wearing diamonds when she was found. Of course, it could belong to the lady of the house. Geilla took several shots of the pearl trying different angles, and even laying her car keys next to it for a reference. She wondered about the remainder of the string. She was about to climb the stairs when she noticed dirty white streaks that appeared to be footprints along the left side of the stairs. Being careful not to step on the prints, she followed them through the kitchen to the rear door. Geilla reached to open the door and saw that it was unlocked. The frame was old and split, but it bore scars where the many layers of paint had been scrapped off as someone had forced the worn catch open. Geilla opened the door gingerly and saw the source of the white streaks. Mr. Nash's hired man had indeed finished laying the patio brickwork, but he had spilled some cement in the process. The powder must have been washed from the bricks in the recent rain, but someone had unwittingly tracked it into the house. Whoever had walked through the house, apparently hadn't noticed that they were leaving tracks. Could that have been because they were walking in the dark? Geilla stepped out onto the patio and looked back into the house. From where she stood it was clear that something had been dragged along the floor. Had it been Elaina's body? Mysie said that dress the police had showed her looked torn and frayed. Could it have been dragged across the bricks? If so, there might still be some fibers caught in the bricks.

Geilla pulled her camera from her handbags and snapped a few pictures. The view was lovely, but she was more interested in the fact that although the driveway circled in front of the house, the handyman had obviously driven around to the back. Could someone else have done the same? If they had, their car would be completely hidden by the house. Geilla put her camera away, stepped back into the house, and closed the door. It would have to be left to the men from the police lab to search the bricks for bits of cloth fibers.

Geilla crept silently up the stairs and went quickly through the few rooms. A thin layer of dust on all the dressers and a trio of spiders in the blue bathtub gave testimony to the fact that the house hadn't been used for a while. Everything seemed to be in its proper place. If there had been a struggle, everything had been put back in order. The last room that Geilla checked was the large bedroom that faced the front of the house. There were two partial footprints on the bare floorboards beneath the window, indicating that someone had stood facing the window. Had someone been waiting when Steven and Elaina drove up?

Geilla took pictures of the prints, and then went downstairs again.

When she noticed the telephone sitting on top of the bookcase next to the stairs, she made a mental note to ask Doris for a list of the calls. She took one last look around then left, being careful to lock the door behind her. As she drove slowly along the narrow road that led into Cornwood, she passed a small bed-and-breakfast cottage and wondered if Elaina had planned on staying there after she left Apbly Cottage. Once she got to Cornwood, she verified that there was a bus that ran from Cornwood to Plymouth six days a week.

Geilla had no trouble finding the pub that Compton had mentioned. It was the only place in town that showed any activity. She relaxed over tea and a light lunch of salad, cheese and crackers. She felt free to savor the robust flavor of good English Cheddar without worrying about hurting Charlotte's feelings. She wished that Kon were there with her. What a pity that even though they worked on the same team, they still often worked separately.

Chapter Eleven

Victor Rhodes apparently didn't feel the need to run an ad in the yellow pages, but a check of the businesses on Oxford Street turned up five importers. Paul concluded that Rhodes must have been in an expansive mood when he named his business *Universal Exchange Ltd.* On Thursday and Friday Kon made repeated attempts to contact Rhodes by phone, but no matter when he called there was never an answer at his office or his flat. Since the office building was closed for the weekend, Kon and Paul agreed that they should keep watch on Steven Compton for a while to see if they could determine the extent of his involvement in Elaina's murder. Compton lived in Richmond, so they moved their base of operations to the Richmond Gates Hotel.

On Saturday they got Geilla's report and the photographs from her visit to Apbly Cottage and decided that they definitely wanted to search Compton's residence. Unfortunately, from what they had observed from their post near the Compton's front gate and their frequent phone calls to the house, Mr. and Mrs. Compton appeared to be spending a quiet weekend at home. Kon and Paul were forced to bide their time until they knew the house would be empty.

Their only relief from surveillance duty was to take turns making phone calls. Kon called Geilla who was staying in Dorkin with E.P. for the weekend. Her visit had freed Mary to take the train to Plymouth to be with Brad.

When Paul's turn came, he called Nea Cortland at her London flat. She hadn't seen Paul for three weeks and offered to come down to Richmond, but Paul put her off. She was disappointed, but not offended. After all, Paul had kept his promise to call her when he had some free time. There was no use resenting the fact that between his job, his demanding mother, and his seven younger brothers, he didn't have a hell of a lot of free time. Nea consoled herself with the assurances she got from Mary and Geilla that Paul wasn't spending his precious free time with any other woman. Although she hadn't told Paul, since she had met him, she wasn't particularly interested in seeing other men.

On Monday morning, while Kon kept watch on Compton, Paul paid a visit to Rhodes' office building. There was very little activity in the building when he arrived and the directory did not show *Universal Exchange* as one of the tenants. Paul noted that there was only one lift servicing all six floors. He wandered through the halls on the first two floors until he came upon a light-colored, wooden double door with a dull brass sign engraved with the words "Universal Exchange, Ltd." and a logo featuring a globe that was so stylized the continents were totally indistinguishable. He tried the door, but it was locked. Further along, almost at the end of the hall by the window, was a single door, but it too was locked. Paul paced off the distance from the window to the double doors and concluded that Rhodes' business occupied a suite of rooms. It cost a tidy sum to lease that much office space even on the less prestigious end of Oxford Street. Carrying a black sample case as a badge of his trade, he tried the door of the office marked Baldwin's Light Fixtures which was down the hall from Rhodes' offices.

The reception area was empty when he entered and he took a few minutes to look around before he stuck his head around a partition and called out tentatively, "Hello? Anyone on duty?" When there was no answer, he called again. "Hello, Baldwin's. Anyone here?"

Suddenly a young girl whose frosted blonde hair was a good eighteen inches longer than her denim skirt came down the hall to Paul's left. She seemed startled to see him standing there. "Oh! Sorry, sir. I didn't hear you come in. If you're looking for Mr. Baldwin, he's not in."

"I haven't come to see him," Paul said quickly. "Actually, I've come to fix Mr. Rhodes' copy machine, but the place is locked up. I thought someone might know whether or not everyone over there is at lunch or taking the day off."

The girl slid behind a desk, sat down, and pulled a long metal letter opener from a drawer. She picked an envelope from the top of the large pile of mail in front of her and began to slice it open. "Day off! That's a laugh! I've never seen them people have a day on!"

Paul had suspected as much, but he pretended to be surprised. "Well, somebody was there long enough to bust the copier."

The girl stopped slicing momentarily and looked up at Paul. "Probably the owner doing his own work. I never saw any office staff over there. If you ask me, he was too tight to hire anyone."

"Maybe he spent all his money on equipment," Paul responded. "According to my work order, he's got a top-of-the-line copier."

"Well, I hope for your sake that he still has it. He had some fancy computers too, but I hear they got repossessed."

Paul shot her an appropriately shocked look. "Where'd you hear that?"

"I eat lunch with a girl on the first floor," the girl said as she took up a rubber stamp and began to assert her authority over the day's mail. "She seen them taking it out. Mr. Rhodes didn't look none too happy about it."

"Well, he's signed a service contract for a year, so I'm obligated to fix his machine. I just can't figure out how to get at it. Has anyone seen him lately?"

"I never wanted to see him even when he was here, but he hasn't been around in weeks."

"Why didn't you want to see him? Was he a grouch?"

The girl brought her stamp down with a vengeful slap and suddenly stopped stamping. "Oh no! He was Mr. Charm—snake charm, that is." The girl looked around quickly and tugged at the edge of her shirt as if she suddenly wished it covered more of her. "He would come in here every day and say the most outrageous things to me. He asked me to go for drinks with him and talked about wanting to hire me," she made a disgusted face before continuing, "and you can believe he wasn't talking about typing or filing. It gave me the creeps, it did. He's got to be older'n my father! Angie down on the first floor—she said the same thing. I always thought dirty old man meant . . . you know . . . old. He was just creepy. I'm glad he's gone." She shuddered as she finished.

"So, I don't suppose you would know how I can reach him. I need to get into his office. I'm new with the company and if I can't fix his copier, my boss won't be happy."

"I can understand that," the girl said thoughtfully. "I can't help you, but the girl down in the leasing office might be able to. He would have

101

to put something on the lease. He might even have used his real address."

Paul brightened and flashed her a smile he hoped was totally devoid of snake-charmer creepy. "I would really appreciate it if you could get me his address."

"Well, I'll try," the girl said picking up the phone.

After a short conversation punctuated by several outbursts of giggling and a lot of "the creepiest," the girl hung up and handed Paul a telephone message sheet with an address and phone number on the back.

"This is great! I really appreciate it. Is there anything I could do for you? You know, some free toner samples or something."

The girl thought a moment. "Did you say toner? Sure, I bet you know all about that stuff. Follow me," she ordered, pulling a key from the desk drawer.

Paul obeyed, making sure he stayed a safe, non-creepy distance behind her. She led him around a partition and down a hall before she stopped and unlocked a door. She pushed it open and turned on a light as she stepped inside what Paul recognized as a storage room.

"See those ten boxes?" she asked pointing to a pile in front of her. Paul nodded. "I ordered the wrong toner cartridges. I have to get a signed authorization slip to send them back, but I don't dare tell Mr. Baldwin how dumb I was. Do you think you could swap them for me? I'd be happy to get even two I could use. He'd sign a new order without blinking an eye, but he'd question a return."

Paul looked at the boxes, trying to estimate if he could carry them without a hand truck. He wasn't concerned about the weight, but he wasn't sure he could carry ten of them without dropping them. "What kind do you need?" he asked.

"You tell me—I thought this *was* the right kind."

"Let me see your machine. I'm sure I can get you the right kind," Paul said, hoping he could deliver.

The girl turned around, squeezed past Paul, and flicked the light off with a careless wave of her hand. "It's down there," she said pointing to a door at the end of the hall. "It's a big nuisance having to walk all the way back there every time I need a copy, but it's the only empty space that's big enough."

Paul waited expectantly for her to escort him, but he quickly saw that she was not about to make another trip even to get him to help her with the toner exchange. "Right," he said at last. "I'll get the model number and see what I can do."

"Great!" the girl responded before quickly disappearing down the hall. Paul had no trouble finding the copier which dominated the small room. He wrote the make and model number on the back of the phone message the girl had given him and went back to her desk. She was slicing more mail, but stopped long enough to ask, "Well? Whaddaya think? Can we trade?"

"No problem," Paul assured her. "You want me to write you a receipt for the wrong lot and carry it away, or do a switch when I bring the right stuff?"

"Let's do a switch. He's seen the boxes and he'll wonder if they're gone. When can you get it?"

"If this phone number works out, I will be back tomorrow or the next day to fix Rhodes' machine—that soon enough?"

"Sure. Can you call me first, in case Mr. Baldwin is hanging around?"

"Certainly. By the way, what's your name?"

"Miss Bremerton, but you can call me Tracy," she said as if bestowing a special honor on Paul. He smiled, figuring he had passed the test and been categorized as "non-creepy." He was also pleased that he now had a legitimate excuse to return to the building and would have an alibi if he were questioned about being in Rhodes' office. "My name's Bill Knott. Sorry I don't have a card to give you, but the company hasn't given me one yet. Maybe they're waiting to see how I work out before they waste the ink."

"Pleased to meet you, Bill. Don't worry about the card. I'm sure you'll get one soon since you're making an extra special effort to fix Mr. Creepy's machine. If it was me, I wouldn't bother, but I guess you haven't met him."

"Well, sometimes we don't get to pick who we work for."

"Ain't that the truth. I don't have my own card either, but you can call me on the main line and I'll pick up," she said handing him a card printed with glossy blue ink.

"Good. See you soon," Paul promised and made his exit.

Paul made several more attempts to reach Rhodes at his flat that same afternoon, but to no avail. He checked again with Doris at British Telecom and confirmed that the phone number and address that he'd gotten from Tracy were the ones she had listed for Victor. Doris suggested that Rhodes might be on a business trip hunting up specialty items to import, but Paul had his doubts.

Doris also gave Paul the news that a check of the phone records had revealed that on the night Elaina died, someone had made a call from Apbly Cottage to the private residence of Kenneth Wobel. I guess Wobel conveniently *forgot* to tell that little bit of information to Kon, Paul mused.

Late the following afternoon, Paul waited while Kon made several calls to Stephen Compton's office under the name Griffin Bordet to verify that Compton was safely occupied in a meeting. Kon felt secure that Compton's secretary, Evelyn, was too intimidated by the fact that he was from Interpol to lie to him. Pulling a pair of blue coveralls over his suit, Kon picked up the metal toolbox Paul had borrowed for him and hurried toward the battered van Paul had rented.

Meanwhile Paul went to his car, which was now loaded with ten boxes of toner, and drove to Rhodes' Oxford Street address. As he pulled into a small space behind the office building, he saw that Kon had already parked. Loading the toner onto a hand truck, he pushed it around to the front of the building and went in. He pressed the button for the single lift and waited briefly in front of the door, feeling good that his pockets were now full of cards identifying him as Bill Knott of Island Business Machines. He had also arranged for Doris to answer the line and vouch for him, should anyone be inclined to call the office number listed on his card.

As he came off the lift on the second floor, he saw Kon polishing the display case hanging on the wall opposite the lift. Having checked with the maintenance company that serviced the building, he knew Kon would have about twenty minutes to complete his work before the real custodial crew arrived.

As Paul pushed his burden out, Kon stepped over to the lift and set the "stop" button to hold the lift in place. He pulled an "Out of Service" sign from beneath his overalls and quickly fastened it across the open doorway using a string suspended from two large magnets. Picking up his toolbox, he dashed around the corner and signaled to Paul who opened the door to Tracy's office and went in pulling the boxes behind him. As Paul disappeared, Kon opened a huge can of chrome polish, set it on the floor beside him, and draped a white cloth over his left arm.

As the strong odor of metal polish wafted through the hall, he pulled his lock picks from his pocket and started to break the code on the shinny chrome-plated lock. To Kon's relief the lock was built for appearance rather than security and presented no problems. With the lift out of order and Tracy occupied, no one noticed him and he quickly unlocked the door and slipped a piece of tape over the latch. He recapped the polish, placed it in the toolbox, and stepped around the corner to retrieve his sign and put the lift back into operation. Checking the hall a final time, he slipped into Rhodes' office without being seen and closed the door. He waited by the door without turning on a light until he heard Paul knock twice and pretend to insert a key into the lock, then he pulled it open and Paul slid in.

The reception area in Rhodes' office was furnished with a built-in counter that faced the door and a low, glass-topped table flanked by two high-backed chairs with wooden arms. An arrangement of silk flowers carefully chosen to match the blue upholstery of the chairs was displayed on the table along with a light coating of dust. Paul surmised that due to the fact Rhodes was three months behind in his rent, the building management had cut off his custodial service. There was very little furniture in the six offices and, as Tracy had hinted, no computers. The atmosphere was one of a grand scheme gone sour.

Paul didn't find a copier, but he was prepared. He went into the office farthest from the door, opened his case and took out a small battery operated tape player. As soon as he touched the "play" button, the appropriate clicking and wheezing of a copier in action hummed through the room. Leaving the imaginary copier to sort a large job, Paul joined Kon in the office that obviously belonged to

Rhodes.

"Find anything?" he asked Kon who was fiddling with the lock on the center drawer of a huge wooden desk.

"Not yet. This lock is trickier than the one on the door, but I'll have it open soon," Kon replied with confidence.

Paul grinned. Kon's ability to make locks yield their secrets to him was in strange contrast to his strong need to keep much of his own life locked away. He wondered if Kon's clients at the bank would feel as secure if they knew how easily Kon could gain access to their safe deposit boxes.

While Kon worked on the lock in the desk, Paul pulled on a pair of latex gloves and began to search the matching wooden hanging file cabinet which had no lock. The top drawer was full of purchase orders and invoices to what appeared to be clients of *Universal Exchange, Ltd.* The addresses and dates on the transactions indicated that Rhodes had been in business at a multitude of locations over the past five years. A quick glance through the files told Paul that Victor had tried his hand at trading everything from china tea sets to Russian-made watches with varying degrees of success. A search through the bottom drawer filled in other details of Rhodes' business and revealed that he had suffered more than the occasional legal problem. As he read through the correspondence, Paul was struck by the frequency of complaints that the quality of goods Rhodes delivered did not measure up to what he had promised.

Paul spent a short time reading the legal records to gain background about Rhodes' business dealings, but when he pushed the files labeled "Z" aside, he found something much more interesting. Lying flat against the bottom of the drawer was a briefcase made of fine quality leather. Paul lifted it out carefully, holding onto the edges and avoiding the handle. As he laid it on top of the file cabinet, he noticed the gold, embossed initials BSW and called to Kon. "I think we've found something to link Rhodes to the problem at Marcolm and Blake. Come take a look!"

Kon stepped over to the file cabinet and even from where he stood behind Paul he could see that someone had sprung both of the clasps in an effort to override the combination locks. It was unlikely that Bennett Shelby Wildridge had been the last person to open the case. Using a pencil, Paul lifted the broken clasps, raised the lid, and fished out several large sheets of paper that had been roughly folded to fit into the case. He spread them open on the cabinet top and counted off three scaled drawings of lens mountings and a thin computer printout of wavelength specifications. Each sheet had been stamped **CONFIDENTIAL** with a rubber stamp that from the tired look of the letters was nearing the end of a long useful life, and a stamp pad that was badly in need of re-inking.

"No doubt Roger will be able to identify these," Paul said.

"We should have them checked for prints," Kon added.

"Definitely," Paul agreed, "and this too," he added, pulling a computer disk out of one of the pockets in the briefcase. "Looks like our friend Bennett made quite a haul."

"Yes, but I wonder why Rhodes didn't take this stuff with him when he disappeared." Kon replied, referring to the fact that Rhodes had not been seen at his London flat for over a week.

"I'd say he was planning on coming back," Paul answered.

"Well, he'll be locked out both here and at his flat if he doesn't pay his rent soon."

"From what I've read in his files, it won't be the first time he had to pack up and move out."

Kon shook his head. "Whatever business he's involved in, I wager it has very little to do with imports and exports. I guess he spends all his money keeping up a front and going to parties. I'm going to get back to work on that desk drawer. I'll blow the damned thing if I have to. Seeing what Rhodes has stashed in here, I doubt he'd report a break in."

"Patience, Kon—don't destroy any evidence."

"All right—I'll fiddle with it again. Plastique is Jack's job anyway," Kon said going back to the desk.

Paul refolded the papers and put them back into the briefcase before he went back to reading more about Rhodes' legal battles. It's a wonder this guy can stay in business at all, Paul thought as he examined Rhodes' files more closely. He's run one shady deal after another. Any time he gets a cash flow coming in, he puts it into some stupid scheme that blows up in his face.

"Got it!" Kon called in triumph a moment later. Paul heard the drawer slide open, but he continued reading while Kon searched. "I can see what Elaina and Victor had in common. Look at this," Kon said holding up a checkbook. Kon passed the book to Paul when he came over to the desk and sat on the edge of it. "Notice the pattern?" Kon asked leafing through a handful of bank statements. "Cash deposits at the middle of every month."

Paul took the statements from Kon who quickly returned to searching through the drawers.

"Dio mio! Here's another account—it's her bloody business account. Christ! This must be the money she was squeezing out of Wobel—one deposit right after the first of every month. Of course! He told his wife he was investing in real estate. What's all this stuff doing here?"

"The break in at Elaina's—it must have been Rhodes!" Paul answered immediately.

"You're right! He went to make a monthly trade, but she had disappeared. Looking at these he must have thought she'd run off with someone else. I can't wait to get his prints checked with the ones we found in her flat."

"Prints are great, but I wish we had Rhodes."

"So do I, but he must be planning to come back. If he skipped the country, he would have taken the drawings with him."

"Yeah, unless these are copies of old drawings. I want to get Roger Dremann's take on all this. Are you finished with the desk?"

"Yes," Kon answered, closing the drawer and checking his watch. "Five forty-five. I would guess that most of the workers have left, but I want to get out of these overalls before someone asks me to collect their rubbish."

"I would say you've collected quite enough today," Paul concluded.

Chapter Twelve

Even before the courier arrived from London with the briefcase full of drawings, Brad had received Paul's report confirming that the unidentified prints found in Elaina's Saltash flat belonged to Victor Rhodes. After Brad reviewed the drawings himself, he left the Duke of Cornwall and drove to Marcolm and Blake. Tony was on duty at the security desk when he arrived, but despite all the recent goings on at the plant, he seemed more interested in his chocolate covered doughnut than in Brad or the briefcase he was carrying.

He's a nice enough young lad, but definitely not well trained in security measures, Brad thought as he noticed that one of the new rotating security cameras he had asked Roger to have installed had come to rest facing into a corner. Brad was about to mention the fact to Tony, but decided to let Roger handle it. After all, no one at the plant knew that he was responsible for having the equipment installed. He nodded silently in answer to Tony's cheery greeting and placing his card against the wall sensor, buzzed himself through the door to the offices.

Since Roger was expecting him, he went directly to his office.

"Yes, yes, Chillingsworth. Do come in," Roger said in greeting although they were alone. "Is this the case?"

"Yes, but it's not so much the case as the drawings that I need you to identify."

"I see. Well, let's have a look," Roger said and moved the marble penholder farther toward the edge of his paperless desk and motioned for Brad to set the briefcase on the dark green blotter. Since the case had been thoroughly dusted for prints, Brad had no qualms about handling it with his bare hands. He let Roger open it and watched as he drew out the papers and slowly unfolded them. Suddenly Roger drew in his breath. "My God! Have we anything left! Where did you get these?"

"I take it this is current information then."

"Some of it. Yes. It's our latest ideas."

"Is it from a project that Wildridge was working on?"

"From the project yes. But these are not just his ideas. This technology was developed by a team of researchers. It represents years of work."

"He must have been selling it along with the other ideas. It was in his briefcase that was never found after his murder. You said some of it was recent. What about the rest of it?"

"This other material is just some ideas Wildridge was working on. It's his theory, really. No one else could make the program run and his output was never reproducible. As for the case, I can't identify it. I never saw him with it. Perhaps his wife would recognize it. I want to know where you found it."

"My men found it in London in the office of a man named Victor Rhodes. Does that name mean anything to you?"

Roger straightened up from his study of the drawings. "Rhodes . . . Rhodes . . ." he repeated thoughtfully. "You did say Rhodes, didn't you?"

"Yes. First name Victor. Do you know the name?"

Suddenly Roger looked dazed and collapsed into his chair. "But it can't be the same Rhodes. Surely it's just a coincidence. It's been years . . ."

"Do you know him?" Brad asked.

Roger shook his head absently. "Not him—his father, Oliver—only his name was Broderick then. The family changed their name after his suicide."

"Suicide! What happened? Did he work here?"

"No. He wasn't an employee. He was one of our suppliers. His company developed the synchronous mounting we used to use to overcome image distortion when our cameras were mounted in moving aircraft. He was a clever man, but his production schedule was erratic and oftentimes he was late with delivery. We had a lot of trouble with him, but he made such finely crafted machinery that we let him a large contract. That was his undoing. He couldn't seem to gear up fast enough. He fell way behind schedule and we had to find another source.

"We had no choice, but it spelled financial ruin for him. I don't know what his mental history had been up to then, but he went on a rampage one night and shot one of our engineers—Joseph Kingsley, who was testing our equipment. Then he killed himself."

"How long ago did this happen?"

"Let me see—it must be at least twenty years. Joseph Kingsley survived, but he was on disability for the rest of his life. He died just a few years ago."

"What happened to Broderick's family? You said they changed their name."

"Oh yes . . . dreadful scandal! The papers were full of lurid pictures of Broderick and his family. His poor wife had a nervous breakdown. The oldest boy had to take charge of her and his younger brother."

"You seem to remember all the details quite well."

"Oh, I kept track of them through it all. I was paying disability for Kingsley. I hoped his family could collect something from Broderick's business, but there was nothing there. I did what I could for Kingsley's family. I paid his medical bills and hired his wife as a bookkeeper."

"Is she still here?"

"No. After her husband died, she remarried and moved to Bristol."

"And you think Victor Rhodes is Oliver Broderick's son."

"Quite possibly. I never actually met Victor. After Oliver's death, I dealt with the older boy, John. He had been in the business with his father. I was going to pursue a lawsuit on behalf of Kingsley, but as I said, there was nothing to gain. Broderick had been drowning in debt for months before he killed himself."

"Do you have any idea where the family is now?"

Roger shook his head. "No. I lost track of them years ago," he replied sadly. "I just can't believe Oliver's family has come back."

"Would anyone else at Marcolm and Blake remember Broderick? Someone who worked with Mrs. Kingsley perhaps."

"It all seems so long ago, I don't think . . . but hold on—Lilla's been here forever and she's a walking tabloid. If anyone knows it would be her."

"Shall we call her?"

"I don't think that would be wise," Roger cautioned. "She would be sure to tell everyone that she got a call from me. It would be better if you went down to her area and talked to her alone."

Brad sighed. "But I'm supposed to be new here. What can I say to find out about something that happened twenty years ago?"

Roger tapped his fingers against the arms of his chair for a few seconds and then his eyebrows shot upward. "Tell her you're looking into some work that Oliver Broderick once did and you need to check if the family still holds the patents."

"Brilliant idea!" Brad replied sincerely, thinking once again that Roger had cleverly covered his real reason for being at Marcolm and Blake. "I'll go straightaway."

Brad found Lilla behind her computer, working on the monthly payroll. She was the perfect source of information, he thought. Not only does she know everyone, she knows how much they earn and how long they've been with the firm.

Lilla greeted Brad with a smile and moments later as he asked a few cautious questions about Oliver Broderick, he felt himself bracing against a flood tide of company history. He listened; he made mental notes; he jotted addresses on yellow paper; he feigned interest occasionally; and murmured his need to attend a meeting once or twice; but it was a struggle to keep from being pulled under by the tidal wave of malicious gossip and speculation that Lilla spewed forth. When at last he pulled himself away, he had a few concrete facts and a dull headache. Roger you bloody coward, he thought bitterly, you knew this would happen.

Along with all the history and gossip Lilla had related to Brad in tedious detail, she had informed him that Oliver Broderick's son, John, had moved to Ivybridge and was going by the name of Rhodes—his mother's maiden name. Lilla also volunteered that John had married, fathered two sons and was working in a pub called The Red Coach. Brad was sure that Lilla could have supplied him with the going price of a pint of bitters at The Red Coach, but as he hoped to get to Ivybridge before Guy Fawkes Day, he didn't ask.

The Red Coach occupied the bottom floor of a large two-story Tudor style building on the edge of town. The spacious car park in the rear gave it a decided advantage over other nearby establishments and, according to Lilla, the food wasn't bad either. After Brad parked, he took a moment to admire the blood-red fuchsia blossoms arching gracefully in the rear garden that was enclosed by a neatly trimmed boxwood hedge. With vicarious pride he noted that the blossoms were not as abundant as on the plants in Mary's garden in Dorkin. But then Mary had a natural talent for nurturing both plants and people.

When Brad paused, he noticed that although the garden was well tended, the building itself was in need of repair. Some of the wooden window frames looked as though they hadn't felt the touch of a paint brush since they were spruced up for the coronation of George VI. Brad blinked as he stepped from the bright garden into the dark interior of the pub. As his eyes adjusted, he became aware of the low wooden ceiling beams, turned black from age and fireplace smoke, and the deep red of the velvet upholstery on the seats of the high-backed benches. The polyurethane coating on the rough-hewn planks of the tables reflected the soft light from the candle-shaped lamps on the walls. Here and there on the walls hung horse brasses of various sizes and shapes.

There were few patrons in sight and Brad made his way past the seats to the bar where a broad-shouldered man alternated between pushing buttons on an old adding machine and cursing under his breath. He seemed totally engrossed and looked up in surprise when Brad addressed him.

"I'm looking for John Rhodes. Is he here?"

"He's either here or you're speaking to his ghost. How can I help you?"

"Actually, I've come about your brother, Victor."

"Victor? Haven't seen him."

"Would you know where I might find him?"

"How would I know? He doesn't work here and he doesn't live here."

"I thought perhaps he had contacted you."

"About what? I haven't seen him in months."

"Are you sure? I need to talk to Victor in connection with a murder investigation."

"Murder!" Rhodes said leaning forward over the bar as if to steady himself. "Who are you? What do you want here?" he demanded and then turned away from Brad before suddenly turning back. "No—I don't care who you are—just get out of here! Go on, get out! I got work to do!" Rhodes snatched up a wet cloth and began scrubbing the bar hard enough to remove the varnish.

Brad stood his ground and reached silently into his vest pocket, pulling out his I.D. "I didn't come here to make trouble for you, Mr. Rhodes. My name is Basil Franklin and I'm with Scotland Yard. I need to talk to your brother. Have you seen him?"

The man continued to scrub the bar, but Brad persisted, "Have you seen Victor?"

Rhodes looked around as if hoping to find a place to hide. "He doesn't live here, you know. I'm not responsible for him."

"I understand that, but he hasn't been seen at his flat in London for days and his office appears abandoned."

"I don't know anything about his business."

"Do you know any of his friends? He's in the export business and was traveling in some high circles."

Rhodes waved his hand impatiently behind him framing the room with his motion. "Does it look like I hobnob with the gentry? He's always managed to party with the best, even when his pockets were empty. I don't mix in his social circles. He don't want to admit his brother is a bar keep."

"Where does Victor stay when he's in town?"

"I have no idea. It's not in Ivybridge. Look! I've told you I don't know where he is so just clear out!"

Chapter Thirteen

As far as Kon and Paul had been able to determine by tailing Compton, he was carrying on business as usual, coming into the office and going home on a regular schedule. Kon had not been able to find much information about Constance Compton, but a search through the files at the local newspaper office turned up the detail that she was a "friend of Kew Gardens." Every Wednesday she worked in the shop or helped with setting up special events. Accordingly, Kon chose Wednesday to search the Compton residence.

While checking on Compton's ownership of a dark blue Bentley, Paul had also learned that Compton's wife drove a light gray BMW. The Compton home, while not palatial, was comfortably situated in a partially wooded area north of Richmond Park known as Richmond Hill Rise. Kon parked his hired car well to the side of the road away from the house. He swung his pack of equipment over his shoulders and adjusted the straps. Most of the gear it contained would not be thought necessary for an ordinary hiking trip, but working with Jack tended to make one gadget-conscious. Kon rotated his shoulders a few times, trying to settle the gear into a more comfortable position and walked towards the gates. Although a storm had been predicted, only a light drizzle was falling and he hoped that the weather was not bad enough to deter Constance Compton from her usual Wednesday appointment. Kon had called Kew Gardens and learned that a school group was scheduled for a tour that afternoon. He hoped the approaching storm would not cause it to be canceled.

As Kon approached the driveway of the Compton's, he slowed his pace. He had noted while following Compton that it seemed to be the couple's habit to leave the huge iron gates open to the road. The two-story stucco house was painted a dark cream color and the large 16-pane casement windows evenly spaced on either side of the double wooden doors gave a pleasant, balanced look to the front. Huddled in the shadow of the main house on the west end was a two-car garage, which from the color of the paint, was obviously a new addition.

There were some low shrubs and various succulents in beds next to the house, but all the trees were set well away from the building.

Hiding himself in the branches of one of the evergreen trees, Kon scrutinized the grounds and peered in the windows using a pair of miniature, high-powered binoculars. He didn't see any motion detectors or any plaques notifying him that the premises were protected by an alarm system, but to be safe he scanned the house with a small, hand-held microwave sensor. Easing his way through the trees and sliding from bush to bush, he made his way to the back of the house where he made a mental note of the location of the various rooms. He saw that there was no porch or shed beneath any of the rear windows and that the wisteria vine clinging to the house looked too young and flimsy to hold his weight. He also noted the drainpipe fastened to the wall near a small window on the east end of the house.

By the time he had circled around to the front door, the light drizzle had changed to a steady rain, and his hair was wet and falling in his eyes. He brushed it back with his hand before he rang the bell. It appeared that no one was home, but he didn't want to be surprised by a live-in housekeeper.

When there was no answer, Kon rang a second time before he reached in his pocket for his latex gloves and lock picks. Then, with a last look over his shoulder, he set upon the lock. It was a standard household variety and, as he had hoped, presented no real problem. Kon pushed open the door quickly and stepped onto the highly-polished parquet floor of the entranceway. The floor was beautiful, but unfortunately, the mirror-like surface showed every ridge in Kon's rubber-soled shoes. Before taking another step, he sat by the door, removed his shoes, and placed them in a plastic bag in his pack. Retrieving a small towel from one of the zippered pockets, he blotted the moisture from his jacket and wiped away the two telltale footprints making sure to take up every bit of grit and moisture.

Hefting his pack once again, Kon took a quick look through the downstairs rooms in his sock feet and headed up the wide staircase. The thick carpet in all the upstairs rooms muffled his footsteps and he could hear no sounds except the faint ticking of the hall clock and the steady rhythm of the falling rain. He made a quick survey of the second floor rooms before going to the Master bedroom and concluded that despite Compton's extended affair with Elaina, he was not estranged from his wife. They still shared the same bed, if not the same interests. Kon hurried around the double bed which was decorated with a floral skirt and a matching duvet and headed for the large walk-in closet. His and her clothes hung neatly on either side of the huge space, with some of hers encroaching on the far end of his side. Kon pulled open a few of the small built-in drawers, but they contained nothing more sinister than lace panties or black socks.

Along the floor on each side of the closet shoe racks displayed footwear of every color and use imaginable. Getting on his knees, Kon quickly checked the soles of Compton's shoes, but he found no traces of cement powder. He was about to leave when he decided to check Mrs. Compton's shoes. She owned so many pairs it was quite a chore to pull each one forward and check the soles, but half way down the line, he found a pair of suede walking shoes that showed definite discoloration. Kon carefully scrapped some of the white powder into a plastic bag. It was quite possible that this pair of sturdy walking shoes could leave a footprint that could be mistaken for a man's. Kon continued to crawl around, checking all of Mrs. Compton's shoes, but he found nothing else of interest in the closet.

As he passed through the bedroom again, Kon glanced at the dressing table and spotted a small wooden jewelry box. He figured that Mrs. Compton kept most of her jewels in a safe hidden somewhere in the house, but he was curious as to what she kept out for day-to-day use. He turned the metal clasp, opened the lid and suddenly another piece of the puzzle fell into place. The single strand of pearls which was coiled carefully into one of the velvet compartments was broken and the clasp was missing. Kon had no doubt that the pearl Geilla had found would match the string in Mrs. Compton's box. Taking out his miniature camera, Kon snapped several pictures of the dressing table, the jewelry box, and the pearls. Before he could replace them, however, he heard the sound of a car coming up the drive. Damn the luck! he thought. I should have been faster. With a quick twist of his wrist he coiled the pearls back into their compartment and closed the box. Then he sprang to the window and peered out. He recognized the gray BMW and knew he had to get out fast.

Tossing his pack over one arm, he left the Master bedroom and dashed down the hall to the guest suite on the east end of the house. Hurrying into the bathroom, he threw open the window and looked out. "Damn you, Compton! Are you too busy chasing women to keep up the maintenance on your house?" he cursed under his breath when he saw that the drainpipe he had planned to use had come loose from the wall.

In disgust, he tossed his pack on the bathroom floor, zipped it open, and pulled out a 50-foot length of Dacron line. Then he zipped his pack closed and slung it on his back. Carefully he looped one end of the line around the heavy metal radiator and took both ends in his left hand. He backed across the room toward the window and pulled himself up onto the narrow sill. He pulled on the line once and then twice. I hope this radiator is fastened more securely than that blasted drainpipe, he thought and slipped his feet over the edge of the sill.

The radiator held, and Kon hung by the window for a moment to push it closed as far as possible without risking having the line caught by the metal frame. I hope the housekeeper doesn't take too much grief for leaving the window open, he thought as he used his large, strong hands and powerful arms to lower himself slowly down the wall. He felt extremely exposed crawling down the side of the house and prayed that the Compton's neighbors could not see him through the trees at the bottom of the back garden. He felt fairly certain that if Mrs. Compton was having a cuppa in either the kitchen or the dinning room, he would not be visible to her.

Rain pelted Kon as he came down the wall and as soon as he touched the ground he began to sink into the freshly turned flower bed. He was up to his ankles in mud by the time he had retrieved and recoiled his line. He slogged through more mud as he headed for the cover of a large stand of Pampas Grass that was growing on the edge of the property. Its wet, lacy fronds slapped him in the face as he peered out to see if the coast was clear. He couldn't see anyone, but decided to keep to the edge of the property and plowed through more Pampas Grass and slunk behind some evergreens as he crept toward the iron gates. He slipped his line under his jacket before making a final dash to the road.

There were no other pedestrians out, but the traffic on the road seemed heavy. He straightened himself and tried to appear nonchalant as he hurried toward the safety of his car. He hoped that no one driving past would notice the mud clinging to the bottom of his pant legs and oozing through his socks.

When he reached the car, he threw his line into the boot and closed the lid with a bang. He unlocked the driver's door, slipped his pack off his shoulder, and literally threw it and himself inside with a sigh of relief. As he brushed his wet hair out of his eyes, pine needles scattered across his chest. He also noticed that his latex gloves were shredded and the knuckles of his right hand were bleeding where they had scrapped against the rough stucco on the wall. "Shit!" he said aloud in disgust. "Why can't I learn to be happy sitting behind my desk like everyone else at the bank? Edgar would like it. Charlotte would like it. Geilla probably wouldn't mind." Oh, sure, he thought as he calmed down, two months of that and I'd be stark raving mad. I guess I'd sooner wear muddy socks than a straight jacket!

Zipping open the backpack, he unrolled a clean dry handkerchief and wiped his hands. He touched his knuckles to his mouth for a brief suck and decided that was all the medical attention they needed. He slipped his wet jacket off and was grateful that, except for where the wet line had rested, his upper body was dry. There was not much he could do about his wet pant legs until he could get the heater going. He pulled his shoes out of the plastic bag and threw them on the floor. Then he reached for the one piece of equipment Jack had trained him to carry without fail—a pair of dry socks. Good ol' Jack! Sometimes all this shit comes in handy, he thought as he peeled off his mud-encrusted socks. As much as he hated to waste anything, he rolled the socks into a ball and dropped them into the paper bag that held the remains of his carry-out lunch. Geilla would have a fit if I put these in the wash, he thought.

Feeling better once his feet were dry, he retrieved his thermos from the back seat and poured himself a cup of coffee. Still hot—Jack's right about this new thermos too, he thought gratefully. Setting the cup on the dash, he popped open the glove box and pulled out a small flask. Twisting off the cap, he poured a liberal ration of whiskey into his coffee. Jack's right about this too, he thought. Those Boy Scouts of his really know how to make the best of a bad situation.

Kon felt confident that the team had enough evidence to give to the police. He just wasn't sure how Brad wanted to go about turning it over. He decided to call in his report to Paul and drive down to Dorkin to visit with Edgar Paul for the evening. He'd probably be awake for a little while and, if not, he'd just hold him and marvel at how beautiful he was. It's easy to be a father now, he mused. E.P. doesn't ask much of me. But some day he will start talking and asking me questions. He will expect me to be wise and all knowing. What am I going to do then? Costa never told me anything about life. He just yelled orders at me and made me afraid of him. I don't want my son to be afraid of me. I want to be as good a father to E.P. as Edgar was to me. Dio mio, I don't know how Edgar managed it!

Chapter Fourteen

Geilla had been trying to check on Mysie by phone, but it wasn't working. She had made repeated attempts, but the phone went unanswered no matter what time she called. After a day and a half Geilla decided that she had better visit Mysie in person. She knew that the Plymouth Police had traced Elaina to Milton Keynes and were aware that Alona was really her child, not Mysie's. Geilla suspected that people from Social Services had contacted Mysie and sent her into a panic and she wanted to be there to help Mysie get through it all.

Geilla drove to Mysie's flat and using the keys that Brad had made from the impressions she had taken earlier, she cautiously let herself in the front door. That key had been easy to identify because Mysie had tagged it with a piece of red yarn. Geilla tried to match the size of the other keys to their function, but she still had to try twice before she found the right key to open the door to the flat. Once inside, she was not surprised that the flat was empty.

She took a quick look around and saw that Alona's pretty blue coat and bonnet were gone. Geilla had not been in Mysie's room before, but she searched through it carefully now. She suspected that Mysie didn't have a lot of clothes, but the closet looked almost bare and there was a pile of hangers on the closet floor, as if someone had pulled the clothes off in great haste. In Alona's room, the dresser drawers were hanging open, but there was very little left in them. Geilla's heart sank as she realized she was too late. Mysie must have received a call from the police and had flown with Alona. But where to? No doubt Davey would know, but who knew where he was. And was Mysie safe with Davey? Kon had learned that Davey was on parole after being convicted of burglarizing a pawnshop.

Since Kon and Paul were still in London, Geilla called Jack who agreed to check out some of Davey's former associates while she went to see Davey's mother. Geilla drove to St. Budeaux and found the address where she and Kon had let Davey off several nights ago.

The place looked even worse in the daylight. Paint was peeling off the fence surrounding a front yard overgrown by a scraggly rose bush and a few geraniums that had turned yellow and gone to seed. The front door, which Geilla could tell had once been a dignified shade of dark blue, was scratched and marred with footmarks from repeated kicking. Geilla surmised that the doorbell was not working and she was correct. She knocked several times and was speculating on the wisdom of trying a few kicks, when the door suddenly opened a crack.

"Mrs. Anslow, my name is Audrey Weeks," Geilla said quickly, addressing the one bloodshot eye that was visible by the edge of the door. "I'm looking for Davey. Do you know where he is?"

The eye blinked a few times before a throaty voice responded, "Wot you want with 'im? 'e's been reportin' regular and mindin' 'is own business."

"Oh yes, I know he's been trying to stay out of trouble, but I'm trying to locate a friend of his and I need to talk to him. I thought you might be able to tell me who some of Davey's friends are. May I come in?"

"You from the shop?" the voice asked, opening the door a little wider. Geilla could smell alcohol and wondered if the woman was sober enough to know what was going on in her own house.

"No. Actually I'm Mysie Platt's aunt. Do you know where Mysie has gone?"

"Don't know no Mysie. Wot she got to do with Davey?"

"She and Davey are friends, Mrs. Anslow. I though she might have told Davey where she was going or that Davey went somewhere with her."

"Davey don't go nowhere 'e ain't supposed to no more. I see ta that."

Geilla sighed, but still hoping there might be something in Davey's house that would give her a clue about Mysie, she pushed onward. "Do you know the names of any of Davey's friends that I might talk to?"

The door opened a bit wider as the woman thought for a moment and Geilla saw that she was wearing a terrycloth dressing gown that was festooned with dozens of pulled threads. She was barefoot and her greasy, gray hair was sticking out in all directions. "Don't know none of 'is friends. 'e don't bring 'em by."

"Would you mind if I came in and took a look at Davey's things. I might be able to find something that would help me. I am really worried about Mysie. It's not like her to go away without calling me."

Mrs. Anslow looked Geilla up and down a few times as if determining how difficult it would be to throw her out if she caused any trouble, and Geilla added quickly, "I promise I won't take anything if that's what you're worried about. I just need to find a name or a telephone number. Won't you please give me a hand to locate Mysie?"

"Oh why not? I was about to get up and about anyway," the woman answered and pulled the door open to its full width for Geilla. "Mind the magazines," she added, motioning to the stacks of papers scattered over the floor.

Mrs. Anslow led the way into the sitting room, hesitating a moment to nudge an empty liquor bottle under the sofa with her foot. Geilla heard a clink as it joined its friends. Geilla glanced around and saw that the entire house was in a terrible state of disrepair and neglect. Her heart went out to Davey. She knew full well what it was like to try to look after a parent who was an alcoholic. How is a boy supposed to stay out of trouble with a hopeless example like his mother always in front of him?

Mrs. Anslow pulled a cigarette from a pack sitting on a side table and lit it with a wooden kitchen match. She waved the pack at Geilla, but Geilla shook her head without answering. Mrs. Anslow wobbled as she led Geilla down the short hall and into one of the bedrooms and Geilla held her breath against the stench of stale clothing, booze and cigarettes.

"This 'ere's Davey's room. But 'e ain't home much," Mrs. Anslow said throwing open the door.

To Geilla's amazement the room was clean and orderly with built-in wooden shelves lining the walls. Although the assortment of knots betrayed the wood as cheap pine, the shelves had been finished with a pleasing walnut stain and were minus the thick layer of dust that coated every surface in the front room. "What a charming room," Geilla commented evenly, trying to hide her surprise. She went to a wooden table and tentatively shuffled a few papers to see if Davey might have jotted down any names or phone numbers. As she moved the papers aside she saw that the tabletop was marred with white water rings and blackened by cigarette burns. She pushed the papers back in place quickly, but not before Mrs. Anslow noticed the marks.

"'e didn't like it when I spoilt that table. It were an accident, but 'e carried on something awful. 'e helped 'is dad build it, ya see."

"I see. Mr. Anslow must be very clever with wood. Does he work as a carpenter or is it just a hobby?" Geilla asked trying to sound casual.

"Oh 'e was good with wood, but not with naught else," Mrs. Anslow answered derisively. "'e worked in one of them boatyards. Not no more though. 'e got 'isself killed in a fall years ago. Davey can work wood too. 'e made them shelves all by 'isself, but I told 'im there ain't no way I'm gonna let 'im work in a boatyard and get killed. 'is old man never left no insurance or nothin'. I told Davey no way was 'e goin' to do that! Not while I 'ad a say!"

"Of course," Geilla agreed. "Any good mother wants to protect her child—when did you say you last saw Davey?"

Mrs. Anslow scratched her head and squinted as if being asked to account for time was an impossible task. "Must 'ave been Sunday. 'e gets half day off on Sunday. 'E brought some take out. 'E knows I don't cook—not that I can't fix a real spread when I get up to it. But I don't seem to 'ave time no more what with house work and the garden . . ."

"Yes," Geilla nodded, faking understanding. She picked through some more of the papers and pulled open a drawer that was skillfully fitted into the table. She shut it quickly before Davey's mother could see that crumpled inside was a long-outdated catalog of woodworking tools. So much for a boy's dreams, she thought. I really have to find him and Mysie before he gets into more trouble with the law. She turned to speak to Mrs. Anslow. "Thank you for your time, Mrs. Anslow. I don't see anything here that will help me find Mysie. When Davey comes back, will you ask him to call me?" she said handing Davey's mother a card with the name Audrey Weeks on it.

"Sure. You wouldn't 'appen to 'ave a few pound I could borrow to lay in some vitals for fixin' Davey a meal, would yer? Just until Davey gets 'is paycheck yer understand. I didn't 'ave time to go . . . ."

"Of course. I know how busy you must be," Geilla answered tactfully. She opened her handbag and passed the woman some bills without looking. It will probably all go for booze, but one can always hope, she thought sadly, once again remembering her father.

While Geilla was talking with Davey's mother, Jack was busy tracking down Davey's friends. According to a newspaper account of the local crime scene, an older lad named Mike Markey and a boy named Hubie Winters had been arrested along with Davey for the pawnshop burglary. The newspaper also mentioned that Mike's mother was known to keep company with the owner of the shop.

At the trial, Mr. Banks the owner of the shop, had testified that he had given a key to his flat, which was over the shop, to Mrs. Markey. He also testified that during the course of an all night visit, Mrs. Markey had become aware that although the front door and windows of the shop had been fortified by an elaborate metal grating, Mr. Banks could ascend from his flat to his shop by way of a secret staircase.

Mrs. Markey had strenuously denied that she had given the key to Mr. Banks' flat to her son, but she did admit that she might have mentioned the secret staircase to him. In any event, a local locksmith testified that he remembered Mike coming into the shop to get a key duplicated. The police had been able to match the paint scrapings on a television set found in Mike Markey's room to the paint on Mr. Bank's wall. Mike was arrested and immediately implicated Davey and Hubie. None of the stolen goods were found at Davey's house, but the fact that his finger prints were found in the shop and that he refused to cooperate with the police investigation earned him a six month term as a guest of Her Majesty at Exeter Prison. It hadn't helped his case that he and his mother had frequently been charged with disturbing the peace after late night screaming matches on the street in front of their house. Their landlord had attempted to get them evicted several times, but Davey had always been able to come up with the rent at the last minute, and in cash which seemed suspicious.

Jack went to visit Mrs. Markey at the St. Budeaux address listed in the newspaper account of Mike's arrest. When he started asking about Mike, she maintained that Mike had been a model citizen since he had been released on parole and had found work as a mechanic's helper at a local car dealership on Edgcumb Street. Jack drove to the shop at normal speed, but gunned his engine and turned into the car park with a squeal of tires. He brought the car to an abrupt stop in front of the glass display windows and jumped out leaving the car door hanging open. There weren't many customers in the showroom and all heads turned as Jack stormed up to the counter and announced in a booming voice, "I'm looking for Mike Markey. Where is that little weasel?"

The manager of the shop was aware that Mike was on parole and had been visited by Mike's parole officer several times, but it had always been low-keyed and conversational. He was startled and thrown off guard by what he thought was a sudden change of approach. "Er . . . Mike's in the back. Is anything wrong?" he asked quietly as he came around the counter.

"It all depends," Jack said holding the manager in a steady stare. "I need to get some answers and I need to get them now!"

The manager held his hands up in front of him as if to show that he had nothing to hide. "All right, go and talk to him. But please, keep your voice down. Mike's doing a good job here and is trying to stay out of . . . "

"Where is he?" Jack boomed again.

"He's in the back—through that door," the manager said pointing to a metal door.

As Jack strode to the door and pulled it open he heard the manager plead, "Why can't you leave the kid alone? He's trying to make a new start."

"Sure, sure," Jack growled, "Mike Markey! Come on out here, you little sneak thief, I want to talk to you!"

No one came forward, but Jack heard a tool drop at the back of the shop. There was tense silence for a moment until the manager called, "It's all right, Mike. I know you're trying to do a good job.

Please come out and talk to this man so he'll leave us all alone."

Jack pulled a notebook out of his pocket and waited. He heard some nervous whispers and then a tall lad with long hair tied back with a rubberband sidled out from behind one of the cars. Jack hurried forward, took him by the arm and pulled him toward the open door of the bay.

"Good to see you got a job, Mike. You been behaving yourself?"

"Yeah. What's the big problem? I didn't do anything."

"You're sure about that, are you?"

"Yeah, I'm sure."

"Good. I wouldn't want to get your boss upset over nothing. Actually, I'm looking for one of your friends, Mike—Davey Anslow. Know where he is?"

"No. I'm not supposed to hang out with Davey no more."

"That's not what I hear. I hear you and he been cooking up some new deals."

"Who said that? That's a lie! I don't know what Davey is up to, but I had nothing to do with it."

"So you're telling me you don't know that Davey's disappeared with a girl and her baby? He's in big trouble, Mike. Kidnaping is serious business. Davey's going away for a long time when we catch him. You'll be in trouble too if you helped him."

"I didn't help him. An' I don't know nothing about no kidnaping."

"Where did they go, Mike?"

"I don't know. Look, I mean it. I swear I don't know. He came here asking for money and I told him I couldn't help him."

"You'd better be telling me the truth, Mike. If not, I'll be back. I may just come back anyway," Jack threatened. Without another word, Jack walked out through the bay doors and back to his car. Davey's a fool if he thinks that Mike's his friend, he thought to himself. First he rats on him to the police and then he turns him away when he needs money.

Jack was disappointed that he hadn't gotten more information from Mike, but he didn't dare try twisting his arm while he was pretending to be a police officer. Jack drove to the address he had found for Hubie Winters, the other boy who had been arrested for the pawn shop burglary. It was not far from Davey Anslow's block. He knew from the look of it that it was Council housing, but the building looked neat and the tiny front garden was well cared for. He opened the front gate, went up the walk and knocked on the door. There was no answer for several minutes and he knocked again, using more force. In reply he heard some banging and then the door was jerked open.

"Will you quit banging the house down or I'll sic the dogs on ya!" threatened a hairy-chested man who was hastily tying a faded plaid dressing gown around himself.

"I'm sorry. I didn't mean to wake you," Jack apologized politely, although he was not at all intimidated by the man.

The man scratched his head and yawned as if he was half-asleep. "You didn't, now. You mean to tell me all that bloody pounding was yer idea of a lullaby? What you want?"

"Are you John Winters?"

"And who would be askin'?"

"Robert Woods. I'm with Social Services," Jack lied and extended his hand.

The man ignored Jack's outstretched hand. "Social Services? It ain't exactly social to wake up a man who works the night shift! Wot you want with me?

"I'm just checking on a report we got about Hubie."

"Hubie? Wot you want with him? He's been behaving hisself. The police are satisfied—why you botherin' him?"

"I was just checking that he had proper supervision. It's just a formality."

"Formality? Listen, we had enough formality from the police. A kid gets into one scrape and people are after him for life. Well, let me tell you, Hubie's a good kid and he gets plentya supervision. I'm here near every day and his mum is here every night."

"I see," Jack said contritely. "Then the message I received must be incorrect. And where might Hubie be now?"

"He's either at school or at that pizza place he works at. He don't have time to get in trouble. You better get your messages straight before you go pounding on people's doors."

"I'll make a note to do that," Jack answered. "And might I ask where Mrs. Winters is?"

"She's at work."

"And where is the pizza place where Hubie works?"

"It's over on Wolseley Road near the railroad station."

"Thank you. And thank you for your time. I'll be sure to put a note in the file that you work nights so no one will disturb you again."

"Yes, do that, will ya. It's hard enough trying to sleep with kids yelling in the street and vans going by."

"Yes, quite—well, I won't disturb you any longer," Jack said and backed away from the door. He raised his arm in a friendly greeting before he turned to leave, and Mr. Winters gave a spontaneous, but limp response and closed the door.

Jack went back to his car and drove to Wolseley Road. He drove up and down and stopped at two places that advertised pizza before he decided that Mr. Winters must have meant an Italian Restaurant called Ricci's. He parked the car and went in being careful to duck his head to avoid getting hit in the eye by the clusters of artificial grapes hanging from the ceiling. A dark-haired waitress wearing a short red skirt quickly appeared and offered him a menu. She appeared genuinely disappointed when he declined, stating that he wanted to see Hubie Winters.

"Another friend of Hubie! Aren't you a bit too old to be knocking about with Hubie?"

"Well, actually I'm with Social Services."

"I knew you didn't come for a meal. I just knew it. Look here, Hubie's old enough to work and he only comes in after school. Don't you come bothering honest people."

"I didn't come to bother anyone. I just came to talk to Hubie. I'm trying to help a young girl—honestly."

"Oh sure. She forget to ask your permission before she had a kid, that it? Well Hubie's not the father. He's just a kid."

"I didn't say he was anyone's father. I just need to talk to him. Please," Jack concluded. He was starting to wish he had pretended to be a cop instead of a social worker.

"All right," the waitress relented. "He's in the back. Don't go upsetting him so he cuts himself instead of the bread." She turned and walked through an opening in the fake grape arbor and Jack followed. They passed the cash register and then she opened a door and called over the sound of running water. "Hey, Hubie—come on out here will you. The pot police want to make sure you're scrubbing fast enough!"

The sound of the water ceased abruptly and a voice answered. "What'd you say, Mrs. Longardi?"

"I said there's a man here to see you." Suddenly a boy who looked about fifteen stepped around a stack of crates. He hesitated when he saw Jack, but the woman put a hand on his shoulder. "If you gonna keep inviting your friends in to watch you work, you gotta talk them into eating some spaghetti, Hubie. Don't keep him from his work," she cautioned Jack before she turned and left. Jack closed the door she had left open and noticed that Hubie looked tense. He stared at Jack for a few minutes, but didn't say anything.

"I'm looking for Davey Anslow. Do you know where he is?" Jack asked abruptly.

Hubie gave a nervous jump, but started shaking his head rapidly. "I haven't seen him lately."

"Are you sure?" Jack pressured.

"Yeah, I'm sure," Hubie answered firmly.

"He's in big trouble, you know. The police are after him about a kidnapping. I'm with Social Services and I need to get to him first to hear his side of the story."

"I don't know where he is," Hubie insisted.

"You'll be in trouble too—as an accomplice. The police don't take kindly to kidnapping. You got off easy last time, but kidnapping's heavy stuff. You and Davey could be put away for a long time."

Hubie blanched, but remained silent.

"I'm just trying to help Davey stay out of trouble, but if you won't cooperate, I guess I'll have to tell the police. If they can't find Davey, they'll have to arrest you. What's your dad gonna say?"

"You got it all wrong!" Hubie blurted. "It weren't no kidnaping. She wanted to go away. She said you blokes was after her baby. Davey was just trying to help."

"Where did Davey take her?"

Hubie bit his lip and looked down at the floor.

"Come on, Hubie. You've got to tell me. They've got a baby with them—think about that."

Hubie shuffled from one foot to the other. "You won't send the police if I tell you?"

"No. I just want to make sure they're safe. If nobody's been kidnaped, there won't be any trouble."

Hubie's chest rose and fell with a huge sigh. "Davey took her to hide out at his gran's. She lives up north."

"Where?"

"I don't know. Weren't none of my business. Davey said he was comin' back."

"How was Davey planning on getting up north? His bike's still at the shop."

Hubie sighed heavily again.

"Do you want to tell me or the police, Hubie? I'm only trying to help him stay out of jail."

"He borrowed Mr. Finch's car. He only uses it once a week. The old coot's so daft we figured he wouldn't never notice the thing was gone."

"How did Davey get the car going?"

"It was no big deal. Like I said—Finch is daft. He locks the garage, but leaves the keys in the car."

"What make of car are we talking about?"

"It an old Triumph—'70 or '71, but the body is like new."

"What color?"

"Red."

"What's the plate number?"

"Hell, I don't know. We weren't going to keep it long enough to pay taxes on it."

"When did he leave?"

"I'm not sure."

"I need more information, Hubie. They could be lost or broken down somewhere."

"Davey came by here the night before last. We got to talking and we remembered about the car. We used to talk about going for a ride some night, but once he and Mike got . . . well, Davey's been trying to cool it, so we never did. "

"Where does Finch live?"

"Same block as Davey. Everybody knows him—been there a hundred years. He keeps the car in a hired garage one street over. "

"How did you get into the garage?"

"Promise you won't tell the police?"

"Come on, Hubie. You're in this with Davey. You either help me or you're both going away. "

"Davey's going to think I'm a ratface . . ."

"Davey could be up for being a car thief and a kidnapper if I can't get him back right away. "

"O.K. We cut the lock. We was going to tell Mr. Finch we saw somebody sneaking around and we scared them off. "

"You boys have a lot of imagination. I hope you're not giving me a bunch of horse shit right now. "

"No! I'm telling you the truth. You got to tell Davey I was just trying to keep him out of trouble. He won't let me hang out with him no more if he thinks I can't be trusted. "

"One more question, Hubie. Does Mike know where Davey went?"

"Hell no! Davey said he went to Mike about a car and some money and Mike wouldn't even talk to him. Besides if he knew, he'd rat for sure. He's all for himself, man. "

"O.K., Hubie. You just sit tight until you hear from me. I'll do my best to get to Davey before the police do. In the meantime, if they show up, don't volunteer that I was here. "

"Don't worry! I'm not going to tell nobody nothin' until I talk to Davey. "

Chapter Fifteen

As Hubie had reported, the padlock on the garage door had been sawed through and the garage was empty. Since it was now Wednesday and, if Hubie was right, Mr. Finch would not realize his car was missing until Friday, Jack decided not to tell him that someone had borrowed his vehicle. If he could locate Davey and Mysie and get the car back by Friday, no one would be the wiser.

Armed with the information about Davey's grandmother, Jack called Geilla to let her know that he was going to pay a visit to Mrs. Anslow. As Geilla had suspected, Mrs. Anslow had used the money she had given her for alcohol and she was far from coherent by the time Jack knocked on her door. In one way her condition made the encounter easier for Jack because she quickly accepted that he was from the police. But getting a straight answer about an address for Davey's grandmother was decidedly more difficult.

Mrs. Anslow made no effort to hide her hostility toward her mother-in-law, Esby Anslow. She claimed she had no idea whether the woman was dead or alive. In the end, however, Mrs. Anslow agreed to let Jack look through Davey's things and did not shadow his every move as she had done to Geilla. He was grateful the boy was so neat compared to his mother, but it still took Jack well over an hour to find an address on an old letter in Davey's room. As Jack scanned the letter he understood why Davey would hie to Esby for help. She undoubtedly was the mysterious source of cash that kept Davey and his mother from being evicted. Jack wrote down the address and carefully replaced the letter. He felt fairly certain that Esby Anslow would know the whereabouts of Mysie and Alona, but since it was already four o'clock and rain was still falling steadily, he debated the effectiveness of driving across the moor to Manaton. He decided to drive to Derriford Hospital and discuss the situation with Bridget.

He had been finding one excuse or another to talk to Bridget since the team had come to Plymouth. In fact, he had been going to visit

Bridget since the previous fall when he first met her in Paris. She had been there for some advanced training for her air rescue squad and he had been on an assignment with the team. He figured that Paul suspected he was involved with someone, but so far no one on the team had met Bridget. Even after all this time, Jack wasn't willing to admit to himself or anyone else just how "involved" he felt about Bridget.

Bridget was on duty when Jack arrived, but she didn't scold him for interrupting her work. She always worked a full shift while waiting for an emergency to come up that needed the air transport squad.

"Hello, Jack. I see that the weather hasn't improved. What's the situation?" Bridget called in her crisp accent when she came into the reception area in answer to his page.

Jack stood by the reception counter trying to let the water rolling down his foul weather coat gather in one great puddle on the floor. "I can't be sure, but it looks pretty certain that Mysie and the kid are with Davey. He stole a car the night before last, and I think he headed for his gran's in Manaton. I was wondering if you could get the chopper so we could go after them."

"Have they been reported missing?"

"Not yet, but there's nobody to report Mysie and Davey's mum is too drunk to realize that he hasn't been home for days."

"Oh dear. Did you call his gran to see if they have arrived?"

"I checked with the phone company, but she doesn't own a phone. Besides, I don't want to warn them that I'm on to them."

"Well, we could make a case that this is an emergency, but with the weather being what it is, I doubt I could get clearance for taking the bird up."

"I'd be willing to try, but I don't suppose they'd let me fly it."

"I doubt it, but I have another idea. Didn't you say the gran lives in Manaton?"

"Yes. I got the address off a fairly recent letter to Davey."

"Well, as I remember, there's a lovely inn there called the Blue Goose. People of all kinds are always wondering in off the moor. Some are on holiday and others are just lost or missed the last bus. The rescue squad used their place as a base one time and I've met the owners . . . nice couple. Let me ring them up and see if they or any of their customers saw Davey and Mysie coming by."

"It's worth a try."

"Sure it is. In a little village like that someone might notice if an old woman suddenly had company. I'll go look for the number. And sit down, Jack. Don't worry about the wet, the chairs are plastic."

Bridget scurried off without waiting for Jack to answer. She was gone for what seemed a long time, and she wasn't smiling when she returned. "I found the number. I thought I had better call since I sort of know the owners. They haven't seen a couple with a little girl, but they promised to ask around. The owner offered to send someone down to talk to Mrs. Anslow, but I told him we didn't want to upset her in case the youngsters are lost."

"That was wise," Jack agreed. "Something might have happened to the car. You certainly have a network of eyes and ears working for you, Bridget."

Bridget smiled self-consciously. "Oh, you get to know a lot of people in my line of work. Folks in these lonely places have to rely on one another. What do you want to do now? My shift's over and I'd be happy to drive out there with you. It's not really all that late even though it is getting dark."

"I want to go now before somebody gets the bright idea to put Mysie on a bus to somewhere else. And I need to see about the car before the old guy Davey stole it from realizes it's gone. The longer we wait the more trouble those kids are going to be in."

"All right then. Just let me get my coat and Wellies and a torch and I'll be ready to go." She glanced quickly at the large face of her watch before continuing, "We can pick up some sandwiches at the market down the street on our way out. They do a lovely cheese and pickle."

"Good idea. I've got a heavy duty jack and a tow line in the Rover."

"Splendid! Be back in a jiff," Bridget said and disappeared leaving Jack feeling once again that she was always one step ahead of him. Would any other woman be willing to go chasing over the moor with me on a night straight out of Edgar Allen Poe? Probably not, he decided, thinking once again that he was very lucky to know a woman like Bridget.

Bridget was true to her word about not needing long to get ready and soon they were headed over the narrow roads to Manaton. Jack wasn't sure what route the youngsters had taken, but since the car Davey was driving was old and stolen, he was betting that Davey would choose the longer route across the moor rather than risk going on the carriageway. The rain was falling in torrents and splashing up again like geysers from every dip in the road. Jack gripped the steering wheel to keep from being pulled off the road, feeling more like he was guiding a boat across the sea than driving a vehicle across the countryside. They made a rest stop at a pub in Princetown and headed on.

Bridget unwrapped the sandwiches, broke off little pieces, and fed them to Jack who gobbled them down, trying not to scatter bits of pickle all down his front. But even Bridget's caring could not make the driving seem like anything other than a tiring chore. Finally as they crossed a cattle grating near a bridge, Bridget called out, "Stop! There's a car back there."

"Where? I didn't see anything."

"It was off the road. It must have slid into the ditch."

"Are you sure?"

"Yes, I'm sure. I just caught a glimpse of something, but it was too red to be a cow."

"All right. I'll go back. I just need to find a place to turn around without landing us in a ditch too."

Jack drove on another five hundred yards before he found a rise that he judged safe enough to use to turn the Rover around. He drove slowly back toward the bridge, but he didn't see anything.

"Is this where you saw the car?"

"Yes, but I didn't spot it when we came back this way."

"O.K. I'll have to turn around again. Jeez I wish this blasted rain would let up," Jack said, staring ahead for a place to turn around safely.

Jack turned the Rover again in a tight circle and crept over the bridge in second gear, while Bridget peered intently out the window. "There it is," she called excitedly just after they reached the north end of the bridge.

"I see it," Jack confirmed. Pulling to the edge of the narrow road, he set the brake and turned on the flashers. "I'll go see if I can determine what happened. You wait here."

"I don't mind the rain if you need help," Bridget put in airily.

"I appreciate the offer, but let me check it out first," Jack said, struggling into his foul weather coat and pulling up the hood.

Bridget smiled at him in the dark, and leaning over she tugged playfully on the peak of his hood and planted a kiss on his cheek. "Such chivalry. Makes me wish I had a lace token to give you."

Jack turned his head and kissed her full on the lips. "Hummmm. If you've got anything lacy, I wouldn't mind seeing it when we get back to Plymouth."

Bridget answered his kiss with her own before pulling away. "Oh, noble sir, I fear I doth distract you from your quest. Out you go now and let this gentle rain cool you off. Here, take this," she added, handing him a torch.

"Cruel maiden!" Jack mumbled as he opened the door.

Bridget watched him walk away noting with alarm how quickly he disappeared into the wet blackness.

Jack was grateful that Bridget's torch had a bright beam, but the light was absorbed by the ocean of darkness and he had to focus the beam directly in front of his feet to see anything at all. He stumbled ahead trying to guesstimate how far he had come. He looked back, searching for the comfort of the Rover's flashing lights, but they too had been absorbed by the darkness. Jack half expected to have to push the darkness aside to move forward, it was so thick, but his feet moved as easily as ever.

After he had gone what he estimated was two hundred yards, and hadn't seen the car, he thought he must have passed it. He raised the torch and waved it up and down and from side to side. He went forward a few more feet and tried again, then once again. On the fourth try, he picked up a reflection from the chrome fender. Heartened, he hurried forward with the torch upraised until he saw the Triumph.

The front end was headed into the ditch at a forty-five degree angle to the road. Jack slid down the low bank and circled the car. The right front tire was flat and the passenger door was jammed against a bush, but he managed to pull the driver's door open. As he guessed, the ignition key was gone. He searched carefully over the dash board, up and down the seat and over the floor in both the front and back, but he didn't find any bloodstains. The windscreen was still intact, but there was no indication whether or not anyone's head had bounced against it recently. Jack finally closed the door again and trudged back to the Rover.

"Any sign of them?" Bridget asked.

"There was nothing in either the front or the back. I hope that means they left under their own power."

"The rescue squad didn't have a record of any call, so let's hope for the best. Would you like more coffee before we start again?"

"Sure. It's so black it feels like it's midnight."

"There's a bus that takes this road. Perhaps they took that when the car broke down."

"I hope so. And it wasn't pouring down rain yesterday. That would make it easier for the little kid. I'm glad I don't really work for Social Services."

"You're worried about the baby, aren't you?"

"Well, sure. Aren't you?"

"Of course. I just didn't realize how much you liked kids."

"I don't have anything against kids," Jack said defensively. "I don't usually have anything to do with them in my line of work. Don't you like kids?"

"Oh yes! I hope someday . . . " Bridget began but quickly lapsed into silence. The men on the rescue squad never wanted to hear what she hoped for her life. They got embarrassed and impatient with anything that reminded them that she was a woman.

"Good. That's settled then. Let's get going," Jack said decisively, leaving Bridget wondering what had been settled.

Chapter Sixteen

Jack had stopped at the Blue Goose Inn when he and Bridget arrived in Manaton shortly after seven, but neither the owners nor any of the patrons reported having seen Davey or Mysie. Bridget managed to get detailed directions to Esby Anslow's cottage, but even with all the help of 'close by' and 'opposite the' it was hard to spot in the pouring rain. After passing by twice, Bridget finally spotted the number when a strong gust of wind lifted a leafy branch that was hiding the small sign.

A short, plump woman with white hair pulled back into a tight bun answered the door after Jack's third knock. Without a word she quickly pulled Jack and Bridget inside and closed the door against the weather.

"My, my, I see it's still bad out there," she said and smiled as if she was satisfied that she had saved the last two souls in Manaton from drowning.

Jack took a minute to control the water running down his foul weather gear before asking, "Are you Esby Anslow?"

"Aye, that's me," she answered openly.

Jack threw his hood back and unbuttoned his jacket before continuing, "Mrs. Anslow, my name is Robert Woods and I'm with Social Services. I've come about a young lady named Mysie Platt. Have you seen her?"

Mrs. Anslow's smile retreated suddenly, but she remained calm. "Oh dear. I didn't expect you so soon. It must be a fearsome matter to bring you out in weather like this."

"I know this is hard, but Davey and Mysie could be in a lot of trouble with the police if I can't get them back to Plymouth very soon."

"Davey's had enough trouble from the police, Mr. Woods."

"I know he's been in trouble and I don't want to add to your worries, but this is serious, Mrs. Anslow."

She nodded. "Aye and I can't let you take him away again. He's a good boy to have such troubles. But nothing can be decided standin' here. Please come in and I'll put the kettle on. You both look half drowned comin' out on a night like this."

"Can I help you with anything, Mrs. Anslow?" Bridget asked, knowing the answer before she asked.

"No dear. I suspect I need to putter about a bit while I settle. Hang your wet things here," she said, indicating a row of wooden pegs along the wall in the narrow entry hall. "Then come in and sit. I'll call the young'uns down." She turned and ambled away slowly leaving Jack and Bridget alone in the hall.

"This is not going to be fun," Jack whispered as he removed his coat and hung it on a peg.

Bridget nodded slipping off her Wellies and peeling off her foul weather gear. When they were down to dry clothes, she and Jack started to plod down the hall in their sock feet. Suddenly Jack stopped. "I think I'd better guard the door. Davey may try to bolt."

Bridget looked surprised but nodded. "You know best." She went through to the sitting room and a few minutes later Jack heard the cheerful chirp of a teakettle. He waited, listening for any sound from the upstairs rooms, but the house was quiet. He heard Mrs. Anslow say something to Bridget, but he couldn't make it out. A moment later she came through the door and saw him. She seemed disappointed.

"Don't worry, Mr. Woods. Davey's not going to leave Mysie and that baby to fend for themselves." She squeezed past Jack and climbed the stairs with a quickness that belied her size.

Jack was prepared to hear shouting or screaming from the second floor, but all was quiet. After several minutes Jack began to wonder if he had misjudged Mrs. Anslow. Perhaps her welcoming smile is part of a premeditated plan to get me to take my coat off while Davey and Mysie escape out a window. He was about to start up the stairs to check out his theory when he heard a door open above him. Quickly he slipped back to his post by the door. Looking up the stairs, he saw two of the most frightened faces he had seen since he had evacuated villagers in 'Nam.

Davey came down first. It was obvious that the fear of being sent to jail again had wrung every last drop of bravado from him. Jack recalled the parole officer recounting stories of the thrashings Davey had endured at Exeter because he refused to take part in harassing one of the young men who had been labeled a faggot. Davey had not been streetwise when he was sent away and even after six months inside, he still could barely hold his own in a fight.

Mysie followed Davey down, clinging to his arm as if she was incapable of moving under her own power. She too looked as if she was on her way to an execution. Mrs. Anslow followed behind the young folks, smiling and urging them on with, "Now go on down and sit quiet. Everything's going to be all right."

Oh boy! I was right about this not being fun, Jack thought as Davey and Mysie inched past him and headed for the sitting room.

"Now, Mr. Woods," Mrs. Anslow began while she was still standing above Jack on the stairs. "I have delivered these children unto your mercy and I expect you to use them kindly."

Jeez! Jack thought with a touch of resentment. I'm not the one who wants to take the kid away. Well, I guess she doesn't know that. "I'm just trying to save everyone a lot of trouble, Mrs. Anslow."

"Let's go in then and see if we can't find a sensible solution," she answered and coming down the stairs, she led Jack into the sitting room.

Mysie and Davey sat huddled together on the old worn sofa opposite the fireplace. Jack took a seat across from them, folding his long legs so he wouldn't kick anyone. Bridget sat in a rocker to the right of Mysie, and Mrs. Anslow hovered, pouring tea. Jack noticed that she was using dark brown stoneware mugs and wondered if she always used them or if she was worried that Mysie and Davey were too nervous to be trusted with her fine china. She passed around a plate of biscuits, but no one seemed interested.

Jack sipped his tea, trying to decide how he should start. Ah hell! I might as well jump in with both feet, he decided. "I guess you kids know you're in a lot of trouble," he began. Two pairs of eyes looked at his for a moment then continued studying the pattern on the braided rug.

Jack sighed. "What did you think you were gaining by stealing Mr. Finch's car, Davey? Were you planning on hiding out here on the moor for the rest of your life? You're still on parole for God's sake. Do you know what will happen if you don't report in?"

Davey shifted his feet and looked at Jack for a fleeting moment, but said nothing.

"Look, I didn't come here to threaten you. I work with Audrey Weeks and her husband and I came to see that you got back to Plymouth before anyone knows that you and that car and that baby are missing."

"You know Audrey?" Mysie chirped in surprise.

"Yes. We're all working to find Elaina's killer."

"How come so many people are interested in Elaina?"

Jack decided not to go into details. "Elaina was involved in some serious stuff, Mysie. There's a lot of investigations going on."

"Are you workin' for the coppers?"

"No. As a matter of fact, I'm not really from Social Services. I'm just trying to keep you out of trouble."

"Why? What do you care about the likes of us?"

Jack shrugged and Bridget cut in before he could answer. "It doesn't matter who he works for, Mysie. His real job is to help folks get straightened out."

Mysie and Davey digested this without comment and Jack started asking more questions.

"Why did you let Mike Markey talk you into robbing that pawn shop, Davey? That wasn't very bright."

"He didn't talk me into it. It was my idea."

"Your idea! Why? Were you bored or looking for thrills?"

"No. We weren't supposed to take stuff. It was just . . ."

"Just what? Just to prove you were a smartass?"

"No! I . . . I just wanted to get my dad's toolbox before Mr. Banks sold it. I kept tryin' to save enough money, but mum was always . . . Hell! It was all I got left from him, ya know. It wasn't worth nothin' to nobody else, but I really . . . Turned out it was gone by the time I went in. I looked all though everything."

"Did Mike know what you wanted in the shop?"

"Yeah. He's the one who told me about the secret stairs. He pinched the key from his mum. We was just supposed to go in and get the box, but Mike saw this big TV and he had to have it. I tried to talk him out of it, but there's no talkin' to Mike once he gets his head made up."

"Aw jeez!" Jack blurted as the cause of Davey's brief crime wave sank in. "Why didn't you tell anyone, Davey?"

"It wouldn't 'ave mattered. Everyone on the block told the coppers my mum and me were no good. She don't keep the place up too good and me . . . well, I make noise sawin' and nailin' at 'ungodly hours'," Davey said rolling his eyes in what Jack guessed was an imitation of indignant neighbors. "I can't help I got to work late a lot and it's a long way home from where I work. None of them neighbors would hire me. Just 'cause my mum pinches a bottle now and then don't mean I don't work hard." When Davey finished speaking he sat, staring at his hands.

"You made it hard on yourself, Davey. When you wouldn't speak up, the cops thought sure you were hiding something terrible."

"I just wanted to get it over with. The coppers kept comin' 'round botherin' my mum. Then she'd start yellin' and the neighbors were hangin' out the windows. The landlord was threaten' to put us out. I thought things would quiet down if I just went away. Everyone acted like I was a criminal anyway, so what did it matter?"

Davey's hopeless passivity bothered Jack. "How old are you, Davey?"

"Goin' on twenty-one."

"Oh, what kind of story are you telling, Davey?" Mrs. Anslow objected immediately. "You're going on twenty-one like I'm going on dead! You just got to eighteen a few months ago. Now don't be making your gran older than she is."

"I'm sorry, gran. It's just easier to get a job if folks think you're older."

"Well, if you want to keep your job you need to get back to town," Jack warned.

"Are the police looking for Davey?" Mrs. Anslow asked.

"Not yet, but as soon as Mr. Finch reports his car's been stolen, they'll be after him."

"Oh, Davey, you didn't tell me you stole a car. I thought you came on the bus."

"I'm sorry, gran. I just couldn't wait. I had to get Mysie out of town real quick."

"Running away never solves anything, Davey. You know that. I think you'll have to go back with Mr. Woods and straighten things out. He's right about you being on parole."

"It ain't that easy, gran. The car went in a ditch. It might 'ave broke an axle or something. There ain't no way I can get it fixed."

"Well, maybe I can help you out a bit. Miss Keegan's been anxious to get herself that last quilt I did up. Might as well make somebody happy from all this trouble."

"That won't be necessary, Mrs. Anslow," Jack cut in. "I can arrange to have the car fixed or towed or whatever it needs."

"That's very generous of you, Mr. Woods, but I can't let you pay for Davey's mistakes. How's he going to learn right from wrong?"

"I think he knows the difference, Mrs. Anslow. I think he was just in a hurry to help Mysie and kinda got confused. I think he only meant to borrow the car. Isn't that right, Davey?"

"Yeah, I was goin' to take it back tomorrow morning, but once it went in the ditch . . ."

"I can get it out of the ditch tomorrow, Davey, but I need to get Mysie back to town before the police come looking for her. If they think she's run away with Alona, she'll be in big trouble. What do you say, will you come back with me tonight?"

"I don't know . . . ," Davey began hesitantly, but Mysie cut him off. "I don't care what you say, Mister whatever-you-said-your-name-is. I'm not takin' Lonie back to Plymouth. If you really cared about her welfare, you'd find that woman who wants to hurt her."

"What woman?" Jack asked in surprise.

"The lady what sent Elaina them nasty letters."

"What letters? I didn't hear about any letters."

"I didn't know 'bout them before, but when I was cleaning up Elaina's room after I learned she was dead I found 'em behind the dresser. I don't know if they fell back there or if Elaina was hidin' them. When I read them they gave me the shivers."

"How many were there? Who are they from?" Bridget asked.

"I don't know—they wasn't signed. Some woman sent them to Elaina's post box. Elaina never said nothin' 'bout them, but maybe that's why she never let me talk to the neighbors too much. She made out like I was Lonie's mum. Maybe she didn't want to scare me. I sure was scared for Lonie when I read them letters. That woman was saying bad things about Elaina too and look what happened to her."

"Do you still have the letters?" Jack asked.

"Yeah, they're back at the flat."

"We need to get them to the police. If this woman is threatening Alona they can protect her."

"I can't tell the police. They don't know Lonie's not my kid. That woman sure knows. I think Elaina was trying to get money outa her husband 'cause he was Lonie's dad."

Jack exchanged a quick look with Bridget before turning back to Mysie. "Mysie, those letters may have something to do with who killed Elaina. Don't you want to find out who did it and see them punished?"

"Sure I do, but I don't want nobody to take Alona away. She's all I got and I love her like she was mine."

"We understand that," Bridget said reaching across and taking Mysie by the hand. "We'll do everything we can to help you, but if you're hiding, it's going to look very bad. The police already know that Alona's not your baby, but they haven't pushed the case with Social Services. If they find out you've run away they will come looking for you. What will you do then? Where will you go?"

"I don't know! But I'm not givin' up Lonie!" Mysie shouted and pulled away from Bridget. "If Davey wants to go back, I don't care. I'm not goin'!"

Jack greeted Mysie's outburst in silence, but after a moment Mrs. Anslow spoke up. "I know you love that baby, Mysie, but runnin' away with her doesn't make sense. I would keep you here, but the police will find out quick enough. You've already drug that poor little thing halfway across the moor in a stolen car and you didn't find any place to hide. Use your head, dearie, it's not safe for a young girl to be running all over by herself, never mind with a baby. I think these folks want to help you. They came all the way out here on a night that's not fit for man nor beast to see that you get back safe and sound. You've got to give them a chance."

145

"We are trying to help you, Mysie," Jack added. "So are Audrey and her husband. They paid the rent on your flat so that you would have a place to stay. They've arranged to have Davey's bike repaired so he can get to work. Do you think they would do that if they weren't on your side?"

"I don't know. I want to trust them, but I'm scared."

"That's natural," Bridget said, "But you've got to think of Alona. What kind of life will she have if you're running from the police? Without money or a job, how are you going to feed her?"

"I don't know! I don't know! Stop bothering me! I don't want to lose Lonie," Mysie cried, her voice raising to near hysteria.

Bridget reached over and took Mysie's hand again. "We'll do everything we can to see that you can keep her, Mysie," she said quietly. "But you have to come back to Plymouth before the police find out you're gone. What do you say?"

Mysie hung her head and was silent. "Come on, Mysie, come with us," Jack coaxed.

After a long pause Mysie nodded and whispered, "O.K. I can't let Lonie starve."

Mysie sat in the back of the Rover with Davey, holding Alona, who was sleeping soundly, on her lap. Jack and Bridget offered encouragement from time to time, but overall, except for the howling of the wind and the occasional lashing of water against the underside of the car, a gloomy silence reigned on the way into town. Although they retraced the route that they had taken to Manaton, they did not spot the old Triumph on the way back. Once Mysie, Alona, and Davey were ensconced in their respective lodgings, Jack drove Bridget home. She invited him in for coffee and he called in a report to Brad. Although Bridget didn't have anything lacy to show Jack, that night the sheets on his bed at the Duke of Cornwall Hotel remained as unwrinkled as the maid had left them.

Chapter Seventeen

In the morning Jack drove Bridget to Derriford Hospital and arranged for a tow truck to follow him out to the Triumph. The axle wasn't broken, but the wheel was bent beyond repair. Fortunately, the garage was able to replace it and by early afternoon Jack knocked at Mr. Finch's door to announce the good news that his car had been located. Jack repeated the news at the top of his lungs for the next forty-five minutes, but the old man didn't seemed to understand. He was more impressed with the shiny new padlock Jack presented to him than with the news that his car had been returned. By the time Jack left, he was willing to agree with Hubie that Mr. Finch was a bit doolally.

When Jack called on Mysie, he found that she had dug out a total of five letters and sorted them by date. He gathered them up and drove back to the Duke of Cornwall Hotel to show them to Brad. Although they had all been mailed from Plymouth, Brad agreed that from the tone and references, they probably had been written by Frances Wobel. After more discussion, Jack went to the train station to find a public phone. It was just after three when he dialed the number for the Wobel residence. A woman answered on the second ring.

"May I speak to Mrs. Frances Wobel?" Jack asked formally.

"This is she," the woman replied in a polite yet business-like tone.

"I have some letters of yours, Mrs. Wobel," Jack said coldly.

"My letters? Whatever are you talking about? Who is this?" Jack caught a touch of annoyance in her voice.

"They're letters you sent to Elizabeth Duncan."

Jack heard a slight gasp before Mrs. Wobel cried, "I don't have the slightest idea what you're talking about. Who is this?"

"Let's just say I was a friend of Elizabeth's. The police might be very interested in what you wrote to her. It wasn't very nice—definitely not ladylike. They might even interpret it as threatening. And seeing that her body was found along the road near your house, they might even try to connect you to her death. That would be very unfortunate, wouldn't it, Mrs. Wobel?"

Jack heard another gasp, and there was a long silence before she asked, "What do you want for the letters?"

"Information. And, of course, a token of your appreciation for not bothering the police with the letters."

"How much?" she demanded.

"First, the information—then we negotiate terms. I don't like to rush a business deal."

"How did you get the letters?" she asked in a tone that told Jack she was becoming angry.

"I'll ask the questions!" Jack snapped. "How did you find out that Elizabeth was blackmailing your husband?"

"I'm not the financial idiot Kenneth thinks I am. I knew he was funneling her money through that fake business of hers."

"How did you learn about her kid?"

When she didn't answer immediately, Jack turned up the pressure. "I'm running out of patience, Mrs. Wobel. Don't play games with me!"

"If you must know—I hired a detective to follow her and my husband. Since he wasn't meeting her, we figured it must be about the child."

"And you never faced your husband with your suspicions? I find that hard to believe."

"I intended to, but then . . . I . . . I decided not to."

"Where were you on the night Elizabeth was killed?"

"I've already told the police. I was playing bridge with some friends in Plymouth."

"I want the names of those friends, Frances. You won't mind if I call you Frances, will you, seeing as how we're going to be business associates."

"What is it you want from me?" she asked in a voice that was close to hysterical. "I've told you I will pay to get the letters back! Just name your price and stop tormenting me!"

"I want the truth, Frances," Jack hissed into the phone. "All of it!"

Jack managed to get the names and addresses of the people Mrs. Wobel claimed she had been playing bridge with on the night Elaina was killed. Then he called each in turn, pretending he was doing a follow up interview for the police. Most of the players stated that Frances had been either in the game or helping in the kitchen until the party ended, as usual, at eleven. However, one woman said that she was glad that Jack had called because after thinking about the evening, she recalled that Frances had left early because she had a headache.

Chapter Eighteen

Paul followed Compton home after receiving Kon's report about his search of the Compton residence and remained on watch until well after midnight when Kon arrived to take over surveillance duty. Then he went back to the Richmond Gates Hotel, set the alarm for 6:30 and threw himself onto the bed. In what seemed like minutes he heard a quiet beeping and rolled over. "God that was quick!" he muttered as he hauled himself up. He stumbled into the bathroom, threw some water over his face and ran his razor over his chin. Then he pulled on his clothes and headed for the station as he had been doing for several days. He arrived just before 7:40 in order to catch the same train as Compton and tail him up to London. The strategy worked because even if Compton remembered seeing Paul on the train, he would have no way to link him to the investigation.

Paul was at the station on time, but Compton was not on the platform. Paul stood with his back to the tracks, pretending to be engrossed in the morning paper he had grabbed on his way into the station. The 7:40 train arrived, a few passengers got off, most of the crowd boarded the train, but still there was no sign of Compton. Paul kept watching the doors to the platform lest he show at the last minute and jump on just before the doors closed. Finally the doors did close and the train pulled away.

Paul paced up and down the empty platform twice, wondering what had happened. At length he decided to sit on the metal bench and really read the paper until the next wave of passengers arrived. People began to drift onto the platform after about ten minutes and then the rush began in earnest as the regulars formed queues in the areas where the car doors would open. Paul studied the crowd for a glimpse of Compton, but he didn't spot him. As before he waited expectantly for Compton to show, but to no avail. The giant metal beast arrived, disgorged its load, ingested the new crowd, sealed them in, and lumbered away with unthinking precision.

Paul tore his ticket in half in frustration, pitched the pieces into the wire mesh bin and drove back to the hotel. He checked at the desk as he came in and found a message that Kon had left while he was out. It said that Compton had made a drastic change of route and driven to Heathrow. Kon stated that Compton had checked in at the Air France counter and that he would stay on his trail. He promised to meet Paul at the hotel once he was sure what flight Compton was on.

What the hell is Compton up to? Had something or someone spooked him? And how does Kon expect to track him through the maze of Heathrow? Paul crumpled the handwritten message and stuffed it into his pocket as he headed back to his car at a fast walk. You'll never make it in time to do anything useful, he told himself as he maneuvered through the snarl of morning traffic.

By the time he got to the airport and parked his vehicle he was sure Compton's plane was long gone, but he walked through the terminal trying to formulate a plan. Suddenly he heard a familiar voice call his name. He turned to see Kon hurrying forward.

"You're not going to believe what just happened."

"Try me. Did you find out where he went?"

"Not exactly, but it shouldn't be hard. The police sent three cars after him. They must have heard he was leaving the country and wanted to nab him."

"Police? What were they after?"

"I couldn't get close enough to hear their conversation, but when I called Compton's office, Evelyn told me she had booked him on Flight 1479 to Paris. She thought it was a business trip, but he was carrying a full load of luggage."

"I forgot about Evelyn. I think she's succumbed to your charm, Kon," Paul said with a grin.

"I think she's scared to death of me, but it has the same result when it comes to getting information."

"Was Compton actually arrested or just taken for questioning?"

"I couldn't hear what was said, but they put cuffs on him."

"Shit! We've got to get to him before he starts rattling on about Griffin Bordet, and Interpol, and secrets."

"Yes, and I think it's time we gave a copy of those pictures from both Compton's house and Apbly Cottage to Ian. Scotland Yard will want to talk with Constance Compton."

"One of them must be lying. What was Compton running from if he didn't kill Elizabeth?"

"I've been thinking about that. I think he was making a break from his wife. I would not be surprised to learn that she set the police on him."

"Vindictive little bitch, isn't she."

Ian McBriad at Scotland Yard was indeed very interested in the pictures from both Apbly Cottage and Constance Compton's jewelry box, and he immediately took them to his superior. It was then he learned of Constance Compton's accusations and the hurried call to Inspector Tomlin in Plymouth that had resulted in Steven Compton's arrest. After more consultation with Tomlin, who agreed to come up to London, the police brought Mrs. Compton in for questioning. As soon as Tomlin arrived, Ian alerted him to the critical new evidence and asked for an official on-site inspection of Apbly Cottage. When Tomlin inquired where the information had come from, Ian claimed an anonymous source had sent it to him. Since Tomlin had never worked with Ian, he was annoyed. Ian's superiors, however, had learned never to question the source of his leads. Without Ian's many mysterious informers, half the homicides in London might have gone unsolved.

Later that day Ian called Brad with a summary of the interviews Scotland Yard detectives and Inspector Tomlin had had with the Comptons. "Mr. Compton was forthcoming with information. He admitted that he drove Spengler to Apbly Cottage, but he's sticking to his story that she sent him to get some champagne and was gone when he returned. A crew went over his car, but couldn't find any evidence linking him to her death."

"I see," Brad replied in response to Ian's summary. "Your information is most helpful, Ian. Did you happen to hear what Mrs. Compton had to say for herself?"

"Actually, her story is rather more involved, but she too denies killing Spengler. She claims she had been suspicious of her husband's affair for a long time. She learned of his planned tryst with Spengler when Mrs. Nash, the wife of the man who had given Mr. Compton the key to Apbly Cottage, rang up to remind her to check the new brickwork. She said she drove down to the Cottage early on Friday evening and parked her car out of sight behind the house. She knew the back door latch was loose and she jimmied it open using a screwdriver she brought with her. Then she waited in the upstairs bedroom for Steven and his lover to show up.

"She confirmed that Steven did not stay in the house when he first arrived with Spengler. After he drove away, she confronted Spengler as she came up the stairs. She admitted there had been some slapping and hair pulling during which Spengler snatched her pearl necklace so hard the string broke. She had been furious and pushed Spengler with so much force that she fell down the stairs.

"Mrs. Compton said she was afraid for a moment that she had actually killed Spengler. She ran down the stairs and saw that Spengler was only unconscious. Her head was bleeding, however, and Mrs. Compton wanted to rush her to a doctor. She said she started to drag Spengler out to her car, but Spengler came to and refused to go. Mrs. Compton said that Spengler told her that she didn't love Steven and had no intention of marrying him. She did not want to be tied down to a civil servant whose career was on a downhill slide. According to Mrs. Compton, Spengler said that she had sent Steven for champagne so that she wouldn't have to tell him face to face that she didn't want to marry him. She claimed that Steven had become violent in the past when he didn't get his way about something.

"Mrs. Compton said she was relieved that she hadn't killed Spengler, but she thought that she should have had the courage to tell Steven the truth. She claims she left Apbly Cottage in tears, not sure whether or not she wanted to stay married to Steven even if he came crawling back to her.

"When he didn't come home on Saturday, she figured that Ms. Spengler had lied and that she and Steven had spent the weekend together. She remained undecided whether she should tell Steven that she knew about his affair and demand that he end it or go to her solicitor and begin divorce proceedings. She claims that she was in a terrible quandary until she got a call from Mrs. Nash telling her that a friend from Plymouth had sent her a newspaper account of a dead woman being found on the road near Apbly Cottage. Mrs. Compton said she immediately recognized Spengler from the description in the paper. She said her indecision turned to fear as she realized that Steven must have killed Spengler when he learned that she didn't want to marry him.

"Mrs. Compton claimed she had expected the police to come knocking on her door any moment to haul Steven away, but, of course, it never happened. She said she was just beginning to imagine that Spengler's death was accidental when Steven declared he was going to Paris for the week and wanted a divorce. She was furious and called the police in a fit of anger."

"That's quite a story. Do you believe it?"

"I'm not entirely sure," Ian replied cautiously. "I must say her story does explain some of the bruises that were found on Spengler's body. According to the ME's report I got from Tomlin, some of the bruises were caused before the fatal injuries."

"Well, I appreciate the report, Ian, but it does seem inconclusive."

"Very. We had to let the Comptons go for now, but we've advised them both not to take any trips to Paris."

Chapter Nineteen

Once Steven Compton was arrested, Kon was no longer tied down on surveillance duty. That same afternoon he drove to Milton Keynes to follow up on the leads to Elaina he had traced through records at Sommerset House in London. The files showed Elaina's parents were both dead, and that she was survived by an older brother named Hollis. He appeared to be more conventional than Elaina, for the records showed that he had a wife and two children. Kon did more checking once he got to Milton Keynes, but the address on Hollis Spengler's vehicle registration was no longer current. Kon tracked him from a moderately priced row house to Council housing, and finally to a single room in a large boarding house.

When Kon rang the bell an extremely short, elderly woman wearing an enormous woolen cardigan opened the door. "May I help you?" she asked in a voice that matched her diminutive size.

"I'm looking for Mr. Hollis Spengler. Is he in?" Kon replied softly to match her tone.

"Hollis? Why yes. I believe he's in his room. Is he expecting you? He didn't let me know. He scarcely has any visitors."

"He didn't know I was coming," Kon answered. "I'm here on a business matter."

"Oh, I see. Would you like to go up or shall I call him down?"

"Perhaps you could let him know that I am here and let him decide. My name is Patrick Weeks," he said and handed her a card.

"Oh. I hope you aren't here to collect money. The poor man's been hounded nearly to death. Not that it's any of my business, mind you, but he's had a bit of bad luck lately. Usually I only let the rooms to students, but he was hard up."

"It's more of a legal matter really," Kon explained, realizing that despite her size, the woman took a protective interest in her boarders. "And I assure you it won't cost Mr. Spengler any money."

"A legal matter, did you say? Oh Lord, has that wife of his gone to court again? He's trying to pay, you know. He loves those boys. He's just down on his luck."

Kon smiled, thinking, if the records didn't indicate otherwise, I would swear she's his mum. She is kind though and no human being should be so alone that no one cares about him. "I assure you," he said aloud, "I'm not acquainted with Mrs. Spengler and I am not here to collect money."

"Well, in that case, would you care to wait in the parlor? No one is using it at the moment and it *is* more comfortable."

"Yes, thank you. The matter may take some time to settle."

"Come this way then," the woman said as she turned and walked across the spacious entry hall. She opened a door and waved Kon inside. The room was large but crowded with a jumble of mismatched sofas, chairs, bookcases, and tables. Despite the lack of floor space the overall atmosphere was cozy and comfortable. The late afternoon light was still visible through the lace curtains covering the ceiling to floor windows on the far end of the room, but it was dwindling fast.

"I'll let Hollis know that you are here," the woman said and quickly retreated back to the hall, closing the door behind her.

Kon went to the window and gazed out at the large walled garden. A tiny area near the house held various bedding plants that were blooming valiantly, but the grass that was farther from the house was long and untidy with weeds sticking up here and there. Kon was still looking at the garden when he heard the door open. He turned and saw a middle-aged man of medium height standing by the door. As Kon came away from the window he noticed that the man bore no resemblance to Elaina. His hair was dark rather than blonde and his chin was stronger and more angular. Kon detected a slight note of defiance in his steady gaze and in his voice when he said, "You wanted to see me."

"Yes," Kon said coming forward. "You are Hollis Spengler, are you not?"

"Yes. I haven't sunk to denying it yet. What do you want?"

"My name is Patrick Weeks and I've come about your sister Elaina."

Spengler looked startled as if the mention of Elaina was the last thing he had expected to hear. "Elaina? God! What's she up to now?"

"I'm afraid she's dead, Mr. Spengler. She was murdered about a month ago."

Spengler put his hand to his head and shielded his eyes. "Well, I have to say I'm not surprised," he said numbly.

"Could we sit down and talk about this more comfortably?" Kon asked.

Spengler shrugged. "Sure. Why not? Mrs. Lund doesn't allow just anyone to use the parlor, you know. She must have been impressed with you."

"I promised I wasn't here to pry money from you."

Spengler smirked and dropped onto the sofa nearest the fireplace. "Yeah. There has been a bit too much of that going on lately."

Kon sat in the chair on Spengler's left. "Had you heard from Elaina recently?" he asked after a long silence.

"Recently? No. It's been years."

"I take it you weren't close."

"Naw. She's a lot younger than me. We even had different dads. My dad died when I was ten. After about two years, mum married again and then Elaina came along a year or so later."

"When was the last time you saw Elaina?"

Spengler rubbed the back of his head before answering, "Must be about three years ago. She just showed up one day, saying she was pregnant, and asking to stay with me and the wife until after her baby was born. I was surprised that she wanted to have a kid. I knew the kind of life she led, going from one man to another."

"But you let her stay in the end, didn't you?"

"Yeah. I had a few words with the wife over that. She and I have two kids of our own and the house we were in was small as it was. But Elaina seemed desperate. She talked like she really wanted to have a baby, but she was scared to go through it all alone. She said she would pay me whatever I asked and I thought having a kid might do her good. You know, settle her down a bit—maybe make her more responsible an' all. So I let her stay."

"How long did she stay?"

"Oh, must have been six or seven months. Say what's all this to you? Are you the kid's father or something?"

"No. But now that Elaina is dead I am trying to determine who is responsible for raising her child."

"Oh bloody hell! And I suppose you found a copy of the will and think you can pawn the kid off on me. Well, I got enough problems already. The last thing I need is another mouth to feed. I'm having trouble scraping together enough to pay child support for my own two kids. My wife has me in court every other day trying to get more money out of me."

Spengler stood up and paced the length of the room and back before coming to a halt in front of Kon. "That woman can't seem to understand what it means to become redundant at my age. I never made a lot of money, but the work was steady and I thought the owner liked me. He sort of talked like he was going to turn the business over to me to run when he retired. I had moved up to supervising the other clerks and taking care of the books, but then the old man up and dies. Next thing I know his son shows up and closes down the shop. It was making money, but he says he can make more money by selling the building. So here I am with nothing after all the years I put in."

"Did you try to find a place somewhere else?"

"Of course I did! I'm not lazy! But who wants a man my age when they can get some kid to wait on their customers? Not that they can do it as well as I can—half the time the kids don't even show up for work on time. And when they do come in, they're smart with the customers. I tried and I tried, but I can't find anything steady. I can do bookkeeping—I did it for years for the old man. But I don't have a fancy certificate to prove it, so no one wants to take me on."

Spengler threw himself on the sofa and buried his face in his hands. The room was silent for a moment until at last he sighed. "I don't mean to sound so bitter, but I'm at the end of my rope. I am sorry to hear that Elaina is dead. We weren't close, but she was my sister. She was a cute little thing and mum enjoyed dressing her up and showing her off. But mum died when Elaina was still a baby and . . . well, frankly, my stepfather was not a good person. He used to slap me around over nothing and I suspect he did worse things to Elaina. After mum died it got worse. I left home when I was sixteen because of the way he was. I guess I should have tried to protect Elaina, but I was only a kid. I didn't really understand what he was doing and Elaina was too young to tell me. I found out later that some of the neighbors thought that he had killed my mum, but I guess the police could never prove it. Why am I telling you all this anyway? What's it to you?"

"It is important, Mr. Spengler—may I call you Hollis? After all this is personal business."

"Why not. It's not fittin' for a man in my position to be particular."

"I'm sorry to hear you are having such difficulties, Hollis, but I'm here to try to help. I believe your statement that Elaina did not have a happy life and I want to see that her child has something better. She deserves to be with people who love her."

"Well, it can't be me! I just can't handle anything else. I know Elaina wanted me to, but things were different then. I can't even support my own kids."

"I can understand that. Tell me about this will. Do you still have a copy?"

"Yeah. I must have it tucked away somewhere. There's two of them actually. Elaina gave me a copy of the first one when she was staying with the wife and me. She said that she wanted to make sure that if anything happened to her, her child would grow up along with my kids. Then she went off to have her baby and never came back. I was a bit put out that she never came to say "good-bye" or "thanks" or even "sod off" after all we did, but she had her own life and I guess she wanted to get back to it. She liked the parties, and the jewelry, and all that glitter—all the things she never had when she was growing up. Then about a year later, she sent me a second will. That one named me as guardian of her daughter until somebody I never heard of turned twenty-one. It mentioned a trust fund that she had set up to pay for the kid's expenses. I never paid attention to all the details and, like I say, there's no way I can take care of anybody's kid right now."

"May I see the will?" Kon asked.

"Now wait a minute. Just what are you after, Mr. . . . er, what did you say your name was?"

"Weeks, Patrick Weeks" Kon answered calmly.

"Are you a solicitor? Just what *is* your stake in all this?"

"I am not a solicitor, but I am acting on behalf of the person who is currently caring for Elaina's daughter Alona. Frankly, Hollis, I am quite familiar with how it feels to grow up without anyone who gives a damn about you. I don't want that to happen to Elaina's child, and I will do all I can to see that she can stay with the person who loves her."

Hollis took a minute to weigh the sincerity of Kon's statement before commenting, "Yeah. It was hell after mum died. Well, I won't stand in your way. I sure don't need another kid to worry about."

"Good. May I see the will to determine what we have to work with?"

Hollis shrugged. "Why not. If Elaina's dead I guess I need to read it again myself."

He stood up and walked to the door. Suddenly he hesitated and turned toward Kon, "I wasn't always like this. Just over a year ago, I would have taken the kid without a second thought. It kills me that I can't even take proper care of my own two." He pulled open the door and went out before Kon could reply.

As Kon waited, he noticed that the light had finally faded. He went to the wall and threw the switch to turn on the small lights mounted on either side of the fireplace. Their dim glow was attractive, but not adequate to brighten the large room so he turned on the large lamp located on the table behind the sofa. Then he went to the window and pulled the drapes closed against the autumn chill.

Hollis was gone for almost twenty minutes and Kon surmised that he was taking time to read the will before he turned it over to him. He was pacing up and down when Hollis entered the room again.

"I been studying this new one and as I make it out, I get custody of the kid and her trust fund and this Platt woman gets the car and jewelry. Sounds like I get the short end of the stick."

"May I read it?" Kon asked cautiously, trying not to appear too curious.

"Why not? Reading won't change what it says," Hollis answered, handing Kon the packet of papers.

Kon sat quickly and studied the papers carefully. Finally he looked up and smiled at Hollis. "My reading of Elaina's will is that she wants Alona to be raised in a family atmosphere by people who care about her. It does not specifically say it has to be you. What would you say if I told you I believe I could work out a deal whereby you and Ms. Platt both can get what you want while staying in compliance with Elaina's last wishes?"

"Whaddya mean?"

"I would have to refer you to a solicitor to work out the details, of course, but what if you agreed to be legal guardian of the child and used the trust fund to hire Ms. Platt to take care of her. In turn Ms. Platt would sign the car and jewelry over to you."

"Back up and run that by me again. I get custody of the kid, but I don't have to take care of her. That doesn't seem quite right."

"Oh, I believe it can be arranged. You see Social Services will want to know that some responsible person of legal age is looking after Alona. You are a blood relative and are named in Elaina's will so they won't question your right to the child. But as guardian, you have a perfect right to hire a caretaker and Ms. Platt is more than willing. She would adopt Alona this very minute if she were not underage."

"I see. But what's the part about a car and jewelry?"

"Elaina collected some very valuable jewelry over the years. She is also reported to own a late model Porsche. Unfortunately, to date neither the police nor I have been able to locate it, but I am confident that it will be found. I wouldn't be surprised to learn that Elaina stashed some cash somewhere. Perhaps if we work together we can find it too. Now, I do believe that Ms. Platt would be willing to turn most, if not all, of these assets over to you in exchange for an agreement giving her care of Alona immediately and full custody in two years when she comes of age."

"Christ! She must really want that kid."

"Wouldn't you do as much to retain custody of your sons?"

"Yeah, I guess I would. I never had anything, but if I did, I'd give it up to keep my kids."

"If I can arrange this for you, you should have enough cash to pay child support, and put a little aside for your sons' education."

161

Hollis was speechless for a moment and then muttered, "I just can't believe it! My crazy little sister coming through for me like this. It's like a miracle."

"Well, there are still a number of legal details that need to be settled."

"Such as?" Hollis asked warily.

"Did Elaina ever tell you who fathered her child?"

"No. She told me the bloke who was paying her rent gave her money to have an abortion, but she didn't want to go through with it. She'd done that twice and she wanted a kid. The way she talked, I don't think the man was one of her regulars, if you know what I mean."

"Do you think she told him about the baby?"

"I don't think she did. I asked her once if she was going to hit him up for money and she said 'no'. She didn't want to settle down. She said it was just a brief affair, but, you know, I think she must have been in love with him. She knew how to use men to get what she wanted, but she never talked about making that guy pay. I think that baby was a love child and that's why she wanted to keep it."

"I hope you're right about that. It will make the legal issues a lot less complicated."

Chapter Twenty

Early Friday morning, while Jack was still at the Duke of Cornwall, he got a phone call from Bridget. "Jack, I've just heard some news I think you should know about," she began excitedly.

"What? Are you O.K.?" he asked anxiously.

"Yes, I'm fine. This is important. When I came in this morning the place was all a buzz about a man that was brought in late last night. Apparently, your friend, Mrs. Wildridge, was out driving drunk and smashed into his car near Crownhill Road. He's in bad shape with a broken leg and a ruptured spleen."

"Good God! What happened to her?"

"Oh, she got off with nary a scratch, but rumor has it she was arrested."

"Arrested! Shit! I'd better tell Brad. Thanks for letting me know, Bridget. You've been a great help with this case."

"I've just got a nose for trouble, Jack."

"That must be what attracts you to me. Listen—I've got to run. I'll call you later," he said and hung up the phone.

As soon as Brad heard the news, he was on the phone to Inspector Tomlin. "Good morning, Inspector Tomlin—Randolph Chillingsworth here," Brad began hesitantly.

"Ah good morning, Chillingsworth. How is everyone at Marcolm and Blake?"

"Well Roger is holding up, but to tell the truth, I'm having a difficult time containing the gossip and the rumors concerning Bennett Wildridge's death. I've just heard a shocking story about Kathryn Wildridge being arrested for drunken driving. Could there possibly be any truth to it?"

"I'm afraid it's more than a rumor, Chillingsworth."

"Good lord! Is she still in jail?"

"Hardly. Her solicitor must have heard the crash, he was at the station so fast. Her daddy isn't going to be happy about this one. She was driving his Mercedes."

"Her father's car! Does he live in the area?"

"The address on the registration was St. Mellion."

"I see. That's north of Saltash, isn't it?"

"Yes. The place is called Fernwood Farm."

"I see. What's her father's name?"

"Lowell Cosgrove. I tried calling, but he wasn't in."

"Well, thanks for the information. You see, since Bennett's death, Roger has appointed me to try and console his widow. It's hard, you know, with no facts to give her. Perhaps I'll give her a call and see if I can be of any assistance."

"I would appreciate anything you could do to calm her down, Chillingsworth. She was threatening to lodge a formal complaint about how rude the police were to her last night."

"I'm afraid I don't have any influence over her, but I will see what I can do."

Brad ran a quick background check on Lowell Cosgrove and discovered that he had lived in St. Mellion for twenty-five years, had been widowed once and divorced twice. Kathryn, his only child, was a product of his first marriage. Currently his four vehicles were all insured by the firm of Talbot & Barnstall. Brad smiled, thinking that he could have learned most of the information from Lilla, but it probably would have cost him the entire afternoon.

He took the now familiar route over the Tamar Bridge and headed north to St. Mellion. Fernwood Farm was hard for even a stranger to the area to miss. A large wrought iron sign which had been painted white arched between two huge fieldstone posts set on either side of the gravel drive. The house was every bit as ostentatious as the one Mrs. Wildridge occupied, but it had the added attraction of a large conservatory attached to the west end. Luckily, instead of a bulldog housekeeper, a more formal quasi butler-caretaker answered the bell.

When Brad showed him a card bearing the name Charles Brenton and the logo of Talbot & Barnstall insurance firm he was admitted immediately.

"I'm sorry, sir, but Mr. Cosgrove's not in. Actually, he's on the Continent at the moment. If you leave your card I will give him your name when he phones in."

"I'm afraid that won't do. You see, I need to settle the matter of a little, shall we say, "incident" that occurred last night. However, I don't really need to talk to Mr. Cosgrove. It's only necessary that I view the vehicle in question and make an estimate of the damage."

"In that case, sir, I believe Mr. Cosgrove's mechanic can assist you. He is in charge of all Mr. Cosgrove's vehicles."

"Excellent! I shan't have to bother Mr. Cosgrove at all about this matter."

"Very good, sir. I'll just fetch the mechanic. If you would be so good as to wait here please."

Brad was left to stand in the formal entrance hall admiring the tapestries hanging on the wood paneling. The light coating of dust on the waist-high combing lent credence to the rumor that Mr. Cosgrove spent much of his time abroad. After a long wait, Brad heard the echo of footsteps on the tile floor and the butler-caretaker returned, followed by a young man who wore his hair falling below his shoulders and his jeans slung below his hips. He wore a long-sleeved shirt, but it was open at the neck.

"This is Andrew, Mr. Brenton," the butler said rather coldly. "I'm sure he can handle any questions you may have about Mr. Cosgrove's vehicles."

"Thank you," Brad answered and nodded. He turned to Andrew and the butler slid away quickly. Andrew grinned. "Old Hartly don't like to see me in this part of the house. I have a room over the garage and I usually keep to the kitchen."

"This is a business matter. I understand that you are in charge of Mr. Cosgrove's vehicles. Has the one that was damaged last night been brought back yet?"

"As a matter of fact, some solicitor phoned this morning to tell me it was towed to Atson's garage in Plymouth. I went down to look at it, and I suspect its useful life is over if you get my drift. Mrs. Wildridge really did a job on it. I guess I shouldn't be saying so, but it's not the first time she's been playing dodgems on the road."

"Is that so? I haven't been called in on the other matters. They must have been minor incidents."

"Well, Mr. Cosgrove likes to fix over the smaller things so as not to bother Talbot and Barnstall."

"I am sorry to have missed Mr. Cosgrove. Do you suppose I could take an inventory of the other vehicles as long as I'm here?"

"I don't see that he would mind. Come out to the garage and I'll show you around."

"Splendid. How long have you worked for Mr. Cosgrove?" Brad asked casually.

"'bout three years," Andrew called over his shoulder as he led Brad down a long hall and out the rear door. Brad followed Andrew into a covered portico that led to a large outbuilding. "The garage is separate from the main house," Andrew explained. "I guess that worked well enough when Mr. Cosgrove had a chauffeur. Once he started doin' his own driving he had this covered thing built. Don't exactly match the house, but it's practical."

"Very sensible I would say," Brad agreed. "How do you like working for Mr. Cosgrove?"

Andrew shrugged. "The farm's a bit off the beaten track, but the money's good and Mr. Cosgrove lets me tinker with me own stuff when I'm not busy."

"So you do most of the repair work yourself?"

"Yes. Mr. Cosgrove trades in for new models so often, he don't run into any major problems." Andrew laughed. "You might say his daughter takes care of the running into things part."

"Accident prone, is she?"

"Very! I don't do body work, so I got to take all the cars into town to get them put right after she's used them."

"That's strange. My records don't show many claims."

"Well, like I say, Mr. Cosgrove likes to take care of things quiet like."

Andrew opened the door to the enormous garage and Brad

followed him inside. The area was well lit from several florescent lights hanging from the overhead and there was a well-equipped workbench along the far wall that would be the envy of many a commercial repair shop. Brad did a quick mental inventory of the vehicles against those listed with Talbot & Barnstall. The Bentley and the Sterling were in place, but the Citron was missing.

"I take it Mr. Cosgrove drove the Citron to the airport."

"No sir. He takes it on the ferry with him. Says it gives him an advantage with the locals."

"It sounds as though Mr. Cosgrove is a shrewd businessman."

"He must do all right to keep this place going and travel round like he does," Andrew agreed.

"Yes, and keep his vehicles in repair. When was the last time Mrs. Wildridge got into a mess?"

"Let's see, last week she put a scratch on the Sterling. That was just a minor thing—no body work—just a paint job."

"And before that?"

"Well now, about a month ago she took the Bentley out one night and did a job on the front end."

"Really? What kind of damage?"

"Broke the front headlamp and dented the bumper."

"Goodness," Brad commented, moving closer to the Bentley. "It certainly looks fine now. Where did you have it repaired?"

"Same place I always use—Atson's. They're over on Edgcomb in Plymouth."

"I'll have to keep them in mind. They certainly do good work."

"That they do. Say, would you like to see how the bumper looked before they replaced it?"

"You mean you still have it?"

"Sure. The shop always gives me the pieces. They know I cut them up for jollies. See them tool racks over the bench? Them's my work."

"Really! They're first rate. You've quite a talent, and I certainly would like to see that bumper."

"Great! I just dropped it in the corner over here," Andrew said and disappeared behind the cars for a moment. He returned carrying a severely dented bumper. "See what I mean? I can't guess what she ran into."

"I do see. I wager Mr. Cosgrove paid for this one himself."

"This one ain't been paid yet. Mr. Cosgrove's been on the Continent for months. I figure she ain't told him 'bout it. Truth be told, I don't think Mrs. Wildridge remembers doin' it."

"Why do you say that?"

Andrew grinned. "I was here when she brought the car back. Hell, I was out back welding and I heard her roar in. It weren't that late, but she didn't bother to put the car away. Usually, she puts Mr. Cosgrove's car away and goes home in her own, but not that night. She just raced in, jumped out, and ran in the house like the devil was chasing her."

"Did you speak to her about it?"

"Me? No. But I saw her the next morning. She had dark glasses on and didn't look none too steady."

"I see. Do you remember what night that was?"

Andrew scratched his head thoughtfully with one hand and hitched his jeans up with the other. "I reckon it was a Friday—same day I got me a new cutting torch. Like I said, I was out back testin' it when she roared in."

"That's very interesting, Andrew. Thanks for showing me around. I think I'll just pop down to Atson's and take a look at the Mercedes."

"Sure thing. I guess T and B will be responsible for this one, seeing how the police were called and all."

"Yes. We do seem to catch the big ones. Well, thanks again for your help. Can I just go out this way and go round to the front?"

"Sure. No sense botherin' old Hartly again."

Brad drove down the long drive, hurried into St Mellion, and found a public phone at the Fox and Goose pub. Luckily, Inspector Tomlin was in to receive Brad's report. After the phone call, Brad decided not to visit Mrs. Wildridge after all. He no longer felt willing to comfort her.

Chapter Twenty-One

Brad left Inspector Tomlin to confiscate and inspect the damaged pieces of Mr. Cosgrove's Bentley, while he drove into Plymouth to check out Atson's Garage. As he pulled up, his first impression was slight consternation. The establishment had an ambiance of light-industrial slum that seemed calculated to discourage all but those desperately in need of auto repairs. Brad parked in the tiny car park on the side of the building and walked around to the entrance. The battle-scarred glass door at the front had a huge crack running diagonally across the bottom portion which was reinforced with a square of unpainted plywood.

He pushed the door open and entered the waiting room. It had the same rundown theme as the exterior of the building. The floor was covered with chipped linoleum, and the walls were decorated with an array of greasy calendars featuring scantily clad women touting the virtues of a variety of pistons and shock absorbers. A row of spine-wrenching, blue plastic chairs with rusty chrome legs lined the wall facing the counter. A sign above the Formica-covered counter boasted, "Expert Brake Work," and by the metallic cacophony coming from the rear of the shop, Brad surmised that someone was hard at work breaking something.

Brad looked around the empty waiting room for a moment and then gave several vigorous taps to the worn bell that was bolted to the counter top. Suddenly, above the din, he heard a deep masculine voice call, "Rhonda? Rhonda? Where are you girl? Check the counter, will ya!"

No one appeared for several minutes and then a tall, thin girl with long, limp, trying-to-be-blonde hair pushed open the swinging door behind the counter and stepped through.

"Hello-and-what's-the-problem," she mumbled in one breath with no apparent interest.

"Good afternoon. I'm with Talbot and Barnstall Insurance," Brad said and handed her a card. "I wish to confirm that some body work for which Mr. Lowell Cosgrove submitted a claim was in fact performed. It's just a routine check."

"When was the work done?" the girl asked, becoming a little more businesslike.

"About a month ago."

"A month! That's old business. Have you got a date?"

"I'm not sure, but it was a Saturday—near the first of the month."

"I'll have to look in the other book," she said, hauling a large ledger from beneath the counter. "Cosgrove, you say?" she asked after a minute.

"Yes, it would have been charged to Mr. Cosgrove, but it was probably brought in by Andrew, his mechanic."

"Oh, one of Andy's, was it?"

"Yes—a broken headlamp and a bumper replacement, I believe."

She flipped a few more pages and ran her finger down a column before announcing, "Here it is—billed, but not yet paid."

"I see. Is Mr. Cosgrove usually late in settling up?"

"Not as bad as some. He's away a lot so he takes his time. We let him be 'cause he's a regular. Brings us a lot of business, he does."

"Yes. He brings T and B a lot of business too. Were many vehicles brought in that day?"

"Oh yes, I remember that one. We was running 'till long after six."

"Really? I hope it didn't spoil your weekend," Brad said leaning over the counter and turning the ledger slightly so that he could read the pages.

"No—we had to rush, but we made it to the cinema in time."

"Good for you! Were they all Bentleys that day?" Brad asked leafing carelessly through the ledger.

"Mostly—that's what we specialize in."

"I see there was one customer who paid in cash. Is that common?"

The girl took a quick look at the ledger. "No. Most people pay by check or credit card."

"I wonder what *he* had done that day?"

"Let's see," she said bending over the ledger. "Now I remember. He wanted us to paint over a scratch on the bonnet. It was just a small one really, but he was very particular. Insisted it had to be finished that very day. Hardly could wait for the paint to dry proper-like—offered us double in order to get it done straightaway. We stand behind all our work, but Ned did a beautiful match job on that one."

"What color was the vehicle."

"Deep blue. And nary another mark on it—except for the mud. He must have been driving in the country. And that's another thing, we don't usually do detailing, but he wanted to have the car cleaned inside and out. I tried to put him off, but he wouldn't have it. He kept offerin' more and more money, until I thought 'what's a little mud, Rhonda girl?' and I cleaned it off myself."

"That's very interesting. May I have his name? I might be able to sign him on as a client."

"You can take his name, but you won't get ahold of that one," the girl said turning the ledger toward Brad.

"Why's that?" Brad asked as he took down the name Jonathan White and the plate number.

"When I was cleaning out the boot I found a real expensive looking earring. It didn't seem right to put it back in there again so I put it in a drawer in here for safe keeping. I was going to hand it to the bloke when he came back for his car, but we was working so late, I popped out to get some sandwiches and Ned settled up with him while I was gone. I tried to call him, but the number he gave was for the Grand Hotel. No one over there had ever heard of him. When I learned that, I was real glad he paid in cash. There was something a bit off about that one," she concluded shaking her head.

"He does sound strange. Well, one can't sign on everyone. Thank you, miss," Brad concluded airily. "You've been very helpful."

She smiled, warming to the compliment. "That's my job! Come again and bring your car."

Brad left the shop and drove straight back to the Duke of Cornwall Hotel to confer with Paul.

"You're right," Paul confirmed after a quick look at Brad's

notebook. "That's Compton's plate number and I think I know how the bonnet got scratched. Hold on a minute," Paul continued calmly and stepped into his room. He came back a few minutes later wearing latex gloves and carrying a plastic bag.

"Well?" Brad questioned impatiently.

"While you were out I had a call from Mrs. Mullins, the woman who lives across the street from that house Compton was letting for Elizabeth. She found this white sequined handbag that I'm sure belonged to Elizabeth."

"Where was it?" Brad asked, taking the bag from Paul.

"Remember I told you about all the dogs she keeps?"

"Yes."

"It turns out one of them had chewed a hole in the plastic bag Mrs. Mullins used to hold the clothes Compton had discarded. Apparently the handbag fell out and slipped under a chair. Mrs. Mullins found it this morning while she was cleaning. When I went over to pick it up this afternoon, she confessed that she was embarrassed about letting the dogs chew the bag and had transferred the clothes to a new bag before she brought it out to me. I never saw the blasted hole!"

"How can you be sure it's Elizabeth's bag?"

"That's even stranger. The bag was empty, of course, but look, the lining in the zippered pocket is worn through. I found a house key in the space between the lining and the outer bag. I plan to send the key and the bag up to Ian to have them checked for prints. What's even more interesting is this gold plated clasp. It's been completely mangled, and I would not be surprised if Ian confirms it has traces of paint from a dark blue Bentley clinging to it."

Brad drew in his breath. My God! She must have been holding it when she tried to fend off the car that ran her down. Have you called Ian?"

"Not yet, but I think it's time. Our friend Compton won't be able to lie his way out this time."

Chapter Twenty-Two

Tony Schaffer surveyed the huge chocolate covered doughnut he held in his right hand and pondered the best course for biting in to get the least amount of icing on his face. Should he nibble daintily from the edge and chew around the perimeter, following the lay of the dough, or should he plunge boldly across the middle and risk getting chocolate in his ears? It was 4 a.m. and he was alone at the security desk. Who would notice if he got icing on himself? The longer he held the pastry the less appetizing it looked and the more he wished he had chosen something more nutritious to hold him through the long lonely hours.

He was glad to be earning a little extra money by filling in for Bert on the night shift. He hadn't thought that staying awake until 7 a.m. would be that difficult, but trying to stay alert when absolutely nothing was happening was becoming a chore. At least during the day people were coming and going and he could busy himself with sign-in sheets and little stick-on badges with the word "VISITOR" in big red letters glaring out from the bilious yellow background.

Tony reached for his coffee with his left hand, took a sip and chomped a big bite from the edge of the pastry. Unfortunately, it started to unwind, dropping bits of chocolate on the visitor's log that lay on the counter. He set his coffee down in disgust and started to reach into the little white carry-out bag for a paper napkin. His awkward, left-handed digging set the bag in motion and it slid across the Formica counter top and dropped over the edge.

Tony cursed through his mouthful of doughnut, and still holding the pastry in his right hand, he got up, opened the door in the waist high partition that surrounded the security area and walked around the counter. As he stooped to retrieve the bag he heard the familiar click of the outside door lock releasing in response to a key card being pressed against the electric sensor. He was startled, wondering which of the select handful of people who had 24-hour access cards was coming in at this early hour. He snatched up the bag, turned to call a greeting, and froze in astonishment tinged with fear.

For a moment he was so engrossed in staring at the long, shiny blade of the butcher knife he scarcely noticed the man who was pointing it at him. Unconsciously he stepped backwards, fell against the counter and dropped his pastry. He watched it roll across the gray carpet scattering bits of icing as it went. It struck him that it was running away and he let out a single hysterical laugh.

The man with the knife jerked at the sound and began to wave the knife rapidly indicating his own agitated state of mind. Tony stared at him in speechless confusion until the man finally shouted, "Open the door!"

For a moment Tony thought of his responsibility as a guard. He was supposed to protect the site, but at the moment he couldn't recall a single piece of useful information from his brief training session with Harvey. The most authority he had ever had to display had been to tell an irritated lorry driver that he needed to take his delivery to the bay doors at the back of the building. He couldn't remember anything being said about what to do if someone pointed a steel blade at your throat. He let go of the counter, not feeling entirely certain that his quivery legs would hold his weight.

"You . . . you can . . . can use the same card," he answered hesitantly, noticing the blue card the man was holding in his left hand. As soon as the words slipped out, Tony remembered the "panic button" mounted behind the counter. If he had been able to get to it, it would have summoned the local police. Well, it's too late now, Tony thought. That knife has already set off my panic button.

The man stared at Tony for a moment in apparent confusion, and Tony took the opportunity to study him. He was wearing a well-tailored suit, but it was extremely wrinkled and his shirt was open at the neck. His hair was disheveled and more than one day's growth of beard sprouted from his chin. His cheeks looked pale even through the dark stubble, but it was the harried look in the man's blood-shot eyes that most attracted Tony's attention. He had seen how staff looked after long weeks of stressing over deadlines on some top-secret project, but it was not like this. This man's dark eyes reflected deep despair and hopeless confusion. He was obviously fatigued, but his eyes burned with almost feverish determination. Looking into those eyes, Tony knew he would never forget them. He knew also that studying the man so closely was his second mistake.

Finally, the man with the knife seemed to gather his wits together enough to understand that the card he had would grant him access to the inner offices. "Lead the way," he ordered in a hoarse whisper that sent a shiver down Tony's spine. He stepped away from the counter and shuffled toward the door. He had always enjoyed the spaciousness of the lobby with its four sets of seating areas, but now the walk to the door seemed endless. Having turned his back to the strange man and his knife, he had no idea what to expect. Even though he pressed his own card against the detector, he jumped when he heard the click as the lock released. Nervously he reached forward and pulled the door open. He was relieved when he felt a hand push him through the door. He hoped that the knife was no longer pointed at his back, but he dared not look.

"Which is Bennett Wildridge's office?" the man asked in the same hoarse whisper as before.

For a moment Tony was at a loss. Bennett Wildridge had not been friendly with him and he had never visited him in his office. But then he remembered that Lilla had pointed out Wildridge's office to him, noting that out of either superstition or respect, no one had touched anything since his death. Lilla had reported that staff tended to skirt Bennett's area or become unnaturally quiet when they suddenly found themselves forced by circumstances to walk by.

"It's in the third bay," Tony finally answered and turned right. The man did not reply, but followed silently behind him as he wove left and right around partitions and along long corridors. Tony knew the building well from making his rounds and his card allowed him access to even the most secure areas. But at this time of night the building was forbiddingly dark and silent. At last they came to Bennett's office. The door was unlocked, but the lights didn't come on when they entered.

They stood in the dark for a moment before Tony said hesitantly, "I guess someone turned off the lights. I'll . . . I'll have to activate the switch."

"Do it!" the hoarse voice ordered and Tony jumped again before turning to his left and flicking the switch up. As the lights blinked on Tony stole a glance over his shoulder and saw that the knife was still pointed at him.

The room was silent except for the hum of the florescent lights. Finally the hoarse voice ordered, "Turn on the computer."

Tony moved forward, sat in the chair in front of the computer and started pressing buttons. When nothing lit up, it dawned on him that everything was turned off at the main switch on the surge protector. Moving slowly so as not to alarm the man with the knife, he bent over and pressed the switch. Immediately familiar beeps and clicks sounded and the screen glowed to life displaying the same logo and request for a password that came up on all the Marcolm and Blake computers. Tony heard the man curse followed by what he guessed was the knife blade striking the back of the chair near his right arm.

"What's the password?" the man demanded.

"I . . . I don't know. Everybody keeps their own."

"Then try something—use Wildridge or Bennett!" the man said irritably. "I've got to get more information out of it!"

Tony started keying in all the various combinations of Bennett Wildridge that he could think of, but after every three failures, he got locked out and had to reboot the computer. He tried and he tried and he flinched as the knife hit the chair after each failure. His hands started to shake and it became harder and harder to key in the right letters. He realized that he was smearing chocolate on the keyboard as he typed, but he didn't dare stop. One misdirected blow of the knife and the keys could be covered with his own blood.

He was becoming confused about which combinations he had tried, but since nothing showed on the screen, he had no way to track the entries. He was so nervous he was about to tell the man to type in his own ideas when suddenly the man shouted, "Enough! Unplug the bloody thing! I'll take it to him. He's got contacts—let him figure it out."

Tony switched off the computer, stood up, and began to sort through the tangle of cords surrounding the computer. After a few exhortations to "hurry up" accompanied by more blows to the back of the chair, he had all the wiring sorted out. He straightened up and turned to face the man. He looked even more distraught than before. The face that had been pale was now flushed in anger. Tony felt his heart pounding, but tried to appear calm. He waited silently, not daring to speak for fear he would say the wrong thing and upset the man further.

The man kept staring at the computer as if he expected it to suddenly blurt out some secret. Finally he seemed to come to a decision and shouted, "Don't stand there—pick it up!"

Tony jumped, but he turned back to the computer and removed the monitor from the top. He picked up the computer and turned to face the man again. The man looked at him in confusion for a moment, his wild eyes becoming clouded with uncertainty. He looked around for a moment as if unsure where he was and then started to brandish the knife and shout, "I'll show him! I'll take it to him. He'll have to make it work. I said I would get more ideas and I will. I've got everything now and it's all in there." His face twisted into a strange smile of triumph as he finished. He stood silent for a moment and then thrust the knife at Tony, stopping just short of his throat. "Carry it!"

Tony obeyed, locking his arms around the metal case and leading the way out the door. He could not hear the man's footsteps on the carpet, but he could sense that he was behind him. Every now and then, as they rounded a corner, he heard the knife rap the metal cap on the partitions. Tony's hands grew sweaty from gripping the case, but he held on. Bay three had never seemed so far from the main door.

He wondered fleetingly what time it was. He prayed silently that Harvey would come in early to check on him. But hadn't he been the one to assure Harvey that he could handle the night shift alone. What's going to happen at night for Christ's sake? Nobody comes in after eleven and tomorrow's Sunday. Everybody will be havin' themselves a nice lie in. How could he have been so stupid? How could he have forgotten the bricks thrown through windows and the slashed tyres on the lorries? It wasn't so much his stupidity that had made him cocky, it was the way that Harvey brushed him aside like a fly when anything important came up. Mr. Willard acted the same way, always smiling at Harvey and agreeing with everything he said.

Well, Harvey *was* experienced, but he wasn't always right. He had let that Saunders woman walk in right under his nose. He fancies the ladies. He probably let her big tits cloud his better judgement, the old fool. Old fool, or not, I sure wish he would show up early. I would willingly put up with his gibes to get this madman and his knife out of here.

Tony fanaticized about Harvey's timely arrival all the way to the front lobby, but his hopes were dashed when he opened the door. The lobby was empty. It was just him and his bony back to protect Marcolm and Blake from this mad intruder. The thought frightened him even more and he hesitated in the doorway of the huge empty space until he felt a sharp jab from the knife. He let out a squeal and leaped forward more embarrassed than hurt. He knew the jab had drawn blood, but he judged his response as pathetic. God, Tony, you are a sissy. No wonder Harvey says you'll never amount to anything.

He wondered idly if Harvey would have even an ounce of respect for him when they found him run through with a butcher knife. No, Harvey would call him stupid. A real defender, like the ones in adventure stories, might be gunned down by a band of professional thieves, but they would never let themselves be prodded with a common kitchen tool. Well, to hell with *real* defenders, whoever they are. The tip of that knife is very sharp and very persuasive.

Tony couldn't remember if the man spoke to him again or just poked him, but somehow he understood that the man wanted him to carry the computer out of the building. The automatic doors opened like jaws when he approached, but he was not grateful for their mechanical manners. The doors he had faithfully guarded were helping this madman take him hostage.

He felt the chill in the air as soon as he came out. Once they were off the carpet, he could hear the sharp click of the man's heels on the pavement, in contrast to his own rubber soles that made little sound. As they walked farther and farther away from the well-lighted entry, Tony realized that the man had parked on the street. Of course, Tony chided himself. That's why I never heard the car. The bright glow of the security lights that had been installed at Mr. Dremann's insistence lit up the sides of the Marcolm and Blake building and illuminated the grounds fairly well, but the street side of the high brick wall around the delivery area was dark.

It seemed as if the computer had grown heavier and more awkward as he carried it and his arms were starting to go numb. He walked several hundred yards along the street and did not see the car until he was almost even with it. Suddenly he felt a hand on his shoulder and he stopped. The man with the knife came around his right side. Tony could not see his face in the darkness, but for an instant he saw a glint of light reflected from the knife. My God, he means to take me with him, Tony thought and suddenly the one thing that had stood out in his mind from his brief training flashed through his mind—if I get into that car, I have very little chance of returning alive.

Out of the corner of his eye he saw the man transfer the knife to his left hand and reach into his coat pocket with his right hand. The keys—he's searching for the keys. It's now or never, Tony, do something!

As the man reached forward to put the key into the lock, Tony thrust the computer against the man's left arm with all his strength. The force knocked the man off balance for a moment and in that instant, Tony dropped the computer and ran. Fear propelled him along the street and his rubber soles provided sure traction. He was not one of the Marcolm and Blake employees who ran regularly for the sake of fitness, but his legs were strong and his lungs didn't fail him as he charged toward the front door of the building. He could hear the man following behind him, but he had a good lead on him. He barely slowed as he reached the door and flung his left shoulder with the key card clipped to it against the detector.

The doors opened immediately as if they had been expecting him and he dashed into the building and dove behind the counter. He pulled his keyboard over the edge of the counter, ducked down and began typing in the sequence for activating the emergency lock down that would immediately seal all the doors in the building. In his panic he could not seem to remember the proper sequence. The emergency lock down was considered so serious Harvey had never let him practice. He typed in every number he could remember, but the doors did not respond. He tried again and again growing more desperate with each attempt. He was terrified and couldn't think straight enough to dredge any more numbers from his memory. He thought of stopping to press the panic button, but he knew the police could never get to him in time.

He was still keying in codes when he heard the doors click open. I should have stood up to Harvey and insisted that he let me practice, he berated himself. Now it's too late. He let go of the keyboard and watched it swing by its cord. He crouched beneath the slight overhang of the counter and held his breath. He couldn't hear footsteps, but he knew the man was close by when the visitors log flew off the counter and fell to the floor behind him. He moved closer to the counter wall and prayed that the man would go away.

He winced when he saw the box of red and yellow visitor's labels crash into the wall behind him. He heard the knife blade strike the counter and then the man screamed, "Come out you stupid son-of-a-bitch! Do you think Marcolm and Blake is going to protect you? Well, they won't, you little fool. They didn't protect Bennett Wildridge and they won't protect you! They're all liars and thieves. All this should have been my father's. He was the one whose ideas kept it going. Do you think Bennett Wildridge's ideas were better than his? I killed him for his ideas and I'll kill you too. It's too late now. I know all the secrets."

Tony listened to the ranting with growing terror, hardly daring to breathe. He had no doubt that the man was a killer and he didn't want to be another of his victims. He berated himself for not acting sooner to defend himself, but he wasn't aggressive by nature. He was used to being friendly and well liked. It was madness that anyone would want to kill him, but the man with the knife was obviously out of his mind.

The man was quiet for a moment and then suddenly the door in the counter flew open and the man rushed at him. Tony dodged, but the blade caught his right shoulder before lodging in the wall behind him. Tony caught a glimpse of the man's face as he pulled back on the knife. It was distorted with hatred and rage, and he knew the man was beyond reason. As the man lunged at him again, Tony yanked the fire extinguisher off the wall and pressed the discharge lever.

The man screamed as the foam hit his face. He backed away for a moment and Tony stood up intending to chase him from the building. But to Tony's horror the man didn't turn and run. Instead he became more enraged and rushed at Tony swinging the knife wildly in huge arcs. Tony had been too occupied to think about the wound in his back, but he knew his shoulder was bleeding badly. He could feel himself growing weaker by the moment and doubted he would be able to hold the heavy canister until it was fully spent. Even if he could stay on his feet, the man with the knife was only angered by the burning chemicals. Whether he could see or not, he kept slashing at Tony with deadly fury. Suddenly in one of his charges the man drove the knife so deeply into the wall that it stuck fast. With a scream of anger, he grasped the handle with both hands and pulled.

Tony knew he had only a moment in which to act. Letting go of the discharge lever, he grasped the neck of the canister with both hands, raised it above his head and brought it down on the back of the man's head with his last bit of strength. The man's mouth opened, but no cry came out as he toppled over sideways. Tony almost fell on top of him from the force of his action, but he rolled away as he fell forward. He lay on his stomach, panting from a combination of fear and exhaustion. He half expected the man to rise in renewed fury, but he didn't move. After a few minutes, Tony pulled himself to his knees and crept toward the man's body.

There was very little blood on the man, but Tony could see that his skull was crushed in. Tony was suddenly both terribly sorry and terribly relieved. He couldn't remember whether or not he had been shaking all along, but he felt himself quivering violently. He had an urge to vomit, but he didn't.

Slowly he crawled away from the body. He was aware that he was extremely tired and felt almost overcome with sadness. He thought of pressing the panic button to summon the police, but he didn't want to face them. How could he explain what he had done? How could they understand how terrified he had been? He was still scared. He crawled toward the phone and pulled it off the counter. There was only one person he would have to call. It was his duty to report that something strange and horrible had happened at Marcolm and Blake. He had never called the emergency number before and it amazed him that he knew it by heart. His hands were shaking so badly he had difficulty dialing.

The phone rang a long time before a familiar voice came on the line, "Roger Dremann here."

"Mr. Dremann . . . please . . . come quickly," Tony sobbed into the phone. "Someone broke in and . . . and . . . I killed him, Mr. Dremann. I'm sorry. There was no other way."

Roger tried to get more details from Tony, but the lad was sobbing so incoherently he gave up. He turned the phone over to his wife with instructions to make appropriate calming noises and assure Tony that everything was going to be fine and that he would be there as soon as he possibly could. While Mrs. Dremann tried to calm Tony, Roger pulled on his pants and shoes and called Brad who agreed to meet him at the plant.

By the time Brad got to the plant, Roger was already inside. He had wrapped a blanket around Tony and was holding his arm around him in a fatherly gesture. Tony was still shaking, but he was leaning against Roger and gripping the sleeve of his coat as if he was desperate to hold on to someone he could trust.

"How is he?" Brad asked, hurrying through the partition in the security counter.

"He's been stabbed several times and he's scared out of his wits. He didn't even know me when I came in."

"Have you called the police or an ambulance?"

"Not yet. I was trying to find out what happened before they get here and Tony keeps insisting that he doesn't want to see the police or Harvey."

"What's Harvey got to do with this?"

Roger shook his head. "Nothing really, but Tony thinks Harvey will make fun of him for being afraid."

"It's no crime to be afraid of a madman. I'd say he's lucky to be alive! I'll get him some tea to steady his nerves." Brad turned and let himself through the door to the right of the security counter. When he returned a few minutes later, Tony was whispering frantically to Roger. Brad handed the cup to Roger, guessing that Tony could not be trusted to hold it steady. Roger coaxed Tony to sip the well-sweetened tea while Brad checked out the body.

"Any idea who it is?" Roger called over his shoulder.

"His face is badly burned by the chemicals, but his I.D. says Victor Rhodes."

"I was afraid of that. Tony said he came to steal Bennett Wildridge's computer. Something about giving it to someone who could make it work. Stupid fool, I had Stanley strip all the files off the hard drive the day Bennett's body was found. But of course! Don't you see? He was selling Bennett's work to CDT and they couldn't make it work. I checked the Bourse de Paris yesterday morning. CDT stock has crashed. Whoever invested in Bennett's theories must have contacted Victor to get their money back. Oh God! Now everything is going to come out about losing Bennett's work. I'm sunk," Roger moaned.

"Not necessarily," Brad countered. "Did Victor actually get the computer?"

"I'm afraid so. He made Tony carry it out to his car. That's when Tony got away. He threw it at Rhodes and ran in here."

"Where is the computer now?"

"It must still be in the street. Why?"

"No one has to know what he came here for. Think about it, Roger. He could have been the one who caused all the accidents. No one suspects you caused them as an excuse to tighten security."

"How did you know?" Roger gasped in surprise.

"I studied the reports. You were always the one who fell or had the rock come through your window. You were very careful that no one really got hurt."

"I suppose it was rather amateurish."

"It doesn't matter. It worked. It made people more careful. Let's capitalize on it now and put the blame on Rhodes. He has a history of hatred for Marcolm and Blake. He could have killed Wildridge just because he worked here. He could have come here to steal Tony's computer in order to get the complete staff listing."

"But he didn't. He had a particular computer in mind."

"You and I and Tony are the only ones who know that. What if we switch computers? Are they the same model?"

"Hell, I don't know," Roger sputtered. "The computer committee moves equipment around all the time."

"It doesn't really matter. Start unplugging this one, Roger. I'll get the one from the street," Brad ordered and he was out the door.

He ran toward the street and looked up and down. There were several streetlights to his left and he could see no cars parked along the curb. It has to be down there, he reasoned and ran to the right. As he had suspected there was only one car parked and the computer lay on the pavement by the passenger door. He picked it up and hurried back inside. Roger had finished unplugging Tony's computer and Brad noted that it was a different make. He lay Bennett's computer on the counter. Then, cupping his shirttail in his left hand and his handkerchief in his right, he lifted Tony's computer and carried it out to the car. He hesitated for a moment and then threw it down and dashed back to the building.

"Tony's starting to lose concentration. I'd better call an ambulance," Roger commented.

"Right. Start telling him to forget about Bennett's computer. Tell him he's got to say the man was after his computer. Tell him . . ."

"I'll tell him his job depends on it," Roger said cutting Brad short. "Get that computer back to Bennett's office."

"Yes, sir," Brad agreed, glad that Roger was warming to the new version of what had happened. Using his shirttail and handkerchief once again, he picked up Bennett's computer and carried it toward the door. Fumbling with his left hand he pressed his key card against the sensor, but as he reached to pull the door open, he noticed the chocolate smudges on the handle. "You and your dammed chocolate doughnuts," he muttered. He set the computer down and cleaned the doorknob with his handkerchief before carrying the computer inside. When he got to Bennett's office, he noticed that the keyboard was covered with chocolate. He gave a quick wipe to the keys and set about attaching all the computer cables. The police had been through Bennett's office at least twice so he wasn't particularly worried about Tony's prints.

It took Brad a little while to re-connect all the cables and by the time he walked back to the lobby, both the police and an ambulance had arrived. Tony had lapsed into incoherent mumbling and Roger was filling in the gory details for the police. They seemed to be convinced by the blood on the wall beneath the counter and on the knife that was still stuck in the wall that Tony had been fighting for his life. The paramedics put Tony on a stretcher and carried him to the ambulance.

Tony had been patched in the emergency room and moved to a ward, but the doctors would not allow visitors while they haggled over whether or not he needed a blood transfusion. Roger and Brad were standing in a waiting room when Harvey rushed in. "What happened? I heard the call on my radio and came straight here."

Roger shot a quick glance at Brad and began to repeat his tale. "Some madman came in and stole the computer off the security counter. He tried to take Tony as a hostage and Tony ended up getting stabbed before he managed to kill the brute."

"Stabbed! Was it bad?"

"He's lost a lot of blood and was severely shaken over the whole affair."

"No doubt. Why did Tony let the guy in during the night?"

"He didn't *let* him in," Roger answered irritably. "The man had Bennett Wildridge's keycard. Chillingsworth thinks he might be the one who murdered Wildridge."

"Holy Jesus! You mean we had a killer running around the plant? Tony must have been scared out of his wits. Can I get in to see him?"

"They haven't let anyone see him yet, but I think it would be better if you didn't go in."

"Why?" Harvey asked in surprise.

"Tony was very upset about having to kill that man. Even killing a madman in self-defense was totally repugnant to him. He was nearly hysterical when he called me. But do you know why he called me?"

Harvey shook his head to indicate he didn't know.

"He called me because he was convinced you would laugh at him for being afraid. He said he was so scared he couldn't remember the lock down sequence to seal the building. You've been way too hard on him, Harvey. After all, he's just a . . ."

Harvey suddenly went pale and held his head with his hand. "Oh Christ!" he moaned in distress. "God forgive me! He didn't forget the sequence—I never gave it to him! He likes to play on the blasted computer so much, I was afraid he would seal the doors by mistake. You know how complicated it is to get the system up and running again once its been shut down. Oh God—he might have been killed. I've got to tell him!"

"Absolutely not!" Roger said coldly. "He's been hurt enough. He's not to know that you didn't trust him."

"Well, sometimes he acts like . . ."

"Like what . . . a kid? Just because he's fond of chocolate doughnuts doesn't mean he's stupid. You have never bothered to train him, have you? Now I understand why he has a locker full of spy novels. He's trying to figure out how he's supposed to do his job." Roger felt himself becoming upset and stopped talking.

Harvey was holding his bottom lip with his teeth. He looked both shocked and ashamed. He didn't have anything against Tony. He just never considered him anything more than a goofy kid.

Roger had calmed himself and began to talk quietly again. "Tony told me that all the while the man was marching him around with a knife at his back, he kept praying that you would come in early to check on him. He knew the night shift was when all the accidents had happened. He was worried that you would laugh if he was killed with a common kitchen knife."

"I'm sorry, Mr. Dremann. I just never realized he took everything so seriously. He was always eating doughnuts and grinning."

Roger sighed. "Honestly, Harvey, if I didn't need you on security, I think I would fire you right now. You may be a good police officer, but you certainly failed Tony. And I failed him too. I promised his mother that I would look after him now that his father's dead."

"I think I know a way to salvage Tony's feelings," Brad put in.

"How? It's a bit late, isn't it?" Roger asked, turning toward Brad.

"No, but Harvey needs to go back and change all the lock down codes straightaway. Then tomorrow he can tell Tony he changed them yesterday, but forgot to tell him. Bert's away so he'll never know."

Harvey thought a minute. "It's a lot of work, but it's the least I can do."

"Thank you, Chillingsworth," Roger said gratefully. "Perhaps I shouldn't have put Tony on the security desk, but I didn't want anyone to get jealous and give him a hard time. Now I'll have to find a different job for him."

"Don't do that, Mr. Dremann," Harvey cut in. "He'll think I asked you to remove him. Give me a chance to train him. I owe him that much."

"I'm not sure Tony will want to do security after tonight, Harvey, but if he does, you'd better train him thoroughly this time. Now go change those lock down codes."

"Right, Mr. Dremann!" Harvey answered instantly and hurried out.

Chapter Twenty-Three

On Tuesday afternoon Brad drove out to Ivybridge to see John Rhodes. He wanted to break the news of Victor's death to him before the police did. The pub was no busier than before and Brad hoped that John was not in financial difficulty. He went to the bar where John was still fighting with the adding machine. "Be right with you," John called over his shoulder, but when he looked up and saw Brad, he turned away growling, "What is it this time? I told you I don't know where Victor is."

"We need to talk, John. I've found Victor."

"Oh yeah, well then go bother him. I'm busy right now," Rhodes said turning back to his machine.

"Victor's dead, John. His body's at the morgue in Plymouth. I wanted to tell you before the police came."

John's hand froze in mid-stroke and hovered over the buttons. "You'd better be telling me the truth you bloody bugger."

"I saw him, John. Perhaps we could sit somewhere and talk. When was the last time you saw Victor?"

Rhodes turned in his chair, wrapped his arms around himself, and tucked his hands deep into his armpits. His jaw locked into a stubborn frown. He rolled his head in a circle on his thick neck to loosen his tension.

"All right," he finally agreed and pointed to a table in the far corner. "We can sit over there."

As Brad walked toward the table he heard Rhodes call into the kitchen, "Madge! Can you come out here for a few? I got to talk some business."

In answer to Rhodes' call a woman that Brad judged to be in her late thirties came out and stood behind the bar. Her reddish-blonde hair was permed into neat, tight curls and she wore deep red lipstick. The combination made her appear perky and attractive at first glance, but as Brad looked at her he saw that her face told of long days of hard work and longer nights of worry. She glanced briefly in Brad's

direction then stood on her toes to give Rhodes a peck on his cheek.
"Sure, pet. Is anything wrong?"

"No. No. Nothing to worry about," he assured her quickly. "Be
a luv and bring us some coffee would ya."

She rolled her eyes, but responded cheerfully, "Comin' up, gov."

Rhodes walked over and sat at the table across from Brad.
"Enough bullshit. Tell me straight out what happened to Victor."

"He was killed while attempting to steal a computer from
Marcolm and Blake."

Rhodes suddenly went rigid and his jaw fell open. He remained
speechless for a moment before beginning, "Holy Jesus! Can't those
people leave us alone? Haven't we all suffered enough?"

"I think you know more than you're telling, John. I think Victor
came here asking for help and you took pity on him like you always
have. I think he told you about killing Bennett Wildridge."

Just then Madge came up to the table with a tray and two cups of
coffee. "John! There is something the matter. What is it?" she asked
with evident concern.

Rhodes looked at her for a moment then lowered his eyes. "It's
nothing, luv. Go keep an eye on the till."

"Are you sure?" she asked drawing out her words. She placed the
coffee cups in front of the men and stood holding the tray against one
hip.

"I'm sure," Rhodes said. He reached up with his left hand and
touched her hip briefly. She waited a moment as if assessing the truth
of his statement and the wisdom of questioning it. When she saw that
he wasn't going to explain Brad's presence, she turned and walked
away.

"Victor broke into Marcolm and Blake Saturday night to steal
Bennett's computer. The police found a button from Bennett's coat
and traces of his cerebral spinal fluid in the boot of Victor's car.
Everyone knew that Victor always blamed Marcolm and Blake for
your father's death. The police have their case, John. I just want you
to tell me the details."

Rhodes sipped his coffee and then sat, drumming his fingers on
the table. He looked over to Madge who was puttering around behind

the bar and shifted his chair so that his back was towards her.

"Victor came here on Friday. At first I couldn't get a straight answer out of him. I could tell he was upset about something, but I couldn't figure out what. He's always having some difficulty with his businesses, but this was different. He was frantic. I could tell he hadn't slept and had been drinking heavily."

"Did he tell you what happened?"

"It took me a long time to calm him down, but he finally told me he had killed a scientist from Marcolm and Blake. I knew he had never gotten over dad's death. He always blamed the company for that, but the story he told me was much more involved."

"Why don't you start at the beginning. Why was he contacting the company after all these years?"

"Damn! This business needs more than coffee. I'll be right back," Rhodes said. He got up and went to the bar. Brad watched as John had a quick conversation with Madge. She was obviously unhappy about being left out of any business that had so upset her husband, but she finally realized that she was causing him more grief by asking for an explanation. John returned with a bottle of whiskey and two glasses. Without asking he poured a measure into one glass and shoved it across the table toward Brad. Then he filled a glass to the brim for himself.

"After dad died I had to sell off what was left of his business. Weren't nothing but a few machines. It was all old stuff. He was good at keeping it running with spit and plasters, but I couldn't manage it. Then mum got sick and I had to look after her. Victor started running wild—staying out all night and fighting with the neighbors.

"We was flat broke, on the dole and going down hill when I had a visit from a cousin on mum's side. Said he wanted to retire early and travel and needed someone to take care of his property. So I said I'd come and try to learn the pub running business and he fetched us all out to Ivybridge. That's when we changed our name to Rhodes. Let me tell you, it weren't no picnic living with him and his wife, but I kept my trap shut and he actually taught me all I needed to know. Best part was, he kept his word and left after two years. Bit by bit I been buying him out over the years."

"Did Victor help you with the business?"

"Not for long. The old guy caught him drinking up the profits. I could see he was heading down the same path as my dad so I talked the old man into setting him up with a business in London. Thought the change would do him good. Didn't work though. He's been in and out of business so many times I've lost track.

"Victor took it hard when dad died. He looked up to dad as some kind of example. What is it they call it nowadays? A role model? Well, I was older and I knew better. I'd worked in the business with dad. Any troubles he had were his own damned fault."

"I understand he was very creative."

"Oh he was brilliant all right—when he was sober. But let's face facts—he was an alcoholic. It wasn't Marcolm and Blake that ruined him. It was demon rum. Victor couldn't or wouldn't face that. Mum must have known, but she denied it. She couldn't face all the publicity. She had a nervous breakdown and then a few years back she had a stroke. I think it was her way of avoiding the truth."

"So how did Victor get involved with Marcolm and Blake again?"

"Best as I can understand from what he told me, it was through his business. He met a French agent at some party in London. The agent knew about Marcolm and Blake research and wanted to get hold of some inside information. He was willing to pay Victor good money and promised him advanced technological help with the details. Victor always had some shady deal going on the side and he knew a woman who was perfect for making the contacts. Apparently she was both beautiful and greedy.

"With the Frenchman's help Victor set her up in business. He bought her lots of expensive clothes and luggage and sent her to Plymouth to meet the scientists at Marcolm and Blake and get secrets out of them one way or another. Bennett Wildridge was her contact at the company. She strung him along with the line that she had friends who could set him up in business. He fell for it and began handing her all of his work. He kept pushing her about starting a business, and she kept stringing him along. When he ran out of his own ideas, he started giving her the work of others at the plant.

"Things was going along fine until this woman . . . I think he said her name was Elizabeth something disappeared. Victor said she could be a bitch about keeping in touch and he was never sure if she was reliable or not. She was supposed to be working for him, but he suspected that she had other deals going on the side. Anyway, when he didn't hear from her for several days, he started getting suspicious. So he came down to Saltash have it out with her. He was paying for her flat so he had a key.

"He snuck in about 11 p.m. so no one would see him. He didn't want any questions or for there to be any traceable connections between them. He always made sure to call her at the flat, but he never allowed her to call him. The woman wasn't anywhere in sight, but Victor found her bankbook showing several large deposits. He was furious. She was supposed to be working for him. She had told him that she had set up a real estate business as a front, but it didn't bring in any money. So he put two and two together and figured she had found another buyer for Bennett's secrets. That's when he searched her closet pretty thoroughly. Some of her luggage and some of the expensive clothes he bought her were gone. He always made sure that she had good stuff—to keep up the image, you know.

"Victor starts to thinking that she ran out on him and took Bennett's ideas with her. First, he's mad that she's got the goods and then he starts to figure that maybe she's run off with Bennett. At that point the only thing he could think of was losing 200,000 pounds. He'd been investing heavily in that woman and now she's gone. He was really in a stew.

"Victor knew Bennett was the contact at Marcolm and Blake, so he took a risk and called him. He told him he was one of the people who was considering setting him up in business. Well, this Bennett bloke—he nearly comes apart on the phone. He told Victor that Elizabeth had been murdered and he was scared out of his wits that the police would think he had done it. Victor was stunned. He instantly assumed that the woman had tried to sell Bennett's material to someone and the deal went sour. The only thing he knew for certain was that he had to keep Bennett away from the police. He got Bennett's home phone number and promised to phone him later that night.

"When Victor phoned, Bennett kept mumbling that he was going to leave town. Victor thought that maybe he could get Bennett to pass him some information before he left. He started telling him that everything would be all right, but that they needed to meet. Victor promised to help him—give him money and things like that. It took him a long time to calm him down, but he finally agreed to meet at the railroad station car park. The plan was for Bennett to bring some materials with him. In exchange Victor promised to arrange for him to get to Paris, and then, after things blew over, set him up in business. Bennett was still anxious to be recognized for his great ideas. Victor's idea was to get his stuff, give it to the Frenchman, and get out of the country.

"Victor went to meet Bennett that night at 2 a.m.— no one was around, but Bennett was upset to the point of being incoherent. He said the police had arrested someone at the plant and they was asking everybody questions. The CEO had ordered security cameras installed all over the place. He gave Victor a few papers, but he said he hadn't dared to copy any more stuff. The light in Victor's car was broken so he spread the diagrams and stuff on the bonnet and tried to sort them out using an electric torch he kept in the boot for road emergencies.

"All the while, Bennett went on and on about having loved Elizabeth and that he had planned to ask his wife for a divorce so that he could marry her. Victor tried to calm him down, but instead they got into an argument. Bennett wanted to go to the police and tell them everything. He thought if he made a clean breast of it, before the secrets got out, he could get off easy. Victor knew he would be implicated in Bennett's confession. His career and all his connections would be wiped out. He tried to get Bennett to change his mind, but he wouldn't. Victor knew that the police might let Bennett off for being a fool, but Victor had a long history of shady deals and he would go down hard.

"Somehow Victor and Bennett got to shoving each other and when Bennett started to walk away, Victor hit him with the torch. Victor cried when he told me, but it wasn't the first time he had lost control of himself. He beat that poor sod to death. Then he put the body in the boot of his car. He was so obsessed with getting more plans he got the keys from Bennett's coat pocket and searched Bennett's car. Victor found Bennett's suitcase in the boot and transferred it to his car. There was a ticket from the car park on the dash and he left it there hoping people would think Bennett had taken the train somewhere. He drove down Wolseley Road until he got below the Royal Albert Bridge and dumped the body in the water. The tide was going out so he thought that was the end of Bennett. He kept the case hoping there were more drawings hidden in it, but he never did find any.

"He went back to London and tried to sell some of the plans to the French agent, but the agent said the company he was working for was having trouble making that last batch of ideas work and he wouldn't give Victor any money. Then Victor went to his office and discovered that all his computer equipment and most of his office furniture had been repossessed and he had been locked out of his office suite. He was desperate to get some cash and he came begging to me.

"I quit giving him money long ago. I have my own family to think about. I just couldn't do it anymore. I've got bills too. Mum isn't getting any better and it's expensive every time she goes in hospital. I told him all that, but he kept begging me. What could I do? He was my brother. I told him to forget about the plans and to get out of the country as fast as possible. I gave him enough money for a ticket on the ferry and promised I'd send some more when he got settled. I've always given him money. Maybe I'm to blame for the way he turned out. He took the money and left. I thought he would be in France or Spain by now."

"That's quite a story," Brad commented slowly when Rhodes had finished. "Of course you do understand that the local police know nothing of Victor's involvement in stealing secrets from Marcolm and Blake."

"Are you sure?" Rhodes asked incredulously.

"Quite—and there's no need for them to find out. They will establish that he had a grudge against Marcolm and Blake, but it would limit the scandal if you didn't tell them what you just told me."

"Won't you have to make a report?"

"I'm not with the local police, John. They have their killer. I doubt they'll spend much time and effort digging up more background on him."

"Well, I won't bring more shame on Victor's memory, but why are you willing to keep quiet? Don't expect me to pay! I can hardly keep the roof over our heads."

Brad looked around and smiled. "Let's just say I like the atmosphere here and would like to see a local lad make good at it."

Chapter Twenty-Four

Kon, Geilla, Paul, and Nea had arrived at Brad and Mary's in Dorkin to relax for the weekend before going their separate ways. Mary had invited Jack, but immediately after Victor was killed, Jack notified Brad that he had some personal business to attend to and he hadn't been heard from for several days.

"So you see, Mary," Brad began when they were all gathered in the living room, "The way things worked out, neither the police nor the press ever got wind of the fact that Bennett and Elaina had been involved in stealing secrets from Marcolm and Blake. When Inspector Tomlin got my report about the dented fender from Lowell Cosgrove's car, he sent a team out to seize it as evidence. While the fender was at the laboratory, Tomlin drove out to see Kathryn Wildridge and confronted her with his suspicions. Fortunately, he did not arrest her for she had a radically different explanation as to how the fender was damaged and the laboratory was not able to find any evidence linking her father's car to Elaina's death."

"What was her story?" Mary asked eagerly.

"Tomlin gave me the gist of it and I pieced it together with what she told me. Kathryn had suspected for a long time that Bennett was seeing other women, but had never been able to prove it. When Bennett called her on the day Elaina was killed, she decided to check up on him. Since Bennett would recognize her car, she borrowed her father's new Bentley. She drove into Plymouth and waited outside of Marcolm and Blake until she saw Bennett come out. Then she followed him to The Three Crowns. The place was crowded and she had no problem mingling with the patrons long enough to see Bennett meet Elaina. Apparently Steven Compton was also there at the time, but neither one knew about the other.

"Kathryn watched Bennett and Elaina until she became so upset she feared she would cause a public scene. Then she stormed out to her car. She sat there for some time while her emotions alternated between feeling sorry for herself and being furious with Bennett. She had a bottle with her and started consoling herself with alcohol. When she finally pulled away, she put the car in first instead of reverse and rammed into one of the bollards along the quay. She was drunk and angry, so she sped back to her father's house and stayed there rather than going home to face Bennett. She's been drinking heavily ever since."

"I guess I can't help feeling sorry for her," Mary responded. "She lost the one man she really loved and she can't seem to find another."

"Well, if she'd stop drinking and get out more perhaps she would meet someone. She's still a very good looking woman," Brad put in.

"Yes, and very athletic too so I hear," Mary said looking straight at Brad as if to say he could hide nothing from her. "But enough of the beautiful Kathryn Wildridge. Tell me about Stephen Compton. What's his story?"

"He finally confessed to killing Elaina when he was confronted with the purse and the story about the paint job on his car."

"Did he say why he went from wanting to marry her to wanting to kill her?"

"Well, I got the story from Ian who never actually talked to Compton. Apparently Compton only half-believed that Elaina was willing to marry him. If you remember, he was furious with her when he saw her with Bennett at The Three Crowns. He calmed down a bit when they were in the car and he went off happily when she sent him into Cornwood for some champagne. But when he got back to the house, instead of finding her in the bath as she had promised, she was on the phone with Kenneth Wobel, arranging for a lift back to town. They had a terrible row and she stormed out of the house to wait for Wobel by the road.

"Compton couldn't believe her sudden change of heart and went after her in his car. He caught up with her at the bend in the drive. He said he sped up meaning to pull across the drive and block her way when she suddenly staggered in front of his car and was thrown into the brush. By the time he stopped the car and went back to her, she was dead.

"Her body was splattered with mud and he doubted that anyone would believe it was an accident. In a panic he put her body in the boot and drove out to Cornwood Road. Everything was quiet and there was no traffic, so he stopped his car and dumped her body into the bushes beside the road. Then he drove back to Plymouth and packed up all her belongings at the house. In the morning he noticed the scratch on the bonnet of his car and decided to have it repaired before he went home. He might have gone undetected but for his thrifty neighbor who recovered Elaina's handbag."

"And the fact that Kathryn Wildridge smashed up another of her father's cars," Mary put in. "Did Inspector Tomlin do any follow up as to why Elaina was sneaking into Marcolm and Blake?"

"He was suspicious for a while, but when the police located Elaina's post box they found the same check from Kenneth Wobel that Geilla had seen. Tomlin told me later that he had talked to Wobel and discovered that Elaina was blackmailing him about the baby. I also coached Roger to stress to Tomlin that Elaina had started dating Stanley and then moved on to Bennett Wildridge even while she was having an affair with Stephen Compton. Roger assured him that her only intent was to garner personal information about various men at the plant. He even insisted that some of his own personal files had been tampered with. After Compton confessed, Tomlin was willing to conclude that Elaina made a habit of preying on wealthy men both for immediate gain and for possible future blackmail. Since we had removed all the links to Marcolm and Blake from Elaina's flat and Victor's office, there was nothing to tie her to Victor or to the plant."

Mary turned to Kon, but before she could speak a maid came in and passed her a note. She read it quickly and stood up. "Excuse me a minute. I have a telephone call," she apologized and hurried out.

Kon resumed playing with E.P., holding him high above his head and watching him smile. Geilla sat enjoying the scene until Mary returned about ten minutes later. Geilla saw her approach Brad for a moment, whisper something to him, and then they both left the room. Several minutes later Mary returned alone and rejoined the group.

"That was Jack. He said he got my message on his answering machine and will come by shortly," she said casually.

"Is he all right? Did he say where he's been?" Kon asked.

"He's fine. We just had a little chat. I'm sure he'll fill you in when he comes. Now, tell me about Mysie and Alona. Were you able to work things out with Hollis?"

"Yes. It took a lot of negotiation, but I worked out a deal between Hollis, Mysie, and Social Services. Hollis will remain Alona's legal guardian, but Mysie has been hired as caretaker and is allowed to tap the trust fund to maintain Alona. In exchange, Hollis gets Elaina's car and all the jewelry."

"Did you finally locate the car?"

"Yes. The police were monitoring Elaina's post office box and found a bill for a hired garage. The car was sitting a few doors away from her flat in Saltash all the time. Apparently she always left it there on Fridays when she was meeting Compton."

"What kind is it?" Mary asked.

"It's a late model Porsche. It should put an end to Hollis' cash flow problems for a while."

"Don't be so modest, Kon," Geilla added. "Kon didn't mention that he was able to find Hollis a job as a new accounts clerk in a local bank. He has a lot of experience with customer relations."

"That's wonderful. What about Mysie? What's she going to do?"

"The money from the trust fund will provide enough for her to live modestly," Kon continued. Geilla is going back to Plymouth on Monday to help her find a less expensive flat. Once she gets settled she wants to go back to finish school and perhaps train to be a hair stylist."

"She's not a scholar, but she's very down to earth and knows how to stretch her money," Geilla added. "And Paul's even lined up someone to mind Alona while Mysie goes to school."

"Oh really? How nice," Mary said turning to Paul. "Where did you find someone?"

"I asked Mrs. Burnell and she was happy to be of service."

"Was she disappointed that she was wrong about Elaina moving to get away from Stanley?"

"Not really, but she was very intrigued to learn of Elaina's double and triple identities. To thank her for her help I drove her to Anthony House in Torpoint and she gave me a deluxe tour of the gardens. She used to be an avid gardener, but she doesn't drive, so I made a few calls to the Cornwall Garden Society and put her in touch with a member who has a car, but hates to go to meetings alone."

"That's great!" Mary said. "Is Mysie still going to see Davey?"

"Yes," Geilla answered. "She liked the fact that he tried to help her keep Alona. She hasn't made up her mind if she wants to marry him, but Alona likes him so that's a big plus in his favor."

"Is he still working at the grocery store?"

"Not any more," Geilla said. "Jack got him a job as a carpenter's assistant with a company that remodels kitchens. He's very good with tools. He's making more money and can move up as he learns."

"Say, Brad," Mary began, "I forgot to ask Jack if he ever found out why Frances Wobel never confronted her husband about his affair with Elaina. Did he tell you?"

"As a matter of fact he did. After he investigated her alibi on the night Elaina was murdered and discovered that she had left the bridge game early, he called Mrs. Wobel again and threatened to tell the police that she was lying. She went into a panic, but she finally admitted that she had left the game early in order to meet with her hired detective. She also confessed that the reason she decided not to confront her husband about his affair with Elaina was that she had begun using her mania for bridge as a cover for the affair she was having with her handsome, young detective. Jack finally wheedled his name out of her and the detective confirmed her story that she was with him the night Elaina was killed."

"So the wronged wife had to bite her lip," Mary concluded.

"Quite so."

"Hummmm, so the handsome detective was having an affair with one of his clients," Geilla remarked, looking straight at Kon. "Well, that settles it! I'm staying on the team whether Charlotte approves or not!"

"What is that supposed to mean?" Kon responded with exaggerated indignation. "Don't you trust me?"

"I wouldn't get into that if I were you, Kon," Paul cautioned with a laugh. "Just take it that she thinks you're handsome."

"Well, that's something," Kon agreed. "What do you think

E.P.?" he asked, lifting his son above his head. "Do you trust your papa to behave?" E.P. laughed and drooled, but didn't comment.

"You're a wise boy, E.P. and much more diplomatic than your father," Geilla laughed as she patted Kon's back affectionately.

The group chatted quietly for a while, passing E.P. around to be tickled and admired, until finally he grew tired and Geilla carried him away for a nap. When she returned, Mary was gone again. "What on earth is Mary planning for dinner?" Geilla asked. "She's been bustling about and whispering to the servants all afternoon."

"I don't know," Nea answered, "but she's been dashing in and out and I haven't seen Brad . . ." Nea stopped suddenly when Mary came into the room leading Jack and Bridget who were holding hands. She stopped dramatically on the threshold and announced with a flourish, "Ladies and gentlemen, may I present Mr. and Mrs. Jack Barrons."

For a moment the room was absolutely silent. Everyone stared at Bridget who stared back nervously and bit her lower lip. Jack tightened his grip on her hand ever so slightly. Then suddenly Nea leaped to her feet and rushed to her, exclaiming, "It's Bridget! Oh, Bridget, this is wonderful! I'm so happy for you both!"

Bridget smiled tentatively and Nea grasped her hand calling, "Paul! It's Bridget! The nurse from the hospital in Paris."

Paul stood abruptly, bounded up to Jack with his fluid stride, and threw several quick punches that fell without force on Jack's chin and arms. "Why you sneaky son-of-a-gun!" he declared in mock outrage. "I knew something was up! I just knew it!" He grinned and slapped Jack on the back before he turned and took Bridget by the hand. "I figured you were special when Jack started making dates over my dead body. I hope you know what a cheeky bugger you married."

"Yes, I know," Bridget said looking at Jack and smiling broadly. "He has a way of sneaking up on a girl and making her do crazy things!"

Paul studied Bridget for a moment and then he understood why Jack was attracted to her. She has the most fantastic smile! And those soft brown eyes . . . she's a hidden treasure all right, worth every trip to Devon.

A moment later everyone was on their feet, crowding around Jack and Bridget, shaking his hand, throwing their arms around his shoulders, hugging her, and planting kisses on her cheeks. She blushed from the attention and her eyes sparkled with delight.

Bridget was a bit overwhelmed by all the attention. Having met Nea once before, she was aware that Jack mixed with a sophisticated group, but she felt acutely conscious of her plainness when confronted by Geilla's stylish beauty and Mary's elegance. Everyone made her feel welcome, however, and fussed over her and Jack until Mary announced that dinner was served.

Mary had sent her small household staff scurrying to transform her intimate dinner with the team members into a lavish celebration. Wine flowed freely as everyone toasted the bride and groom. It was a boisterous meal, capped with a towering dessert hastily put together by stacking all the cakes Brad had garnered from bake shops as far away as Kingston and Richmond.

Although the colors of the individual decorations varied widely, they blended into a single theme of happy celebration. Bridget was astonished at its size and Jack declared it a masterpiece of engineering. Bridget was nearly overcome by a laughing fit when Jack lifted her onto a chair so that she could reach the top of the cake. Together she and Jack cut hearty slices from the topmost layer and passed them around to their friends who enjoyed seeing the pleasure that Jack and Bridget had from one another's company.

When everyone was exhausted from laughing, Mary stood and nodded to Geilla and Nea before saying, "Well, ladies, I think it's time we left the gentlemen to their brandy."

Bridget looked perplexed for a moment, but quickly composed herself and followed suit when Geilla and Nea stood. In silence the women filed out of the dinning room and followed Mary into the study. They had barely seated themselves on the soft wing-back chairs when a maid appeared with a cart holding a silver coffee service and several cutglass decanters. "Would you like cognac or a liqueur with your coffee, Bridget? I know Jack is rather found of Cointreau."

"Then I suppose I should try it," Bridget answered cautiously.

The maid departed silently and Mary served coffee to everyone.

"Do you really keep the tradition of sending the women away after dinner?" Bridget asked quietly.

"Oh no! Not for tradition's sake. It just gives us a chance to talk girl talk and gossip about the men in our lives. I hope you don't mind leaving Jack for a few minutes."

"Heaven's no. I shall have to get used to it. I have to go back to Devon in a few days."

"How sad! Can't you stay at Jack's flat?" Geilla asked.

"Not if I want to get to my job on time."

"I see," Mary put in. "You two haven't really had time to iron out all the details yet. I'm sure Jack will be happy with whatever arrangement you work out. He does have an airplane and he loves to fly."

"Have you thought about finding a job in London?" Geilla asked.

"No. To tell the truth, I haven't had time to think about anything practical. I know you probably think we rushed into this, but we have known each other for over a year."

"We don't think anything of the kind," Mary assured her quickly. "I believe Jack would be afraid to get married if he thought about it very much. He obviously decided to follow his heart and he's made a splendid choice."

Bridget blushed. "Thank you. Thank you all. Jack was afraid that you would all be upset that he made such an important decision without telling anyone. I didn't even tell my mum and dad until afterwards."

"Well, we shall have to arrange a party for you and Jack. We can have it here if you would like. I've always wanted to hold a wedding reception in this house. You can invite your parents and they can stay with us. The train stops in the village."

"I can't imagine a more lovely party than this, but I would like my folks to meet all of you."

"Splendid! We'll pick a day tomorrow, before Brad sends everyone off on another assignment."

Late that evening, as everyone retired, Nea went to her room alone. Although Paul had spent the night at her flat on more than one occasion and everyone on the team was aware of their relationship, he preferred to maintain a conventional front when they were staying at Brad and Mary's. The pretense bothered her a little, but she went along with it. She was beginning to learn that despite all his sophistication, Paul held some very conservative views.

Nea changed into her nightgown and slipped under the covers, half hoping that Paul would join her. But he didn't come. She lay awake thinking over how happy Jack and Bridget were and wishing that she and Paul could have a more permanent arrangement. She was willing to settle for just living together for a while, but Paul hadn't even suggested that. She tossed and turned some more and then decided that perhaps a glass of milk would help her get to sleep.

She got up, put on her robe and slippers and padded quietly into the hall and down the stairs to the kitchen. Since Mary maintained her home as a refuge for the team members who came and went at all hours, she always kept her refrigerator and her larder stocked with everyone's favorite food and drink. Nea poured herself a glass of milk and was about to turn off the light when Mary appeared. "Couldn't you sleep either?" Nea asked.

"No. I think I'm too excited to sleep," Mary answered gaily.

"About the party? It was wonderful!"

"Thank you. It was fun wasn't it. But that's not why I'm excited."

Nea caught a hint of the strange smile on Mary's face as she poured a glass of milk for herself. "What is it? You've been keeping secrets all day."

Mary laughed quietly. "I wasn't going to tell, but . . ."

"What?" Nea encouraged.

"Brad was so inspired by seeing Kon and Geilla with little E.P., and Jack and Bridget together that he's finally agreed that his life wouldn't fall apart if we had a child."

"Oh, Mary! I'm so happy for you!"

"I just hope it's not too late."

"Nonsense! You've still got lots of time."

"I hope so. I've been happy watching E.P., but it's made me realize how much I've wanted a baby of my own. When I mentioned it tonight, Brad didn't give me any of his usual arguments. I know he's not as eager as I, but he'll be a good father."

"I'm sure he will. He looks after everyone on the team. Oh, wait till Geilla hears the news! She'll be delighted."

"Yes. I really must tell her." Mary gave Nea a friendly hug and then slowly withdrew her arms. "Well, I guess we should get back to bed. It's been a long day."

"Yes, but a very happy one."

Mary turned out the kitchen light and followed Nea down the narrow corridor leading to the entrance hall. Suddenly she touched Nea on the shoulder and whispered, "Did you hear that?"

"Hear what?"

"I thought I heard the front door open."

"Do you think someone is trying to break in?"

"Never! Brad has the place locked like a fortress. It must have been someone going out."

"Maybe someone else couldn't sleep or maybe Jack slipped out for a cigarette."

"I don't think so. Bridget said he's quit and I haven't seen him smoke for months."

"Well, now you've made me curious. Shall we wait and see who comes in?"

"No. Let's go to the window. If they haven't made for the woods, there should be enough light from the security lamps for us to see them."

"O.K.," Nea agreed and the two hurried to the window in the entrance hall.

"It's Paul," Mary declared as she recognized the man on the lawn. He was performing a series of striking, kicking, and turning movements in slow motion.

"Whatever is he doing?" Nea asked in astonishment. "It's after midnight! Why on earth is he practicing karate at this hour?"

"Shhh," Mary warned. "He's not practicing. He's performing a coda. Do you see how slow and smooth the movements are? It's very precise and formal . . . almost like a ritual."

They watched in silence for a few minutes. "It's beautiful, but why is he doing it in the middle of the night?" Nea asked.

Mary sighed, held her lower lip between her teeth, and shook her head.

"What is it, Mary? Tell me."

"My guess would be that Paul's upset and is trying to calm himself."

"Why is he upset? I thought we all had a fabulous evening."

"It was fabulous, but Jack's marriage will mean a big change for Paul. Don't you see, he's lost both of his mates and it's bothering him."

"I hope he doesn't think I'm going to push him into getting married! I would like to, but . . ."

"He may be afraid of that."

"Then I'd better go out there right now and straighten him out," Nea said and started toward the door.

"Please don't do that," Mary warned. "Paul would be mortified if he even knew that you were watching him. He has to work this out himself."

"But where does that leave me? Don't I have a say?"

"Of course you do, but not right now. Let him complete the ritual and gain control again. Then he'll be ready to talk."

"Oh great! Why can't he just walk around the block when he gets upset like everybody else?"

"You know he's not like everybody else, Nea. Isn't that why you love him? Give him time to adjust to this new situation. He loves you. I know he does."

"You may believe he loves me, but I'm not sure. He's never actually said it and suddenly I feel as though our relationship is going backwards. I'm getting tired of waiting, Mary."

Mary took her hand and squeezed it gently. "I know. Believe me, I know. Just be patient a little longer."

"Oh, all right. I'll do it for you, Mary, but sometimes I feel that I need to punch and kick a few things myself."

"That's understandable. If it weren't so late I'd set you up with some bread dough and let you pound on it. Let's just go to bed and deal with things in the morning."

Mary awoke early the next morning, but she lay quietly, listening to Brad's breathing and letting her thoughts float happily over last night's decision to try for a baby. It was a joint decision, she reminded herself. It was not a matter of gaining Brad's acquiescence by wearing him down. He had even laid out a plan, in his supremely organized manner, of how long they should try for a child of their own before they would consider adoption. Their house was big enough, and they could afford schooling. Brad was always so thorough about any undertaking, but that was one of the things she loved about him. Just one of the tiny details she loved about him.

Mary finally gathered her thoughts together and pulled herself out of bed. She needed to get an early start on the day's activities, so she showered and dressed quickly and made her way down the stairs. She was surprised to see Nea standing in the entry hall, fully dressed with her luggage at her feet. "Nea, dear, wherever are you going at this hour?"

"Back to London. Could you drive me to the station?"

"Of course I will if you wish, but why are you leaving so soon? Something's happened between you and Paul hasn't it," she said touching Nea on the shoulder. Looking into her face, she could see that Nea had been crying. "Come and have some coffee and tell me all about it," Mary coaxed.

"Coffee isn't going to help, Mary!" Nea answered impatiently, but then she apologized. "I'm sorry. There's no sense making you miss your coffee just because I'm miserable."

"It's not the coffee that helps, dear. It just gives me time to find out why you're so upset. Come along—I think you're a candidate for chamomile tea actually."

"I've had it with wimpy herb teas! That's Paul's choice—not mine. I'll have the real thing. And pull out the stops on the cream."

"Yes, m' lady. Your wish is my command," Mary said seriously. She led the way into the kitchen, plugged in the electric teakettle, and set about measuring the coffee.

"Let me help you," Nea offered, but Mary waved her to a chair by the sturdy oak table.

"No thank you. You just sit and stay away from my crockery until you calm down."

Nea laughed in spite of herself and sat until Mary brought the drinks and joined her.

"Well?" Mary asked after a few minutes of absolute silence. "What did our 'Mr. Perfect' do now?"

"I guess I do owe you an explanation," Nea started, "but this is the last time I'm going to cry on your shoulder. I'm through with him—finished—once and for all!"

"Please . . . start at the beginning and don't leave out any details."

"All right . . . after we watched Paul do his little dance routine last night, I decided to go to bed and see if a good night's sleep would make matters seem any clearer. I got into bed and turned out the light, but I couldn't sleep. I kept tossing and turning. Then about two-thirty, I heard a knock on my door. I was half-hoping that it would be Paul, and it was. He said he had to talk to me immediately. I invited him in and . . . oh, Mary, he was drunk, or as close to drunk as I'd ever seen him."

"Did he say anything?"

"He asked me to marry him, but I told him no!"

"Oh, Nea! Why?"

"You know I have been hoping that he would make a commitment, but the way he did it . . . he said he had analyzed our relationship and felt it was best that we get married. Then he said that any kind of ceremony would be fine with him as long as he didn't have to convert to anything he didn't believe in. It was as if he didn't want anything to do with planning the wedding. He just wanted to get it over with as quickly as possible. It was more like a challenge to some karate tournament than a marriage proposal! He never even said that he loved me," Nea sobbed.

"Of course, he loves you! That's what made it so hard for him. He can't admit he needs anyone. You can't imagine how deeply he feels for you. Did he say anything else?"

"Well . . . he did apologize about not having a ring. He said it was only an outward symbol anyway and that he didn't need one. He said my pledge was all he needed."

"He said that? But that's beautiful, Nea. It's a tremendous breakthrough for Paul to admit he *needs* anything!"

"I knew you'd stand up for him! You always do. I don't want a *breakthrough*! I want a husband! A full-time husband—not someone who comes by when he has nothing better to do. I don't think Paul has time for a wife, between his work and that family of his! I've never even met them. What if they don't like me? His mother sounds really old-fashioned. What if he expects me to be like her and stay home? And another thing, I'm not going to be a . . . a . . . a brood mare like her and pop out a baby every year!"

"Oh, Nea, did you and Paul ever talk about having a family?"

"No. But if he wants to have seven or eight kids, he'll have to find somebody else to have them!"

"Now calm down. Tell me this—do you still love Paul? Do you truly want to spend your life with him?"

Nea sat silently, biting her lip and dabbing at her eyes with a handkerchief. "I do love him. That's why it hurt so much when he acted like he didn't really want to get married. I don't know, Mary. I'm confused. I just want to go home and think things out by myself."

Mary sighed. "I can see that you're very upset, Nea," she began thoughtfully, "but if you leave now, you may never see Paul again."

"Well, what am I supposed to do? Hang around and pretend nothing has happened?"

"I don't want you to pretend anything. But please don't go back to London alone. Let me talk to Paul . . . I know," Mary added, holding up her hand to silence Nea's objection. "He's a grown man and should be able to speak for himself, but sometimes he needs help. You must realize that he's probably had more practice hiding his feelings so that he can negotiate with terrorists about hostages than he has opening his heart to a woman. Let me talk to him. If I can't talk some sense into him, then I'll drive you to the station and I'll never say another word about him. Is it a deal?"

Nea sipped her tea and shook her head. "Why does he have to make things so difficult? This is supposed to be the happiest time of our lives."

"It doesn't always work that way. You don't know how hard Paul had to work to get Kon and Geilla together. I'm only asking for a little while . . . please."

"Oh all right! But this is absolutely the last time I'll let you talk me into giving him another chance."

"Good. Just wait here while I work on him. Are you sure you don't want some chamomile tea?"

Mary put two mugs of coffee on a tray and went to Paul's room. She knocked on the door and called out, "Paul? It's Mary. I need to talk to you."

She knocked again more firmly and suddenly Paul opened the door a crack. He was wearing a robe, but he was barefoot. He looked bleary-eyed and very hung over. "What's up, Mary? Is there some problem?"

"Yes, and you're the cause of it," Mary responded with more than a touch of sarcasm.

"Me? What are you talking about? Oh, God!" he groaned and put his hand to his head. "Couldn't this wait until later? I've got a terrific headache."

"Well, have some coffee and sober up," Mary said, pushing the tray at him and squeezing into the room. "I'm here to tell you about the headache you're causing me."

"What are you talking about? You seem upset. What happened?"

"It's Nea. You've made her very unhappy and she's about to leave for London."

"Oh, and what am I supposed to do about it? She's a free agent," Paul said calmly. He set the tray on the dresser and picked up one of the mugs of coffee.

"For God's sake, Paul, wake up! If she leaves you'll never see her again. Swallow that stupid male ego of yours and talk to her!" Mary held her hand in front of Paul's face, holding her thumb and forefinger about a quarter of an inch apart. "You were that close to working things out and gaining a real life partner, but you ruined it!"

"I'm sorry, but what business is it of yours?"

"I'll tell you what business it is of mine. You say your job is helping people straighten out their lives. I have the same job, only I don't have to run half way around the world to do it. You and Kon and Geilla bring enough troubles right to my doorstep to keep me busy. I thought you and Nea were finally working things out and now this! Really, Paul, you exasperate me!"

"Me? She's the one who ruined everything! I asked her to marry me last night and she turned me down!"

"Nea said you were drunk. How could you even think to approach her when you were drunk?"

"I wasn't drunk! I admit I had a few drinks before I went to talk to her, but only to get up my nerve. We had never talked about getting married and I was afraid she might say she wasn't ready. I was right! She acted like she needed ten years to think about it. I just wanted to do it and be done with it."

"Getting married isn't something you rush to get over with, Paul! Don't you know how important a wedding is in a woman's life? People plan these things months, even years, in advance. It might not be important to you, but it *is* important to Nea. She may want to have a more traditional wedding."

"Maybe I'm not really ready to get married. Until last night when Jack walked in here with Bridget, I thought things were going along just fine. Then it hit me that without Jack around . . . I don't want to get tied down with a big family, Mary. My parents never went anywhere and after my father died, my mother had all those kids and no money. I need more freedom! I couldn't stand to be stuck in some cheap flat with a bunch of squalling kids."

"Did you ever stop to ask Nea if she wanted a big family? No you just assumed she would. Well, you're wrong! For your information, she doesn't want a big family either. And you don't have to live in a cheap flat. You make plenty of money. If you'd stop sending most of it to your mother, you'd have enough for whatever you want. And as for kids being squally, E.P. is a very quiet baby and he's an absolute joy to have around."

211

Mary sighed heavily. "Honestly, Paul, for a person who analyzes situations to death, you haven't given the most important matter in your life any thought. Why were you so anxious to get the wedding over with?"

Paul didn't answer immediately. He put his coffee down and went to the window. Mary watched as he ran his hand through his hair several times and sensed that whatever reason Paul had for wanting to hurry his wedding, it was still on a subconscious level and difficult to put into words. When he finally spoke it came out half way between a groan and a whisper. "I didn't want Nea to be subjected to my mother's inspection. I've seen how she treats my brothers' wives. I was hoping Nea and I could get married quietly and I wouldn't have to tell my mother until afterward. She has a tendency to take over. You don't know what a circus she would make of things if I told her before hand. Nothing I do is ever good enough for her. No woman I picked would measure up. I didn't want Nea to have to face that."

"Why didn't you explain that to Nea?"

"I couldn't. I guess I'm a coward, Mary. Why else would I be afraid to admit that after all these years I'm still tied to my mother's apron strings."

"Oh, Paul, you are hardly tied to your mother's apron strings. You're the most independent person I've ever met. Has it ever occurred to you that the reason your family clings to you is *because* you are so strong and so rational? Just answer me this, do you love Nea or not?"

"Of course I love her! Why else would I want to marry her?"

"But you never actually told her you loved her, Paul."

"I thought she was smart enough to figure it out. I don't go around proposing to every woman I meet! Nea was always so independent she's just what I need."

"So you admit you need her! Why didn't you tell her?"

"I thought I did. Look, I was nervous. I . . . I don't remember what I said."

"You must talk to Nea, Paul. Tell her how you feel about getting married. Work it out with her. She'll understand. I know she will."

"It's too late, Mary."

"It's not too late, Paul, believe me. Get cleaned up and go talk to her. And get her a ring—it doesn't have to be an expensive one, but not too small either."

Paul hesitated and Mary shook her head. "Listen to me, Paul. Nea *is* different. She cares about you. How many other women would put up with all your antics? Don't let her get away."

Paul suddenly grinned. "You're right, Mary! Damn it! Nea and I are the ones who want to get married. To hell with my mother! We'll do it the way we want."

"Good," Mary said firmly, "but don't forget to invite her to the wedding once you've got all the details worked out. I'm sure she would be hurt if her first born got married and didn't invite her to the ceremony."

Mary turned to leave, but Paul suddenly called her name and took her hand. Slowly he raised it to his lips and kissed it. "I wish my mother was as wise as you, Mary."

Mary smiled, but remained speechless, too overcome with emotion for words. Perhaps I've had children for years and never recognized it, she thought contentedly.

About the Author

Barbara A. Scott was born and raised in upstate New York and graduated from Union University. After her marriage to a fellow member of the local Judo Club, she and her husband overhauled, sailed, and lived aboard a 65-foot Bahamian Ketch on the Chesapeake Bay. She has traveled extensively in Europe and spent five years in an international community in Saudi Arabia.

In addition to writing, Ms. Scott has a hectic, full-time day job. She is a member of the Sacramento Publishers Association, California Writer's Club, Mystery Writers of America, serves as vice-president of the Sacramento Chapter of Sisters in Crime and leads a mystery reading group which meets in the Sacramento area.